CW00953872

The Fossil

& other stories

by Richard Ilnicki

ISBN: 978-1-54397-376-1 (Print)
ISBN: 978-1-54397-377-8 (eBook)

Table Of Contents

I would like to dedicate this book to my two brothers, Victor and Stephen. These two men are men "after God's own heart." Their lives manifest the love of Christ as husbands, fathers, brothers and friends of the Bridegroom.

"The only gift better than a book is time enough to read it"

R.A. Ilnicki

Forget not that "Your body follows your mind. Where are you taking yours?"

R.A. Ilnicki

Que's Complaint

Que recently said he didn't want to have nothing to do with his doctor. He was speaking rather casually, and here is exactly what he said, "I ain't gonna have absolutely nothin to do with no doctor." He'd said this to his very best friend, Repo, down at the filling station across from the high school. "I've just about had it right up to exactly about here," he continued while placing his flexed first two fingers right below his smooth, clean shaved chin. "And I'll tell you something else, Repo. I expect you might agree with what I'm saying about doctor S. He kinda gives me the creeps. Even with those horn rimmed, thick, coke bottle glasses he appears to be able to see right through you. And he always carries that little flashlight around so he can look deep into your eyes at the drop of a hat."

Que, who was 5 feet 8 inches tall and weighed 215 pounds, mostly muscle, always had a little flashlight in the back pocket of his overhauls along with an open-ended wrench. He always referred to Dr. Szyrpka as Dr. S. Que wore his jet-black hair in a pony-tail pulled back very tightly revealing a scar that ran directly across his forehead from ear to ear. His skin had a shiny, oily look without the sign of even one wrinkle. His brown eyes resembled two roasted almonds. He had the rough handsome look and natural tan of a native American Indian. He was always very friendly and easy to understand.

Repo was watching Que who was about to light the glue he'd layered onto the surface of an inner tube. Que would then apply a hot patch to the tube. Next, he'd smoothly secure the patch using a roller designed specifically for this purpose.

"Que, now you know Doctor Szyrpka isn't a bad man, and he's a good doctor too. He's been in this town for thirty years, and he has helped a lot of people. Furthermore, you know damn well he cares about you, and what is best for you. He always has and always will," Repo said while watching Que very closely.

"Well, yeah, yeah, but he seems to be against me. I don't think he cares for my kind. You know what I mean, Repo? Sometimes I think he just plain old has it in for me. You know what I'm saying. Don't you?" Que asked Repo, who was watching the blazing glue. Once that glue was good and hot Que blew the flame out and stuck that patch directly onto the exposed helpless nail hole just waiting to be made whole. Sometimes he felt like a doctor; one who really cared. He took a lot of pride even in the smallest task he performed at the filling station

"As far as I know he's always been there for you, hasn't he?" Repo responded with a tone of certainty. Repo stood six feet six inches and weighed 182 pounds. He lived on Moon Pies, glazed donuts, Pepsi, coffee and cigarettes. He was a good basketball player but usually got crushed under the boards and had a difficult time playing full-court. He had poor posture. He had 20/20 vision and always wore sunglasses. He suffered from male pattern baldness due to the loss of the androgenic hormone, testosterone. Consequently, he had developed a horseshoe ring of hair circling the back of his head and temples. The result was a head of prematurely gray hair ridiculously styled in an obvious comb-over. His skin was about as white as a ghost's.

"Well, yeah, yeah, Kinda, but I still don't know why every time I see him, I'm already in the hospital. I swear it seems he has something against me. I never caused him no harm," Que said while examining the hot patch he'd just secured to the tube. "Oh yeah, I did see him once when he came out to visit my mom when she got real sick. He did seem pretty nice that time."

"Well, you sure got a point there, Que, but did you ever give any thought as to why you were in the hospital in the first place?" Repo asked.

Repo liked to hang around the old gas station and drink black coffee from his 16 Oz. jug that had a worn Cleveland Brown's logo on it. When he wasn't drinking coffee, he would be drinking Pepsi while playing the pinball machine. He usually hit at least once a week, but then he'd put the winnings right back in. He worked for his father's towing company. He had been born with a severe angulation of the spine known as kyphosis. His nickname was "The humpback." This condition did not, however, seem to adversely affect his basketball skills, although it did keep him out of the army. He walked like an ape, and his long arms dangled about six inches below his knees. He did a lot of square dancing, and he particularly enjoyed striking the heels of his black leather cowboy boots against the shiny wooden dance floor. He had quite a few different cowboy shirts but preferred the black one with silver buttons. He seldom wore anything other than Levis. He'd occasionally chew tobacco. He could hit the spittoon from four feet away.

"Well, hell no. I just thought he musta put me in there for some reason. I've never been to his office. I couldn't make an appointment unless I was willing to pay cash. He said he didn't take charity cases. I'll bet you've been to his office more than once. Haven't you?" Que asked, now looking up at Repo while holding the inner tube around his right shoulder like a firefighter would hold a fire hose. He wore the same dungarees every day; the kind with shoulder straps. He liked the medium blue ones with vertical gray stripes. The t-shirts he wore beneath were Steelers black and gold. He liked The Steelers, but he had never been to a game. He didn't hate the Cleveland Browns, but he didn't like them either. Que found it difficult to hate anyone or anything, but he did occasionally lose his temper.

"Hell no! I've never been to his office. Why would I?" Repo asked. "Are you fuckin crazy or somethin!"

"I don't know. I was just curious. Heck, you said he was such a good doctor. So, I just figured you musta been there one time or another. If he's such a good doctor, why don't you go see him?" Que asked while walking towards the tire mounting machine. "I know you have insurance, and cash if you needed it."

"I've never needed to see him. That's why," Repo answered sharply.

"So, are you sayin you've never been sick. Hell, I've seen you when you've been plenty sick. So sick I've heard you say you was sick as a dog," Que said while carefully placing the tube inside the tire. He hadn't been looking at Repo while talking. He wasn't ignoring him; he was just preoccupied with the tire.

"Yeah, but not that sick. Not as sick as you. If you know what I mean," Repo replied defensively while moving closer to Que. He was now within a foot of him. He was smoking a cigarette and appeared rather imposing with the dark glasses, the weird comb-over and his half-cocked Cleveland Indians baseball cap. His razor sharp, thin black mustache and Fu-Manchu beard were sort of freaky, kind of scary, kinda like a lecher might look. Behind his back a lot people said he gave them the heebie-jeebies, a man not to be trusted. A few of his acquaintances said he reminded them of Dracula, the white skin and all. He seemed to despise people indiscriminately. He really didn't have one true friend, and he didn't even seem to care.

"Hey, don't get so fuckin close. Are you crazy or somethin? Don't you know this tire iron can snap off and smack you in the goddamn face. Get back a step or two. Don't you got no brains," Que said angrily while handling the tube and tire cautiously. Repo's remark, "Not as sick as you," bothered Que.

Repo frequently said things that bothered Que, things that seemed intentionally demeaning. Sure, they were friends, alright, or so it seemed, but Que frequently felt like Repo considered him kind of retarded. A lot of times he couldn't tell what Repo really meant when he would make fun of him then appear to apologize almost in the same breath. Repo was hard for Que to read. He liked him alright, and he may have been his only real friend, but there always seemed to be that lingering, haunting 'but.' Repo was the only man who could bring the worst out of Que.

Que rarely, if ever, used profanity. His mother had taught him as a child that profanity was the sign of ignorance, and she had made it abundantly clear that profanity would not be tolerated. However, there was something mysterious about Repo that caused Que to see red, and the profanity just seemed to roll off his tongue. Repo knew precisely which buttons to push that would drive Que over the edge, and it was also at those same moments when Repo would remind Que of his mother's admonition to refrain from profanity. This admonition would further boil Que's Indian blood. The result was that he would begin to hate himself as much as he hated Repo.

Que had a way with tires and inner tubes. He could change a tire in less than two minutes using the four-pronged tire iron. There had never been a lug nut he couldn't snap loose. He had powerful wrists and huge muscular forearms. He also knew more about tires than any man in town. If you had a question about tires, he was the man to see. Funny thing, though, as much as he loved tires, he never sold tires. He did burn tires, however, but only if absolutely necessary. He collected bald eagles, and his mattress was supported by about twelve rejects he picked-up along the way from sundry junk yards. He had a dream that someday he would visit the Goodyear Tire & Rubber Company in Akron, Ohio. He knew a lot about the rubber plantations in The Amazon, but he knew he would never be able to go there, but Akron was not out of the question. He was the only person in town who could use a tire as a hula hoop and keep it up for minutes; he was that powerful and unknowingly, sometimes, quite humorous. He liked to laugh, and he liked to make people laugh, but he didn't like it when people laughed at him.

"All right! All right! Don't get so damn excited. You're liable to take one of your fits, and you know where that will land you," Repo said with a hint of arrogance while lowering his sunglasses to reveal his brilliant green eyes. Que didn't appreciate what Repo had just said, although he was right. There are certain forms of excitement that he knew his brain couldn't tolerate, and even though he wanted to smash Repo in the face with the tire iron he managed to control himself. Dr. S. had advised him to be wary of what he liked to call 'cerebral overload.' Que would have preferred to hear something like, "The straw that broke the camel's back." To him, medical jargon was high fallutin bullshit.

"Look, Que, you must remember something about yourself. You're not normal, and besides being abnormal you're also potentially very dangerous to yourself as well as to others," Repo said while taking a few steps backwards. "Look, I consider you a friend, and a good one at that, but I've been watching you lately and you are exhibiting signs that, to me, portend catastrophe if you don't get some help. You're awfully close to hospital material."

Que didn't respond initially. He just kept working on the tire while avoiding eye contact with Repo. "Oh, so I guess you've been spying on me. Is that it?" Que asked smartly. "What the fuck does 'portend' mean, anyway!" he continued.

"Of course not. I've never spied on you, but I have observed some of your obviously bizarre behavior lately. I've also had a few of the teachers at the high school tell me that you've been hanging around the Dairy Queen, again. I thought the Dairy Queen was off limits for you," Repo said while studying Que's body language. "Someone, I won't say who, also told me they saw you dressed-up like a boy scout hanging around the girl scout cookie table at the middle school. And another so-called friend said she saw you feeding bread crumbs on fish hooks to the pigeons in the park, again. And, if that isn't enough, Bobbi Joe Johnson said she saw you streaking the other night. She said you ran right out in front of the school bus that was carrying the football team and cheerleaders to the Monongahela High game last Saturday night. Furthermore," Repo was about to continue when Que angrily interrupted him.

"Hearsay! Hearsay! Fuckin bullshit! Everything you just said is a pack of lies!" Que yelled as he released the finished tire, picked it up and slammed it to the ground on its edge. The tire bounced at least eighteen inches into the air, came down hard against a huge wrench then rolled into the oil pit, which the guys had nicknamed "The Snake Pit." There was no hydraulic lift available at the time, so the mechanics had to descend into a pit to do oil changes, etc.

"Why is it that everybody seems to be against me? Why can't they just leave me alone? I've never hurt nobody. I'm sick and fucking tired of everybody accusing me of things I've never done. I hate this fuckin town! If I had my way, I'd torch this sorry fuckin place and every sorry prick in it, and I think I'd start with you," Que said angrily while heading towards the Snake Pit to retrieve the tire, but not before he gave Repo a threatening stare. Repo just stood still and didn't say a word. He just continued to smoke calmly while exhaling through his nose. The draft in that part of the garage caused the smoke to waft upwards and encircle Repo's head. He looked rather ominous and somewhat mysterious at that moment. It was if he had just become a character in a B rated horror movie.

Que made his way down into the pit. Above him on the lift was a new, red and white 57 Chevy. He'd balanced the tires a few hours earlier and had given it an oil change. It was his brother's car. It had been labeled "The Snatch Wagon." His brother had started his very own rock band, and every girl in the town was after him. Sometimes Que would set the band's instruments up on the stage before the concert and then watch the crowd of screaming girls from behind the curtain. His brother's guitar was off limits, but once, when his brother wasn't home, Que took it out of the closet and began to play it. He made believe he was up on stage, and all the girls were screaming for him. As their screams grew louder and louder some of them began to faint while others removed their panties and threw them onto the stage.

While Que was in the pit retrieving the tire Repo stealthily moved to one side of the pit. He was watching Que's movements very closely. Que was too absorbed with getting the tire to consider where Repo might have been. Just as he was about to get the tire Que looked up and saw Repo's boots. He didn't give it much thought; Repo often spoke to him while he was in the pit changing oil or working on a brake job. While in the pit Que noticed that he hadn't properly tightened the oil pin after the oil change. He momentarily forgot about the tire and reached into his back pocket for his wrench. With both hands above his head to address the problem his feet were suddenly drenched with some liquid. This was precisely the kind of opportunity Repo had been looking for that day. For some unknown reason, he wanted to cause Que harm, mentally and emotionally.

The distraction with the oil pin was a perfect opportunity for Repo to act. While Que had his hands over his head Repo intentionally and carefully knocked over a barrel of waste oil that had been cut with acid. He'd aimed the oil splash directly towards Que's boots. It was easy. The fluid spilled into the pit and soaked Que's boots. The caustic fluid immediately began to eat away at the shoe leather without harming Que's skin. It happened quickly, and it happened exactly as Repo had planned. The damage was immediate and serious.

"Que! Que! Hey Que, watch out. I just accidentally knocked over that barrel of waste oil. Get out of the pit immediately! Don't step into any of that shit and get the hell out of there before you or your boots are eaten alive!"

Que hadn't the slightest opportunity to react except to quickly look down at his boots. He immediately thought of his mother.

Que's mother had been on disability for the past twenty years ever since Que's father had been caught between the couplers of two railroad cars. His dad worked as a night watchman for the P&LE Railroad. The coupler's severed his body into two distinct sections; the upper and lower body, a perfect transverse plane. In spite of the gruesome nature of his death, his body was put together, and at his wake he was mourned in an open casket. Que's mom suffered thereafter from chronic, debilitating, clinical depression and had to quit her job at The Big Boy Drive-In restaurant. While in the pit and observing his acid eaten shoes Que's mind began to gradually implode like a simmering Black Hole.

Que's mom had saved her change in a jar until she had enough money to buy Que a new pair of black, shiny, high-top boots. Boots that Que had set his eyes upon down at the Army/Navy Surplus store. The boots had been used, but they still looked good enough for him. He knew he'd never be able to afford them, but he still fantasized about them. Most of his shoes at one time or another had cardboard inserts for soles.

The evening of his most recent birthday he opened his one and only present from his mom. He always told her he didn't need any presents; she was his present, and he'd always remind her how precious she was to him. So, as always, he reluctantly opened his present. When he saw the boots, he was stunned. At first, he said nothing. He couldn't speak. The boots his mom had purchased for him were not the used ones from the Army/Navy Surplus store. These boots were brand new. His mom had saved enough money to go right down to Kaufmann's, the best store in Pittsburgh, and buy her son the finest boots available. She had also added two pairs of expensive socks; the socks portrayed the Pittsburgh Steelers logo.

Que looked at the boots then at his mom; she was smiling broadly and proudly. Que would do just about anything to bring a smile to his mom's gentle face. She'd not had too much to smile about since his dad's death.

Que removed the boots from the shoe box and examined them closely. These boots were brand new. Tears welled up and spilled from his heart through his eyes down his cheeks. His mom also cried. He put the boots on then laced them up and walked around the room. He felt as if he were walking on a cloud. He then put his mom's favorite 78 rpm record on the Victrola, and they danced to the sounds of Glenn Miller. That night, as was their custom on very special occasions, before they retired, they smoked the Lakota Peace Pipe. This night Que also asked his mom to recite the legend of the Lakota Peace Pipe.

When Que was very young, he would frequently ask his mom to recite to him the legend of the Lakota Peace Pipe. He'd heard the story more than once but never got tired of hearing it. When he grew older, he could almost recite it word for word, but from the lips of his mom the legend became reality. His mom may not have had much education, but she was smart in a very special way.

"Long, long ago, two young and handsome Lakota were chosen by their band to find out where the buffalo were. While the men were riding in the buffalo country, they saw someone in the distance walking toward them. As always, they were on the lookout for enemies. So, they hid in some bushes and waited. At last the figure came up the slope. To their surprise, the figure walking toward them was a woman. When she came closer, she stopped and looked at them. On her left arm, she carried what looked like a stick in a bundle of sagebrush. She was beautiful. One of the men said, "She is more beautiful than anyone I have ever seen. I want her for my wife." The other man replied, "How dare you have such a thought. She is wondrously beautiful and holy-far above ordinary people."

"The woman approached them and said, "Come. What is your wish?"

"The man who had spoken first went up to her and laid his hands on her as if to claim her. Suddenly from above came a whirlwind, then a mist which hid them. When the mist cleared, the other man saw the woman, but his friend was a pile of bones at her feet. The man stood silent in wonder and awe. Then the beautiful woman spoke to him. "I am on a journey to your people. Among them is a good man whose name is Bull Walking Upright. I am coming to see him especially. Go on ahead and tell your people that I am on my way. Ask them to move camp and to pitch their tents in a circle. Ask them to leave an opening in the circle facing north. In the center of the circle make a large tepee, also facing north. There I will meet Bull Walking Upright and his people."

The man saw to it that all her directions were followed. When she reached the camp, she removed the sagebrush from the gift she was carrying. The gift was a small pipe made of red stone. On it was carved the tiny outline of a buffalo calf. She gave the pipe to Bull Walking Upright, and then she taught him the prayers he should pray to the Strong One Above. "When you pray to the Strong One Above you must use this pipe in the ceremony. When you are hungry unwrap the pipe, and lay it bare in the air. Then the buffalo will come where the men can easily hunt and kill them. So, the children, the men, and the women will have food and be happy."

The woman also taught them how to behave in order to live peacefully together. She taught them how to pray to Mother Earth. She taught them how to decorate themselves for ceremonies. "The earth she said, "is your mother. So, for special ceremonies you will decorate yourselves as your mother does—in black, red, brown and white. These are the colors of the buffalo also. Above all else, remember that this is a peace pipe that I have given you. You will smoke it before all ceremonies. You will smoke it before making treaties. It will bring peaceful thoughts into your minds. If you will use it when you pray to the Strong One Above and to Mother Earth, you will be sure to receive the blessings you ask."

When the woman had completed her message, she turned and slowly walked away. All the people watched her in awe. Outside the opening of the circle she stopped for an instant and then laid down on the ground. She rose again in the form of a black buffalo cow. Again, she laid down and then arose in the form of a red buffalo cow. A third time she laid down and arose as a brown buffalo cow. The fourth and last time she had the form of a spotlessly white buffalo cow. Then she walked toward the north into the distance and finally disappeared over a far-off hill as though having become one with the earth and the sky.

Bull Walking Upright kept the peace pipe carefully wrapped most of the time. Occasionally he called all his people together, untied the bundle, and repeated the lessons he had been taught by the beautiful woman. He used the pipe in prayers and other ceremonies until he was more than one hundred years old.

When Bull Walking Upright became feeble, he held a great feast. There he gave the pipe and the lessons to Sunrise, a worthy man. In a similar way, the pipe passed down from generation to generation. "As long as the pipe is used," the beautiful woman had said, "Your people will live in peace and will be happy. As soon as it is forgotten, the people will perish."

Sharing the peace pipe this night was particularly special for Que. The beautiful and mysterious woman in the legend reminded him of his mom, full of wisdom, understanding, knowledge and love. She loved to recite famous Native Indian quotes for him to live by. That night she gave him two new ones, "'Man does not weave this web of life. He is merely a strand in it. Whatever he does to the web he does to himself.'" ""Peace and happiness are available in every moment, and peace is every step. We shall walk hand in hand. There are no political solutions to spiritual problems. Remember, if the Creator put it there, it is in the right place. The soul would have no rainbow if the eyes had no tears.'"

Que loved his mom more than anyone in the whole wide world. Despite her depression she was always there for him. She'd recently been diagnosed with macular degeneration. She couldn't see things very well directly in front of her, but she always kept her peripheral vision on her only son. She pretty much knew where her boy was at all times. She made his breakfast, lunch and dinner every day and always laid out his medication. She instinctively anticipated his every need and happily met each one. Her uncanny intuitive sensitivity always surprised him. It was the little things that filled him with so much joy. No one could possibly ever have a mom as special as his mom. To him she was an angel sent to him by Wakan Tanka, The Great Spirit.

The intentional oil spill initiated by Repo soaked Que's new boots in a mixture of dirty oil and acid. Que's knee-jerk reaction was to immediately seek revenge, to leave the pit, to attack Repo, and perhaps even to kill him. Instead, he purposefully retrieved the tire, but as he ascended from the Snake Pit all he could see were the tears of his broken mother. Tears she shed when she saw the smile on his face as he ran his hands along the leathery flesh of his new boots, boots that were now being subtly eaten alive by the sinister liquid. Once again Que had the opportunity to react either violently or exhibit supernatural control. He wanted to yell, scream, paint his face, do a war dance and kill, but he didn't. He thought about the night he received his magnificent gift and called upon the wisdom of his people. He prayed a special prayer for peace that would pass all understanding. "Oh, Great Spirit, help me always to speak the truth quietly, to listen with an open mind when others speak, and to remember the peace that may be found in silence."

Que came out of the Snake Pit and deliberately walked past Repo without looking at him or saying anything. As much as he wanted to kill him, he didn't want to lose control of his faculties. To a degree, but not entirely, he knew what he was capable of when he lost control. However, Repo wasn't content with the dastardly deed he had just committed. For some reason, this day, he wanted to torture his best friend. No one would ever know, but there was speculation that something horrible, something humiliating had happened to him the night before in the back seat of his black Buick. The Buick was found abandoned at Overlook Mountain. Just like in any small town the rumors ran roughshod through the curious population while tearing certain families into opaque blood-stained shreds.

"Hey, Que, what the heck just happened to your new boots? Holy cow! They appear to have begun to actually melt away while still on your ugly flat feet," Repo said sarcastically while slowly following Que. Que had previously bragged to Repo about his new boots. He told him all about the night he had opened his surprise birthday package. He'd even asked Repo to feel them the first day he wore them. He told Repo they were the best present he'd ever received in his whole life. He'd never been as proud of any gift as he was of his special boots. Que had tried to enlist in the army, but he had been rejected because of his flat feet; just one among a few other very good reasons why he could not enlist. Repo was the only one he had told about his flat feet, but Repo told the whole town. People sometimes kiddingly referred to Que as "Flatfoot." He'd become accustomed to it and usually just laughed when he heard it. Repo's remark today, however, especially hurt him. Perhaps he felt the denigrating remarks had been directed towards his mother.

Que didn't respond to Repo's statement about his boots. He just wanted to get on with his work. In the meantime, the leather of his boots was being slowly eaten away by the oily mixture. "What would his poor mother say," he thought. He couldn't bear the thought of explaining to his mother what had happened to his new boots. Maybe he'd leave his boots at work and walk home barefoot. Maybe he would tell his mom that he didn't want to wear them out. He wasn't sure what to do, but he was sure of one thing. He wanted to kill Repo.

When Repo recognized that Que intended to remain silent, he got upset. He wanted a rise out of Que, and he would settle for nothing less. "Hey, Que, you're probably not used to wearing shoes where you come from. You probably spent the better half of your life half-naked. Why don't you leave your boots behind and walk home barefoot? I'm sure the cold won't even affect you. Isn't it true that most savages seem to adapt to the elements as they grow up?" Repo said as he followed closely behind him.

Que remained silent while Repo continued his denigrating language attempting to upset him. Que almost responded when he heard the word "savages," but he didn't. He just thought of his mother. He knew if he was put away one more time it would probably be the death of her. Furthermore, the last time they smoked the peace pipe his mom made him promise to never under any circumstances harm anyone ever again. He promised, but Repo was severely challenging his promise.

"Hey, Que, is it true that you are a half-breed? Part Lakota and part dumb Pollock? Isn't it true that you and your mom have shared baked dog meat from time to time? I wonder what ever happened to that little Cocker Spaniel that used to live a few doors down from you," Repo continued while closely following Que into the front of the gas station.

Que's blood was beginning to boil, but he called upon the spirit of his great-great uncle, "The Man Who Loved Horses." A man who spent most of his life defending the Black Hills, the land of The Sioux. Que knew he would be home soon. He was about to shut things down for the night. He didn't want to go to jail or the hospital, so he began to close early.

"Hey, what do you think you are doing, Que?" Repo asked. "You've got at least an hour to go before you close, and, besides, I want to play the pinball machine. Que still did not respond. He began to close things down.

He closed out the register, turned off all the gas pumps, turned off the compressor, cooled the pot belly stove, pulled the plug on the pinball machine, shut off all the lights then removed his boots; the sight of them made him sick. He loved his mother and thought of her love for his father. Repo just stood there and silently watched him. He wasn't sure what to say, but he wasn't through. "Hey, I want to play the pinball machine!" he said loudly and defiantly. "You can't close just because you want to go home early. I'll tell Mr.Castellucci you closed early when I see him next time. I'm a good paying customer."

Que grabbed his set of keys. He then motioned Repo towards the door. Que didn't say a word. He just went to the door, opened it and invited Repo to leave. At first Repo did not move, but then Que said, "Repo, if you know what is good for you, you will leave peacefully." The way he said it and the way he looked, convinced Repo to leave, but not before another of Repo's denigrating remarks.

"So, what are you going to do if I don't leave? Scalp me?"

Repo reluctantly left, but not before he gave Que a subtle shove. Que locked the door from the inside and stayed for a few minutes then left and locked the door from the outside. He began the two-mile walk home in the snow in a pair of old worn out shoes. Before he had gotten very far along Repo, who was now inside a tow truck, yelled one more time, "Que!" he yelled. "I think you come from a long line of horse thieves, including your great-great grandfather, He Dog. If it were up to me, I'd march every last one of you up to Saskatchewan in another "Trail of Tears."

The remark about 'horse thieves' felt like an arrow that had just been shot into Que's back, but he didn't turn around. He just kept walking with his head down. As always, he was anxious to see his mom. She'd have something ready for him even though he would be home early. He wasn't exactly sure how she would respond when she saw his partially frozen feet. He was proud of himself for not having attacked Repo. On the way home, a few friends stopped their cars and offered him a lift, but he refused.

When he got to the footbridge, he was within 150 yards of his house. Que loved the footbridge that spanned the railroad yard. He'd often stood and watched with excitement the roaring steam engine locomotives pass right beneath him. He loved to be engulfed with the smoke from the engine's smokestack shooting up between the wooden floor of the old footbridge. The footbridge connected two distinct towns, one much older than the other. The one where his father was born bordered the Ohio River. It was a family, a village of Pollocks, Hunkies and Ukrainians; the other, where the streetcars and buses ran, was mostly Italian. Que found it rather odd that there were no colored people on either side of the tracks. They all seemed to be living happily up in the projects. It was like a different world up there, a world that Que identified with. He was one of only a few white men, half white, anyway, who felt safe spending time up there. Repo always jagged him about the colored girls, only he didn't call them 'colored' girls. He preferred using a more denigrating term.

When he got home his mom was surprised. He was early. The first thing she noticed, of course, was his frozen feet; they were blue. Alarmed, she asked him what happened to his new boots. As planned, he told her he didn't want to wear them out by traipsing back and forth the two miles to and from work. He said he felt as if they were also her boots, and he wanted to preserve them for the rest of his life. When he wore those boots, he felt loved and somehow powerful, almost invincible. He'd not told her, but the first day he put them on he went into the back yard and did a 'ghost dance.' He said he would keep the boots at work and wear another old pair to and from. This way he could brag about them to his friends and customers. The shoes he was wearing could hardly be called shoes; they'd been worn to a frazzle. He might as well have been barefoot.

She was overcome by his foolish remark. She wanted to chastise him, but instead she began to cry and threw her arms around him. "Oh, my son, my son, my only wonderful son. It was a foolish thing you did, but I know you, and only you would do such a thing. I know you wouldn't lie, but I think there must be another reason you aren't wearing your boots. Your heart is as big as the sky, but you aren't a fool, and neither am I," she said while the tears fell slowly down her high cheekbones. Her skin was the most beautiful light oxblood color a white man had ever seen. She'd had quite a few proposals since the death of her husband, but she politely refused each one. No one could ever compare to her husband. She did not want to be disappointed or to disappoint another man; it wouldn't be fair, she thought.

Que's mom got a tub of warm water ready for him. He spent the next hour soaking his feet in a solution of honeysuckle, jasmine and Arnica Montana, also known as Leopard's Bane until his feet came back to life. Surprisingly he didn't lose any of his toes. She lovingly rubbed his frozen/

burnt feet with kukui nut oil to heal the frost bite. She then wrapped his feet in soft white linen that had been soaking in chickweed oil. That night while his mom stayed in her room and read, he listened to the radio until it was time to go to bed. As much as he wanted to, he just couldn't tell his mom the truth. She agreed to discuss it the next day.

At about midnight, while Que and his mom were sound asleep, Repo revisited the gas station. Before Que locked the place that night Repo had used the men's room, but before he came out, he had unlocked the window that opened to the outside. He'd watched Que remove his new acid eaten shoes then replace them with an old pair. He'd set his eyes on Que's boots and devised a plan to steal them. He was certain Que would not double-check the men's room window.

When he arrived that night, he climbed in through the unlocked window and entered the front room through the bathroom. It was easy for a man as thin as he was. Que would never have been able to get in; he was far too big and broad at the shoulders.

Once up-front Repo grabbed Que's boots that he had left next to the still warm potbelly stove, with boots in hand he exited the same way he had entered. Now that he possessed the boots, he could put his plan into action. He got into his dad's tow truck and drove to Que's home in "The Bottoms" Repo arrived at Que's home shortly after midnight. He cautiously crept up to the window of Que's mom's bedroom. Que's mom always slept with her window open even in the dead of winter. Repo had been to Que's home plenty of times for lunch and dinner and other occasions. He knew the house very well, as well as the behavior of the two somewhat unusual occupants. Repo quietly placed the boots on the floor just inside the window of her bedroom. He then gleefully made his way home. He wasn't sure what to expect the next morning, but he knew it would prove to be a very interesting day.

In the morning Que got up at his usual time to the smell of coffee and a home-made breakfast. After his breakfast, he put on his overalls and his old beat up "good for almost nothing" shoes, but before he did, he stuffed some thick cardboard in them to serve partially as soles. He gave his mom a hug and kiss then left for work. Luckily this day he caught the Dingy at the base of the footbridge which dropped him off about only one mile from the gas station. He made the last mile on foot. By the time he got to work the cardboard soles were soaked and already worn out.

After Que left for work his mom cleaned up the kitchen then sat down for her daily devotions. She then went to the bathroom to take the prescribed medications for her heart, blood pressure and depression. She'd suffered two heart attacks in the past year and one mini stroke. Her doctor had told her to take things very easy and not to ever get overly excited about anything. She'd also been advised to lose some weight. She stood 4' 10' and weighed 166 pounds. Losing weight had always been a challenge for her and her son because their diets consisted mostly of simple carbohydrates. They ate meat, of course, but not that often and not that much. They received very little financial assistance for their medications.

Que's mom had been doing quite well except when it came to her son. She always worried about him even when things appeared normal. The last thing she ever wanted was to see him hospitalized again. Keeping things under control was the order of the day. Woodville was worse than the State penitentiary. If you were crazy when you went in, you'd be crazier when you got out.

After she took her medication, she went to her bedroom to take a rest, but before she did, as always, she went to her window to look out at her favorite tree. It was a weeping willow. She loved that tree and had spent plenty of nights sitting beneath it while observing the night sky. She'd come to know the stars very well, and she especially loved to observe the moon in its mysterious phases; that is when she spotted the boots. At first, she thought she was seeing things, and it frightened her, but then she picked-up the boots. She examined them closely. They were barely recognizable, but sure enough they were Que's new boots. She had sewn a name tag into each boot and added, "I love you, son," beneath Que's name; it was his Indian name, Wathohuck which means "Bright Path. She didn't know what to make of the situation. Why were the boots in her room? How did they get there, and why or how had they been destroyed? Why hadn't her son mentioned the boots? Why had he lied to her? What was going on? She was frightened, and her blood pressure immediately spiked. She felt her chest begin to tighten involuntarily. Her head began to feel funny. She was certain her son must be in big trouble. He had never lied to her in his life. She had to contact him. They didn't have a phone and neither did either of their neighbors. When she looked outside at the Weeping Willow tree it had begun to snow; it was coming down pretty hard, but she knew there was no alternative. She had to make her way to the gas station where her son was probably just opening. She was still clutching the boots and thinking of her son's poor feet. "Oh, my son, Que, what have you done? What is wrong?" she lamented with a broken voice. She got dressed in her best winter coat, grabbed the boots, placed them in a brown paper bag and headed out the door to the gas station. The snow was thick, wet and falling heavier than she'd ever remembered, even in North Dakota.

When Que got to the gas station, he noticed one of Repo's father's tow trucks. This was a curious sight. So, he went up to the truck and noticed Repo sound asleep on the front seat. He knocked on the door and woke him. "Hey, Repo, what are you doing here this time of morning? You never get up this early. Are you crazy or something? It's freezing out here. Come inside and get warm while I start a fire in the pot belly stove and make some coffee," Que said kindly.

Que had the capacity to forgive someone even before they asked for forgiveness. Repo truly had become his best friend, and he figured something very bad must have been bothering him otherwise he would not have treated him so horribly. He'd never ever remembered him being so mean. Maybe

Repo needed someone to talk to, and he didn't know how to do it or who to go to. Repo had always said that his father was never available; he was too busy. Que had always been taught that friends are more important than things. Repo, on the other hand, always seemed indifferent to the needs of other people. He had a reputation for being deceitful, selfish and arrogant. He thought he was always right even when proved to be blatantly wrong. He didn't have any real friends, other than Que, and he didn't care. He liked Que because Que was considered crazy. He got a kick out of communicating with someone who had a mental illness. He found Que to be fun and non-threatening, and he liked to hang out with him, especially down at the gas station where he always made fun of the customers. For some unknown reason Repo was suffering from an inferiority complex and spending time with Que always made him feel superior.

Repo, startled by Que's knocking and kind invitation, got up. He'd been in the truck most of the night waiting for Que's arrival. He followed Que inside and waited for some coffee while the stove began to heat up. Surprised by Repo's presence Que had not immediately noticed that his boots were missing. After he got the fire started and had begun to brew the coffee, he went through his regular opening procedures. He waited on a few regular customers who needed a fill-up, then grabbed a cup of coffee. While sipping on his coffee he was surprised by Repo's silence. By now Repo would have been going-on about some local gossip, the national or international news, sports or some other trivial matter. Que was curious as to why he had been in his father's tow truck instead of his black Buick, but he didn't ask.

All Repo could think about were the boots. When would Que realize they were missing? How would he react? He'd never been more anxious and couldn't wait for Que to discover that his boots were missing.

The snow began to fall even harder making it difficult for Que's mom to maintain her footing. She didn't own a pair of decent shoes. She wore moccasins fashioned by a Chiricahua/Apache squaw from New Mexico. The soles of the moccasins were made of the heavy skin from a buffalo's neck. This was the same material used for Indian shields. It wasn't tanned, but it was dried into rawhide. It was tough and very durable. This Chiricahua/ Apache squaw used an awl that was a six-inch sliver of bone, polished to a fine, slender point at one end for leather piercing. It was rounded at the other end to fit into the palm of the hand for pushing through tough animal hides. This Chiricahua/Apache squaw could have used a steel awl to do her work, but she preferred to do it the way her grandmother did it just like the other Plains Indian women.

Even though this pair of moccasins was knee-high and durable it wasn't long before mother's feet began to get soaked. Her thin black dress, she didn't think a woman should wear pants, was housed beneath a knee-length coat made of buffalo hides and horse leather. These hides had been meticulously sewn together by the same Chiricahua/Apache squaw from New Mexico. It couldn't be proved one way or the other, but she was rumored to have been a distant relative of either Geronimo or Cochise.

Que's mother, despite the cruel weather, was determined to bring her son his damaged boots. She deliberately placed one foot in front of the other and held tightly to the boots and her small bag of special herbs, stones and animal parts called a wotawe. The wotawe represented a special source of magic. The magic power itself was referred to as wakan. Even if she were to die at the end of this journey her son would get his boots back. Her weak heart was indeed breaking, and tears mixed with wet snow covered the skin of her beautiful and flawless oxblood face. It wouldn't be long before she would see her wonderful son, and the mystery of the boots would be solved. The moon was still hanging low in the sky, but the sun was about to rise. Que's mom smoked a peace pipe. She'd brought it with her.

Repo was upset that Que hadn't realized his shoes were missing. He was tempted to say something, but he didn't. Finally, after his second cup of coffee, he said his feet were still freezing, and that he was going to take off his shoes and place his feet nearer to the potbelly stove.

Que then realized that his feet were also still cold and freezing, and that it would be a good idea to put on his boots. Even though they had been partially destroyed they would be safer and warmer that those he was wearing. He looked for his boots where he thought he had left them. The previous night he had deliberately placed them on an empty Pepsi crate just behind the potbelly stove. When he realized they weren't where he was sure he had left them, he grew worried. He thought perhaps he was wrong, and that he had put them somewhere else. After all, he was quite upset and somewhat confused by what had happened between himself and Repo. Maybe he had put them somewhere else. Repo was now watching him very closely but still didn't say a word.

Que couldn't believe his boots were not where he was certain he had left them. He had wanted them to get dry and warm by the heat of the quiet potbelly stove until morning. He didn't want to appear panicked in front of Repo, so he kept quiet and began to look elsewhere. He thoroughly covered every square inch of the front office area; it really wasn't an office. It was a small room where a few items were housed in a small glass case; things like small bags of Wise potato chips, Wrigley's chewing gum, Bazooka bubble gum, Snickers, Mallo-Cups, beef jerky, cigars, cigarette lighters, rubbers, etc. The small cash register was also behind the counter. Cash was the only medium for conducting business, but a few of Mr. Castelluci's customers could buy things on credit, even the gas. Que was responsible for keeping the ledger. He did good job. He had a knack for remembering names, and he could be trusted.

Que's inability to find his boots was beginning to drive him crazy. He even looked in Mr. Castelluci's private office; a decision that made him believe he was losing his mind. He hardly ever went into that office even when Mr.Castelluci summoned him. To him it was off limits. He looked again behind the potbelly stove, thinking the boots might suddenly appear where he knew he had left them. He'd become frantic and almost oblivious to Repo's presence. Que was in trouble, and if he didn't find the boots things might get ugly.

"Repo, watch the front. I need to go into the garage and check the bays," Que said anxiously, but he still did not mention the boots. Que's confusion and manic behavior caused a sense of sinister satisfaction to flood Repo's cruel mind and wicked heart.

"OK, Que. What's the problem? You are behaving rather crazy. What's up?" Repo asked while casually pouring another cup of coffee.

"Nothing. Nothings up. I'll be back in a minute," Que said as he headed out the door. When he got outside, he began to rummage through the garage and the bays like a man possessed. He began to throw things and turn things upside down. He could feel himself heading towards the edge of darkness. He grabbed a hammer and began to pound the carpenter's bench. With each blow, he began to scream for his boots. "Where the fuck are you, boots! Where are my fucking boots! Boots, where the fuck are you! My boots! My boots! My mother's boots, where are you hiding! Come out, come out, wherever you are! Boots! Boots! Boots!" Que, who very seldom used profanity, except in Repo's presence, began to experience an introspective meltdown. He'd been warned more than once that when he became a danger to himself or to another person the hospital was right around the corner. The angrier he got the more he hated himself. He began to berate himself mercilessly, calling himself a fuckin idiot who deserved to be treated like an animal. The inwardly projected venom was driving nails into his skull and wooden beams into his eyes. "Is it any wonder people consider me a retard. I am the epitome of an asshole who deserves to be ridiculed. I should be locked up; make no mistake about that. The only jacket I should ever be caught wearing is a straightjacket." Que wanted to kill himself when he thought of his mother's sacrifice to get him his special boots. And now, they had not only been almost completely ruined; they were lost! And he was responsible. He wished he were a dead man. "Why was I born, anyway? I've been nothing but a burden to everyone I've ever been associated with. Why had I not been one of the lucky ones who'd been aborted or had come back in a body-bag?"

Que's mother was continuing her lonely journey through the wind and snow. Her face was being mercilessly whipped by relentless sheets of sharp wind. She should have worn a scarf to protect her face, but when she looked out her window the weather didn't appear that bad. It had quickly gotten progressively worse. Thank God, she had decided to wear her deer skin gloves, otherwise she may not have been able to hold onto the bag and boots. The boots were well protected. She had wrapped them in plastic before she placed them in the paper bag. She was about forty-five minutes from the garage when she felt a sharp pain in her chest. She stopped momentarily until the pain subsided. Beneath her buffalo skin coat, she was sweating profusely. She'd also suddenly become quite thirsty, so she gathered some snow into her gloved hand and put it into her mouth. Steam appeared to be rising from her head. She had a vision of her son on top of a mountain in a tree. He was precariously sitting on the end of a limb and dangling his feet above a fire. The flames were licking at him, but he was just out of their reach. At the base of the tree an old Indian and old squaw were sharing a peace pipe. Out of nowhere a black crow appeared and softly landed on her son's head. When he tried to shoo it away it quickly dug its sharp claws deeply into his skull. Mysteriously, the crow did not draw blood, but its claws penetrated Que's brain for about a minute, causing a disruption of normal neurotransmitter sequential firing. It withdrew its talons then flew away carrying what looked like a long gray noodle.

Que's self-hatred had not diminished with the blows of the hammer. He remembered hearing somewhere that he had previously been put away because he had become a danger to himself and to others. After he'd been shot-up with a few doses of anti-psychotic neuroleptics he recalled hearing, for the first time, the term, Baker Act. Everyone in the town, thereafter, knew he was a certified screwball, and they treated him as such. The third time he was put away it was after he had doused one of Mr. Castelluci's customers with gas. The customer had come in to get his Cadillac filled-up with "High Test." Que inadvertently began to fill it up with "Low Test." When the customer recognized what Que was doing, he began to scream at him. He called Que a moron and made a reference to Que's mom, implying that she must have mated with a buffalo to produce such a lame-brained, boneheaded, poor excuse for a son. The dousing took place while the man was still seated behind the wheel in a white silk suit. After a thorough dousing with "Low Test," Que ran into the garage to get a lighter. The man had jumped out of the car and began to run down the street. Que pursued him with the lighter threatening to set him on fire. Que could not catch him, so he returned and tossed the lit lighter into the front seat. The Cadillac went up in flames. Que was put away and introduced once again to Thorazine.

"I don't deserve the boots! I don't deserve the boots! I don't deserve the boots! I'm an idiot! I'm a danger to myself and others. Maybe I should hurt myself and someone else as well. Maybe I should scalp someone to show them just how crazy I really am," Que began to rant again while swinging the hammer over his head. He began to do a war dance then calmly placed his hand on the bench and crushed his thumb with a vicious blow from the hammer. After he crushed his thumb he looked up, and he saw Repo staring at him through the window from behind the private counter. Repo was smoking and the smoke appeared to be encircling his head. Que could have sworn that Repo had two horns growing out of both sides of his head. At first Que thought he was looking at a buffalo, but then when Repo came into clearer focus Que recognized him as what the devil might look like. The vision seriously disturbed Que. Something was bad wrong, and he knew it. Repo was enjoying himself. Que's behavior took his mind off his abandoned black Buick, and what had happened in the back seat.

When Que came back inside, he seemed to have immediately calmed down. Repo nonchalantly asked him if he had found what he was looking for. Que didn't answer; he just went into the men's room to bathe his swollen, bleeding thumb While in there he noticed that the window he was sure he had locked the previous night had been left open. He also saw muddy footprints from a pair of shoes that had left a distinct cat's paw emblem on the tile floor. He'd, as always, mopped the men's bathroom floor before he closed. It was one of Mr. Castelluci's pet peeves. He liked clean bathrooms. The snow was blowing into the room so he closed and locked the window. When he returned, he eyed Repo suspiciously but, he said nothing.

Repo, unable to maintain his silence about the boots, finally asked Que a question, but it wasn't about the boots. He asked Que about his thumb and what had happened. Que said he had just accidentally hit it with a hammer. Finally, after about thirty minutes of small talk Repo said he was sorry about what had happened to Que's new boots. His apology caught Que off guard.

"Thanks," Que answered.

"No problem," Repo responded. "Que, I don't want to be nosy, but what is it that you seem to have been looking for? I was watching you through the window, and you looked quite upset, almost mad. Is there anything I can help you with?" Repo asked while lighting up another cigarette.

"Look, Repo, I guess it won't hurt to share my concern with you. I've been looking for my boots. I have no idea where they might be. I purposely left them here last night, because I didn't want my mother to see them in their ruined condition. I knew it would break her heart, and I didn't want to cause her any anxiety. She's not well, you know," Que said as he dipped his swollen thumb, hand and all, into the Pepsi machine. The machine wasn't really a machine at all. It was a case full of various types of pop filled with ice cold water. You would grab the pop of your choice and pay over the counter. Que's favorite drink was Dad's Old-Fashioned Root Beer. It reminded him of the sarsaparilla, a beverage flavored with sassafras and birch oil, his mom would occasionally make.

"Que, all I know about those boots is that you left them here last night right before you closed. I saw you put them right on top of that Pepsi crate behind the potbelly stove. I am certain, because after you left, I peeked in and saw them sitting there." Repo said innocently.

Que was curious as to why Repo would stay behind then look inside to check on the boots he had almost destroyed. Maybe he knew something about the boots that Que didn't. Repo's voice sounded almost anxious; it was as if he couldn't wait to talk about the boots. His tone made Que feel he probably knew something about the boots but was reluctant to share it. Que was no genius, but he had a degree of perception that belied his intelligence. He could read people. It was one of the good things about his manic mind. Sometimes those deranged neurotransmitters acted like radio antennas or the sensitive receivers that emerged from the heads of ants. He was a pretty good judge of character. He always liked Repo, but he also thought there was something sleazy and deceitful about him, nevertheless, he was his friend, and Que needed a friend. His mom once read him an anonymous quote that said, "A man who has one true friend has more than his share." Que never forgot it.

"So, you're saying you actually saw the boots on top of the Pepsi crate. Is that right?" Que asked.

"Yes, exactly. I definitely saw your boots sitting on top of the Pepsi crate last night after you closed the place." Repo answered. He sensed that Que's voice was ever so slightly suspicious about his response.

Que took his hand out of the pop cooler and wrapped it in an oily chamois. He then poured himself a cup of coffee with his right hand and drank from his special cup using his right hand. Que was left-handed. He then pulled up a seat next to Repo. Que sat on a newly arrived box of Quaker

State motor oil. While sipping his coffee he asked Repo if might have any idea where the boots might be.

Repo wanted to say something cruel, but he didn't.

"Gee, Que. I really have no idea. How could they have been there last night and now be gone? How could they have disappeared into thin air? Your guess is as good as mine," Repo answered sounding sincerely dumbfounded. For some strange intuitive reason, consistent with his insight into human behavior, Que did not believe Repo. "Que, are you sure you aren't losing what's left of your mind?"

Que didn't respond. He just casually sipped his coffee then politely asked Repo to remove his sunglasses. Repo was seldom without his sunglasses even in the dead of winter. Que wanted to see his eyes.

"Why do you want me to remove my sunglasses?" Repo asked.

"I just want to look into your eyes while I ask you a few more questions," Que answered.

"Like what?" Repo asked. "Like, what kind of questions?"

"Like, where's your black Buick? Like, why were you here so early this morning? Like, why were you asleep in your dad's tow truck waiting for me to open the garage? Like, why did you stay behind last night and peek through the front window to check on my boots? How's that for starters?" Que asked. "Take off your sunglasses," Que said sternly.

"All right. All right. Don't get so pushy," Repo responded angrily. He took off his sunglasses. "I have nothing to hide. Be my guest."

"OK, now look me square in the eyes," Que said. Repo looked Que square in the eyes. Que just stared at him for about a minute before he spoke. He watched Repo swallow nervously and blink. He didn't seem able to look Que square in the eyes for more than a few seconds.

"Repo, do you know where my boots are?" Que asked casually. His brown eyes looked menacing. Repo felt as if he had just been stripped and was standing before Que completely naked and without excuse. He couldn't respond. It was as if his tongue had been tied in knots. So, he stared back at Que and said nothing. He held the stare uncomfortably for about 10 seconds then said, "Hell, no. I don't know where your stupid boots are. How would I know where your boots are? What do I look like? Some kind of a magician or something? Do I look like Houdini or Svengali? Am I a mind reader? Maybe if you close your eyes and think hard enough, I can pull your ugly boots out a hat just like a rabbit." Repo then jumped up off his chair and told Que that he thought he was crazy. "How in the name of God can you possibly think I know where your boots are! If you don't know where your boots are how do you expect me to know where your boots are? Maybe you stuck them in the potbelly stove and don't remember. You know, you really don't have a very good memory ever since they removed that radical retarded rebellious part of your brain."

"I may not have a very good memory, but let's just say I have a funny feeling that you may have a good idea where my boots are. Call me crazy if you want to, but I think you know exactly where my boots are," Que said confidently and in an unmistakably incriminating tone of voice. He moved slowly closer to Repo and began to stare him down. He then placed his hands gently on Repo's shoulders and held him. This was behavior uncharacteristic of Que who had sworn to never touch another man in the least threatening manner. He'd learned his lesson long ago when had almost crippled a man who had threatened Mr.Castelluci's daughter with bodily harm. But this time it was different. He somehow knew that this was about his poor mother, not his boots.

Que tightened his grip on Repo's shoulders then moved his hands slowly towards Repo's throat. Que was as strong as a bull. He'd once ripped a telephone book into two just to prove a point. He could also hold a ten pounds, Thirty-Six Inch sledge hammer straight out parallel to the floor by the handle. His wrists and forearms were like steel that had been forged by a Pittsburgh blast furnace.

30

"Don't worry, Repo; I'm not going to hurt you. I just want the truth. Now please don't lie to me. I know you were here last night, and that you climbed in through the window into the men's bathroom. Don't ask me how I know. I just know.

Now, please tell me where I can find my boots," Que asked while slowly tightening his grip.

"If I don't tell you, what are you going to do? Scalp me?" Repo asked indignantly.

"Probably not, but I must say it occurred to me yesterday when you ruined my boots. You have no idea what those boots mean to me. You have no idea how hard my mother worked and saved to get me those boots. Repo, I don't know much about your mother, but I know one thing. She never made the kind of sacrifices for you that my mother made for me. You've always had pretty much whatever you wanted. No sacrifices were necessary on your behalf. You've been spoiled. Your black Buick was a graduation gift from your dad. I don't hold that against you; I never have, but my mother and her love are all I have. I'm afraid that if someone deliberately did something to harm my mother, I'd need to be held accountable for my actions even though I'd probably have acted insanely. So, tell me. Where are my boots?" Que asked as he relaxed his grip on Repo's pencil neck.

Once Que released his grip, Repo pushed him off very quickly and quite violently. He knocked Que backwards about four feet towards the door. Repo wasn't that strong, but he had just experienced an adrenaline rush. After he caught his breath and stopped choking, he answered. "You idiot! If you want to know where your stupid boots are just ask your sorry excuse for a mother. She knows where your boots are. Now let me out of here before I call the cops, you mad, retarded, half-baked, half-breed," Repo yelled while once again placing his right hand to his injured throat.

Que's anxiety was contributing greatly to Repo's sinister nature. Even though Que was Repo's best, and possibly only, friend, he still was deriving a great deal of pleasure from Que's manic behavior. Outwardly Repo was friendly and gregarious, but inwardly he was curiously and almost frighteningly introspective and lonely. Repo was a loner. In some ways, he resembled a prowling lone wolf, only he was behind the wheel of a Buick and not hiding in the forest. He prowled indiscriminately seeking those whom he believed he could devour. His victims were usually young and gullible. He also had a way of keeping things quiet.

"My mother! Did you just say that my mother knows where my boots are?" Que asked Repo in an anxious and surprised voice of unbelief. This reference to his mother and his boots in the same breath coming from Repo caused an intuitive sense of alarm and fear. He wanted to desperately check himself lest he do something he might regret for the rest of his life, but his mother his mother.

"Yeah, you heard me, "Big Little Retard Man, "You, pitiful excuse for a brave who can't hold his firewater and is afraid of horses. Your mother probably did it with a donkey inside a tepee, and out came a perfect little ass except for his brain. They nicknamed him Que from day one because he resembled a question mark. Before you go for your tomahawk, 'winkte,' I'll bet you three scalps that your mother knows exactly where your precious boots are," Repo said in the most denigrating and humiliating voice he could muster.

The ugly remarks Repo made about Que's mother caused a serious discharge of misfiring neurons, but the subsequent remarks about him and the ultimate insult of referring to him as a 'winkte' was more than Que could stand. The Sioux referred to a 'winkte' as a "two-souled person," by which was meant a man with womanly qualities. A 'winkte' was not a hermaphrodite, as some would have it, but an effeminate man-in fact, a homosexual. That just about did it, but then Repo added more fuel to the fire. He obviously wanted Que to do something stupid, something that might send him back to Woodville, the psyche hospital up on the hill just outside the city limits.

"What do you suppose people say about a man your age who still lives with his mommy? A man who obviously has never been kissed, who has never been on a date, who pulls his pants down in front of little girls and boys and, whose refrigerator always contains at least one pound of raw calf liver?"

Repo's mother got pregnant when she was seventeen. At that time abortions were not being legally performed, and as much as she wanted to have the baby, her boyfriend at the time, Repo's father, didn't want to have anything to do with a baby, and he certainly did not want to get married. So, he arranged to take her up to the "Hill District" to visit a notorious Haitian woman. This woman was said to be able to abort an unborn child using a coat hanger. After a painful bloody mess and $20.00 the procedure didn't work. Repo's mom and dad got married and nine months later Repo was born.

Que did not lose his mind, but he did see red, and the drums along the Mohawk were incessantly beating. He lunged towards Repo and grabbed him by the throat; only this time he began to squeeze Repo so hard that he could not respond. Repo fought back, but to no avail. Que was too strong to begin with, but now he was filled with prehistoric power resembling a Neanderthal fighting with a wild boar. Repo, however, moved their struggling locked bodies behind the counter in front of the main window. Que shoved Repo's head through the window shattering the glass. While still holding onto Repo with their bodies hanging half way out of the window, Que spotted a mysterious body making its way to the station. The person was covered head to toe with snow and looked like a walking snowman. However, Que recognized a familiar pipe sticking out of its mouth and the pattern of smoke signals swirling around the person's face. Was he imagining things, or could this be his mother?

When Que's mom recognized him, she began to move as fast as she could towards him. It was obvious to her that her son was in trouble. Something was dramatically wrong, and she knew intuitively that it had something to do with the boots. As she began to move faster towards him the snow was impeding her effort. The resistance, the snow was about 8 inches high, and the sight of her precious son, began to drive her heart rate up to a dangerously high level. The blood vessels in her head began to swell and were about to burst. The pain and the impending morbidity of her actions could not stop her. Her entire being: mind, body and soul were about to infarct, but this was her son, her one and only son, and he was in trouble. He needed her.

His mom was now within fifteen feet of him. She called out to him, "Usta la shondai, untye a bowtye. Sela lamachthanee. Tieshocja thanai Hua Hua." The words of his mother struck his heart like a friendly arrow launched from the bow of Crazy Horse. He immediately released his grip on Repo's throat, jumped over his limp body out of the broken window, and ran towards his mom, who had fallen into 8 inches of snow face down. She was clutching to the bag of boots with all her might. She'd dropped her magic bag earlier but had never realized it.

When Que reached her, he turned her onto her back. She was breathing heavily and about to give-up the ghost; this was a cliché she often used when referring to a person who was close to death, and Que appreciated it because of the historical significance of The Ghost Dance. Que began to wipe her flushed, semi-frozen face and to smooth her wet hair. She opened her eyes momentarily and seemed to smile. He clutched her body tightly to his chest and kissed her cheeks. Que was certain his mom would not die. She couldn't. She shouldn't, and he wouldn't let her. She was trying to speak, but she couldn't because Que was holding onto her weak body too tightly. He slowly released her and set her body gently on the snowy ground. He studied her beautiful face. This was not the first time he'd seen an angel with big brown friendly eyes, prominent cheekbones and flawless brown naturally tanned skin. She died in his arms, but before she did, she told him she had brought him his special boots. She told him how they had suddenly appeared in her room at the base of the window. The last word out of her mouth was "Repo."

After Que had released his grip on Repo and had run towards his mom, Repo grabbed the phone and called the police. He immediately asked for Sergeant Anthony Pasquale. "Tony, this is Repo," he said.

"Repo, what's up?" Sergeant Pasquale asked. Pasquale was a friend of Repo's. They played on the same basketball team, and they had been known to arrest teenage girls on false pretenses like "Going through a stop sign or a red light," then demand sexual favors to avoid giving the girl a ticket and having their parents notified. Pasquale was an oily, olive-skinned, typical dago whore with an obese, frigid wife and three beautiful daughters. He ran the numbers racket in town.

"Que is at it again. He is in a state of mind that makes him an immediate danger to himself and to others. I am afraid of what he might do. Tony, trust me on this one. If you don't get here quickly something regrettably horrible is about to happen," Repo said in a most urgent and alarming voice. Tony wanted some details, but Repo gave none. He just said that they had better send a squad car and an ambulance down to the gas station immediately, if they knew what was good for them. He said to be sure to come with a partner and to make certain there were at least four paramedics, and not to forget the straight-jacket.

Repo watched from the window as Que held his mom with one hand and opened the bag containing his new boots with the other. Que immediately put two and two together and realized that Repo had broken into the gas station last night and had stolen his boots. Somehow, he had delivered them that night to his house and left them where his mom would find them. While pondering why Repo would do such a thing after he had already destroyed them confused Que. But, he didn't spend much time trying to figure out why. All he knew was that his mom was dead. She had walked two miles in a blizzard to bring him his boots and had died doing so. Her heart had given out due to the physical and emotional stress. That much was obvious, and Repo was responsible. Que placed the boots and the peace pipe on his mom's stomach then picked her up and began to walk towards the front room of the gas station. The snow was very deep, and he had to take one careful giant step after the other. He was careful not to fall. The tears bleeding down his cheeks were hot, and his throat was partially closed off. His heart had just been irretrievably broken. His life had suddenly lost its meaning. The pistons banging against the sides of hardened skull were about to shatter any semblance of sanity, and he would no longer be responsible for his actions once his skull collapsed.

Repo was now at the opened door watching Que's approach. His first instinct was to run, but he wanted to get a closer look at Que's busted face. So, he waited for Que to bring his mom inside. Repo was firmly holding a tire iron in his right hand.

Que got his mom inside, but before he laid her down, he firmly told Repo to grab the paper bag that contained the boots and the peace pipe. Repo didn't hesitate; he grabbed the bag and pipe. He realized he was now holding Que's new boots. Que made a makeshift bed for his mom and laid her next to the hot potbelly stove. He wanted her to get warm. He again wiped her face and smoothed back her thick, black, braided hair. He opened her buffalo coat, made her comfortable then massaged her stiff frozen hands.

While Que was kneeling beside his mom, he looked up at Repo who was holding the boots in one hand and the tire iron in the other. Que then spoke calmly while addressing Repo, "Repo it is a good day to die." The look on Que's face, the busted face Repo longed to see, told Repo that something very, very bad was about to happen. He began to wonder how long before Sergeant Pasquale and the paramedics would show up. He knew his life was in danger, so when Repo looked back down at his mom and bent down to kiss her, Repo struck him directly on the top of his head with the tire iron. He then bolted out the door, carrying the boots with him, and headed for his father's tow truck, but not before he threw the peace pipe into the potbelly stove.

The blow from the tire iron lacerated Que's scalp, and the blood began to flow down his face. However, he did not seem in the least bit phased, and he ran after Repo, who had made it to the tow truck faster than a Snowshoe Rabbit. Que wasn't one bit slower. He got to the truck and almost pulled the truck door off its hinges. His face was a bloody mess, and so were his hands from wiping the blood out of his eyes.

Pasquale had hung up the receiver after Repo's call, then returned to finish a few hands of poker with the boys. He was having a very good day; he'd won the majority of the pots and wasn't about to stop to Baker Act some helpless, innocent Indian who'd recently had a lobotomy at the skilled hands of Dr. Walter Freeman. The kid wouldn't hurt a fly. Besides, Repo had been known to exaggerate while making mountains out of mole hills. Pasquale would get to the gas station when he was good and ready.

Que grabbed Repo, who was clinging to the steering wheel of the truck and yanked him free. He then dragged him through the thick deep snow into the second bay of the garage. He wrapped his arms around him and applied a bear hug that could have killed a brown Kodiak bear. He squeezed Repo so tight that his eardrums burst, his nose began to bleed, his eyes almost popped out of their sockets, and he began release a putrid smelling foam from his mouth that resembled cobra venom. After every ounce of breath had been squeezed out of Repo's body Que let him fall to the ground like a limp rag doll. He then went into the next bay and moved a 50 Gallon drum of grease. Beneath the floor where the drum had been sitting Que had fashioned a hiding place where he kept a special tomahawk and knife. The tomahawk and knife had been given to him by his grandfather, a close friend of Geronimo. He returned to where Repo lay dead and carefully positioned Repo's head against the concrete floor.

When Que was six years old, he liked to play "Cowboys and Indians." Of course, he played an Indian. When he would capture a cowboy, he would remove his play rubber tomahawk from his leather belt, raise it above his head and threaten the cowboy with a deadly scalping. The cowboy could always be heard by the other boys screaming, "Don't scalp me, Chief Que! Please don't scalp me, Chief Que!" Que put the tomahawk and knife down carefully then went out into the snow and washed his head and face thoroughly using the snow. He entered the front of the building to check on his mom. After making certain that she was comfortable he said a prayer then went into the men's room to examine his face. What he saw he didn't like. It wasn't so much the severe laceration inflicted by his friend, Repo, that was still bleeding, it was the scar that ran across his forehead from ear to ear. The scar was a constant reminder that his brain had been scrambled by an unsuccessful full-frontal lobotomy. The good news was that his unsuccessful lobotomy had been followed up shortly thereafter by a visit to Dr. Walter Freeman's office.

Dr. Walter Freeman had become known as the Henry Ford of psychosurgery. He didn't invent the procedure, but he turned it into an assembly-line process, streamlining it so it could be done more efficiently, more cheaply, more quickly and on more patients. In his life-time it has been estimated that Freeman performed more than 5,000 lobotomies, and people taught by him may have done more than 40,000. In one year, Freeman visited hospitals in seventeen states. He also made presentations in Canada, Puerto Rico, and South America. On one five-week driving tour of America, he visited eight states and performed 111 lobotomies. He made these tours driving a specially outfitted car that he called "The Lobotomobile." The first one was a custom-fitted Lincoln Continental. Later he chose a van. Besides carrying photographic equipment to make records of the surgeries, a card catalog of patients' records, a Dictaphone to make notes while driving, and his instruments, he also carried a portable electroshock machine. Freeman became so adept at performing prefrontal lobotomies that he could perform one in less than fifteen minutes. Sometimes he performed a simultaneous two-handed lobotomy, severing both lobes at the same time with a flourish-just like he had impressed his medical students by using two hands to write on the blackboard at the same time.

While studying his face in the mirror Que had a flashback to his visit with Dr. Freeman. He didn't remember much, but he was later told that he had been the recipient of the classic Dr. Freeman trans-orbital lobotomy. The new procedure did not need to be done in a hospital. There was no cutting, no drilling, there would be no surgeon, no anesthesiologist, no hospital stay and almost no recovery time. Que was stretched out on a table. Electroshock was administered, then his skull was punctured by a Uline ice pick. The ice pick was driven alternately through each orbit of his eye then swung back and forth across his frontal lobes in a determined manner to scramble his brain adequately to produce the intended result.

Freeman performed the first trans-orbital lobotomy in 1946. He used an ice pick on his first patient. He saved the ice pick. It's in the Washington, D.C. archives. It says "Uline Ice Company" on the handle. Later, Freeman introduced orbitoclasts in place of the ice-picks. "Orbitoclast" was the name Dr. Freeman coined to refer to his personally designed lobotomy knives.

After the operation Que was nauseous and he had a horrible headache. He was dizzy and he moved like a zombie from Dr. Freeman's office to Repo's waiting black Buick. The next day he had two black eyes, and he was still nauseous, but he felt calm and relaxed.

Que left the men's room and was about to return to where Repo was laying on the cold concrete floor, but before he did, he kneeled beside his mom for the second time. He noticed that her eyes, which he had gently closed earlier, had somehow reopened. He shut them for the last time.

Now he was kneeling beside Repo with the tomahawk in one hand and the knife in the other. He didn't spend much time thinking about his relationship with Repo. He just couldn't figure out why Repo had turned on him, and why he had wanted to destroy his special boots. So, he just raised the tomahawk with his injured left hand and brought it swiftly and forcefully down across Repo's forehead. The blow caused a deep gash exposing Repo's skullcap. He then took his knife and with his right hand began to carefully scalp him. He ran the blade from left to right creating a deep incision around the perimeter of his skull beginning at the point where the tomahawk had split him open. The sharp blade thereafter slid easily through Repo's flesh from front to back and side to side. The messy, bloody scalp dangled from Que's hand in a somewhat bizarre fashion due to Repo's comb-over. Que swung the dangling scalp back and forth for about thirty seconds before he examined Repo's exposed brain. It looked dark in there to him, and he wondered what made Repo tick. He wanted to plunge his hand into the soft convolutions, but he didn't. He just knelt beside him and stared at his face. His eyes were open. Que did not close them as he had his mom's. The raging inferno Repo had ignited in Que's bosom had now been doused, but the ashes of his mom's death would remain.

When Sergeant Pasquale and the paramedics finally showed-up they found Que sitting in the front room of the gas station. He had handcuffed his left foot to his mom's right foot. He was sitting on an empty Pepsi crate. He had Repo's scalp in his hand, and he was wearing his new boots.

Que did not resist, but the paramedics played it safe. They shot him up with a heavy tranquilizer, removed the handcuffs to separate him from his mom, then placed him in the back seat of Pasquale's squad car. The paramedics attended to his mom and Repo while waiting for additional help. Once the detectives and additional medical help arrived Pasquale pulled out of the driveway of the gas station. Just as he was pulling out with a semi-conscious Que in the back seat on their way to the hospital, he noticed something very strange. It was Repo's father arriving with his son's black Buick in tow. He was being followed by a Pennsylvania State Trooper.

The next morning Que woke up in Woodville, the infamous hospital for the criminally insane. His precautionary restraints had been removed, and he was able to aimlessly wander the halls with the rest of the zombies.

While these men moved from place to place, they didn't walk; they shuffled. They moved as if they were ships without rudders until some kind intern took them by their hand and brought them safely back to shore. Their almost involuntary movements would later be cruelly described as "The Thorazine Shuffle."

Que recognized a few patients from his previous visits. Some were in wheelchairs, some on walkers, some moved with canes, some were confined to bed, some actually walked, but they all had a number of things in common. Their faces looked like either soft, jaundiced, stretched, blanched dough or buttermilk pancakes that had not been flipped. They were all once newborn babies full of hope and promise.

Their eyes looked like glazed bottomless pools full of forgotten hemorrhaged memories floating mostly face down. Some of the memories looked like black and blue subdural hematomas due to head injuries. Others resembled herniated expressions that had been rudely ruptured by the caustic of relentless criticism that engendered self-loathing, poor self-esteem, and a poor self-image. Most patients dangled in limbo like galactic imploded black holes where neither space, nor time, nor matter existed. If time, as we know it, did exist, it had forgotten them. Some labored hard beneath pile driving memories that had stuck to the roofs of their mouths as guilty reminders of having been born out of synch with the rest of society. These were hideously dark places their tongues could not reach, though not as troublesome as the fish bones stuck in their throats by friends and family members; constant reminders of the first time they had to swallow their pain like medicine and to do so without objection for the good of themselves, their family members and society. A gray-blue discoloration graced their drooping eyelids. They were either constipated or suffered from diarrhea. All had altered consciousness and had experienced psycho-motor retardation along with neurological movement disorders. These disorders frequently found them in catatonic states manifesting either muscle rigidity or ballistic dystonic states that mimicked karate-like shadow boxing. Most of the men didn't have much to say, at least anything that was of any consequence, except when they were in therapy, and even then, they were never able to get to the root cause of their problem without either breaking down into shards of sharp glass like a fallen, helpless Humpty Dumpty or left floating in mindless meaningless puddles of denial that often gave way to bitterness, resentment and self-hatred. That is precisely why, among a myriad of other reasons, they found themselves participating in the "Thorazine Shuffle" while, once again, being housed in "One Size Fits All" chemical straightjackets.

Que finished his breakfast then shuffled back to his room. After about an hour of waiting he was eventually visited by Doctor Szyprka. Doctor Szyprka had Que's chart in his left hand and a flashlight in his right. He barely acknowledged Que's presence then quickly examined Que's eyes with his flashlight, asked him to stick out his tongue, checked his pulse, used the stethoscope to check his breath sounds, made some notes on Que's chart, then sat down on the chair next to the bed.

After about fifteen minutes of chit-chat Dr. Szyprka was about to leave when Que registered his complaint.

"Doctor S, why is it that the only time you ever visit me is when I am in the hospital?"

The Escapee

The reason most escapes were attempted in broad daylight was due to human energy levels. Energy levels were the benchmarks by which every action, good or bad, was measured, and percentages were meaningless because no one had ever escaped. There was always a lot of talk about it, but very few attempts had ever been made. When energy audits were conducted the expectations were always higher than when the previous audit had been conducted. Conservation was tantamount to success, and that is why 'energy exchanges' were so important, and why it had been deemed more important to receive than to give. That is also why some of the weaker members were always on the giving end. Under our present circumstances "might seemed to make right," seemed, to make right.

The energized state of an inmate was always rather obvious. His behavior was perceived as if he had just received a mega ton jolt of BTU's; a jolt that exponentially increased his energy level thereby characterizing him as a superior quantum mechanical being. In this system there was very little 'give and take.' It was mostly 'take' even though it was sometimes difficult to distinguish between what actually represented giving and/or taking. Occasionally quantum leaps and bounds in energy consumption were experienced, but they were never systemic; they were always extracorporeal and even sometimes synthetic.

They said the effect of spending too much time in the sun could result in a case of sunspots, those darkened, irregular areas on the photosphere capable of turning a man black and somewhat lethargic, not exactly a desirable condition when compared to the plethora of arrogant and bigoted auroras, the high-energy atomic particles that are a more awesome and a much more eerie natural phenomena. One would do well to never appear lazy, and skin color could be a dead giveaway. As a result, natural sunlight, while necessary to get sufficient vitamin D for the promotion of proper bone growth, was rationed. Sun rays captured in tin cans were available on the black market, but being caught with one of these cans was tantamount to opening up a can of worms, maggot food, as it was euphemistically referred to in the camp.

At night there obviously was no visible sun, and the sun was the energy source required to restore an individual's strength. No sun, no conversion of four hydrogen atoms into a single helium atom, and, thereby, no energy from nuclear fusion. In fact, escapes at night were not only foolhardy but almost impossible. It was never a question of being seen; it was only ever a question of getting out, because if one could get out, even if it were just getting out into the heavily guarded courtyard, one minute in the sun would create enough kinetic energy to think rationally. The rays of the sun would kick-start the dormant neurotransmitters and enable one to put up a fight with the brain trust of Dr. Hydrocephalus. However, even though guns were not permitted as a means of subduing prisoners who might attempt escape, the guards had a more potent weapon. They controlled the shadows, and they were absolute perfectionists when it came to casting them. They knew exactly how to keep a prisoner in the dark who might be considering escape.

Dr. Hydrocephalus had discovered a way to turn a flashlight or spotlight into a shadow-light. Not even his most brilliant scientists had ever been able to determine how he had developed such a miraculous invention. They'd disassembled the shadow-light down to its simplest components and could never comprehend how it worked. All they ever ended-up with were a bunch of bolts, screws, nuts, filaments, metal, plastic and glass, but no logical means of producing shadows. No matter what approach they took to disassemble then reassemble the shadow-light the parts they always came-up with resembled those of the common flashlight. Dr. Hydrocephalus had offered any man who could duplicate his shadow-light 1000 volts of their favorite energy, but he never had to award the energy because no one had ever come close to duplicating the famous shadow-light. One beam of the shadow-light was more powerful than the most sophisticated laser and could expose every nerve ending, muscle, bone and organ in the human body and transmogrify a man into a an anatomy chart. Just one pass of the shadow-light across a man's forehead could instantly invoke a soliloquy by him during which he would begin to tell the unbridled truth about himself. No questions need be asked. He would just begin to ramble on until the shadow-light was passed across his forehead in the opposite direction. Occasionally, when the light was just right, you could see shadowy figures, objects of incredible fascination, walking casually among the men. Sometimes the shadows danced their way into the compound, huddled together in the middle of the yard, got on their knees, held hands and prayed for someone to haunt, based on his level of abstract energy. Many an inquisitive inmate had become possessed by a particular shadow he would never be able to shake, a shadow he would have been better off never having cast. If two shadows ever became attracted to one another and the interception of their radiation had become nullified they might become sexually involved and produce a ghost. Two ghosts occasionally became intimately involved and produced a ghoul. Yes, ghouls had been spotted in the cemetery where the energy depleted souls of departed iconoclasts had been laid to rest. These morbid, loathsome grave robbers were not a threat to the living, and they were tolerated and sometimes even welcome at group sessions; occasionally one of them might lead a séance.

The doctor's bizarre brain trust was composed of men, most of whom had I.Q.'s of 150 or better, and who had been endowed with superior physical characteristics, as well as minds that were capable of moving mountains.

These Mensa Society-type men handled intellectual debate like hydra-headed monsters who would thrust and parry then divide and conquer. We knew better than to debate them, but they had an uncanny way of baiting you and then drawing you to your death; they moved like Black Widow Spiders in drag whose distended bellies were full of deceit, and who were able to capture gullible men full of envy, lust, naivete and pride. It never failed to amaze me how many men would debate with these intellectual giants only to be humiliated and stripped of any semblance of intelligence.

Once one of the most brilliant inmates nicknamed Hercule took on these intractable, mythological monsters, but he was soundly defeated. His philosophical position of 'parsimony,' better known as Occam's Razor, or the principle that "The simplest explanation for a phenomenon is most likely the correct explanation" was shredded into an infinite number of particles and found to be almost laughable by the brain trust. He was especially humiliated when he attempted to support his position by quoting St. Thomas Aquinas who said " If a thing can be done adequately by means of one, it is superfluous to do it by means of several; for we observe that nature does not employ two instruments where one suffices." Antediluvian, Neanderthal, archaic, prehistoric, folderol, infantile, were just some of the words they applied to his thinking. They pointed out to him that as long ago as the 20th century epistemological justifications based on induction, logic, pragmatism, and probability theory had become more popular among philosophers. Quite frankly, they informed him, that science, itself, tends to prefer the simplest explanation that is consistent with the data available at a given time, but history shows that these simplest explanations often yield to complexities as new data becomes available. The reasonableness of parsimony in one research context may have nothing to do with its reasonableness in another. It is a mistake to think that there is a single global principle that spans diverse subject matter.

Hercule was not convinced by their logic and refused to recant. Furthermore, he referred to the Trust as a bunch of eggheaded ostriches who had buried their swollen heads beneath the sands of empirical evidence, narcissistic men who insisted on climbing The Tower of Babel and whose thoughts ran along circuitous exponential patterns. Thereafter, Hercule, was relegated to cleaning out the numerous septic tanks of the compound with his bare hands. Nevertheless, and in spite of overwhelming odds, some fools still came forward from time to time to challenge this constellation of men who hung out in the equatorial region of the southern sky by the necks of their telescopes like a herd of quantum entanglements living on the cusp of the razor's edge.

So with these facts and stats on hand and intellectual failure seemingly inevitable I crawled into the tunnel, my soon to be womb or tomb. I would either emerge newborn or as a mummy wrapped in silk pajamas. It was high noon. I had been digging this tunnel with my spoon for about six years. It had taken me that long to dig the 1000 yard tunnel because I barely had enough energy to chew my food and considerably less energy to swallow it. It is a wonder that we had any energy left at night at all based on the system developed by the quintessential narcissist, Dr. Hydrocephalus; a system designed to build his grand city, a metropolis based on Nebuchadnezzar's Hanging Gardens. He drove his taskmasters like Pharoah, and they in turn drove us like Hebrew slaves. Rebellion was out of the question. Our numbers were far too small, and as a race we could not proliferate like the Hebrews. Births in the camp were extremely rare. Adoption was the method advancing the cause. Kidnapping was also employed to add to the numbers. Births, if any, were by natural selection and dictated by butchers in white coats, iron-fisted men who loved to feast on barbecued afterbirths.

When we slept we always had to sleep on our backs. This was easy to do because we were strapped down in such a way as to always be facing east. We were never uncomfortable, however, because of the elixir provided eighteen minutes before bedtime. One of the inmates by the name of Curie said he thought the elixir was synthetic L-tryptophan, a precursor to serotonin, a neurotransmitter involved in a number of somatic functions including sleep. In the morning when the sun came up a peep hole was opened in the ceiling to let a diffused ray of light into our individual rooms. The beam was focused directly towards the center of our foreheads where the magic disc had been subcutaneously implanted the day of our arrival. I later discovered that the disc was fashioned like a pine cone and located in a pocket near the splenium of the corpus collosum. This is the major site of melatonin biosynthesis. The effect of melatonin on humans and the exact function of the pineal gland remain unknown, but there is evidence that inhibition of secretion from the pineal gland is associated with the onset of puberty.

This suspicious implantation of the mysterious disc may have had something to do with the preponderance of grown men roaming the compound like overgrown children. They all dressed the same and had taken an oath of allegiance to Dr. Hydrocephalus. Each had blond hair and blue eyes and spoke in very high pitched tones. They also spoke a second language known only to them and to Dr. Hydrocephalus that sounded like Pig Latin but was much more sophisticated. Their square looking heads were rather large for their bodies and looked like sophisticated transistor radios with ears that appeared as rather large knobs. I discovered one day that these knobs, the external auditory canals which these men possessed, were capable of housing 7,000 inner hair cells, twice the number of the average person. A normal youthful ear can hear ten octaves of sound, spanning a range from about thirty to twelve thousand vibrations a second. These men could extend the octaves to as many as thirty and the vibrations close to one hundred thousand. We were convinced that these men could hear through the thickest of walls. Frequently they would ask us what we had been whispering about from across the one hundred yard courtyard where they had been nonchalantly standing. Furthermore, there wasn't an ectomorph among them.

There was never more than one man in a room at any given time except on Sundays. This was our proverbial day of rest when stronger prisoners were paired with the weaker ones in an attempt to exchange stored energy.

We were told this would be an excellent way to be our brother's keeper. Otherwise, certain weaker inmates whose cells were low might die. We knew better, however. It was just another way to save money and to demean us. I had developed a reputation as the strongest man in the compound, and I never had to take another man's energy, but I had to always give up some of mine. I did what I had to do for the survival of the camp, but I didn't like it.

My vision of setting the prisoners free had never changed, and I would pay just about any price to make my dream a reality. We had not been born to live unnatural lives; the result of some bizarre theory of natural selection that would render us worthless, helpless, hopeless and devoid of any common spiritual bond. There was much more to life than living in an anabolic state where metabolism was expected to grow exponentially and where men were judged by their resemblance to cytoplasms, and where it might be possible to see men with minus body fat percentages training personal trainers who would then be training other personal trainers. Catabolism was a four letter word.

The day I got down into the tunnel I knew I had just this one chance to be free. If I got caught I would spend the rest of my life confined to an oblong black box, and I would be sustained by artificial light, except for the days of the month when the moon would be full. The artificial light was filtered through a mask which the man would be required to wear while in the box; it diffused light into geometric patterns. The mask had a small circuit board made-up of bipolar cells given to rapid cycling; these cells represented atomic building blocks for matter that could corral radical velocities predisposed to consume the speed of light. This provided the power for the intermittent repetitious emissions of messages designed to redeem us. There was no guarantee, however, that you could survive the ordeal and/or be redeemed.

Occasionally a man would be set free from the confines of the box, but only after he had submitted to an intellectually induced mental metamorphosis and emerged with imaginary wings and a spirit of abject humility. No one ever wanted to be sent to the box. It was the proverbial 'kiss of death' as far as one's imagination was concerned. Picture a grown man whose brain stem auditory evoked potential had become silenced by a shunt plunged into his neck and whose eyesight had been impaired by induced macular degeneration, a man who could only see peripherally in a maze with neither left nor right hand turns. Picture a zombie in striped prison attire with the affect of a buttermilk pancake.

On those nights when the moon was full the ominous looking box would be brought outside the camp and hung by a thick bungee cord from an old oak tree. The recalcitrant occupant hung there looking like a butterfly in the pupa stage. The lunar light of the full moon was a subtle way of torturing those who were hungry for the real thing, the light of the sun.

Something about the moonlight could drive a man crazy; it could turn a genius into a lunatic. It was as if the lunar tides were pulling his brain stem with an irresistible force, a force designed to separate him from his real personality, his hippocampus and the ability to remember. One inmate who had failed in his attempt to escape described his time in the box this way, " The pull of the tide was like experiencing a transorbital lobotomy while awake and watching the removal of your scrambled frontal lobe along with the real you, later to be lapped-up by the beckoning undulations of The Black Sea." The interesting thing about being in the box was that you were never looked upon, and you could either be dead or alive. In other words, according to Dr. Hydrocephalus, you were living in a state of superposition. The principle of superposition claims that while we do not know what the state of any object is, it is actually in all possible states simultaneously as long as we don't look and check. It is the measurement itself that causes the object to be limited to a single possibility. Of course, this was just one more of the good doctor's quantum hobby horses he would ride hard then put up wet.

Once in the tunnel one of my companions repacked the dirt and covered the hole. I began to slowly crawl my way to freedom and the ultimate freedom from the confines of the camp. I believed I had stored up enough energy from the sun to complete the journey. I had also gathered additional energy drawn from mutated plant life, fish eggs and some confiscated gonadotrophic hormones derived from the loins of a lamb without spot or blemish. I kept this extra energy in a stainless steel canteen. Breathing was difficult, but I had anticipated the problem by furrowing holes up through the earth every ten yards. I expected to reach daylight in approximately eight hours. My determination had become electric based on my potential to achieve absolute zero, a temperature of -459.67 F, and to emasculate Dr. Hydrocephalus by possessing 'absolutely' no thermal energy.

The size of the tunnel was such that I could only inch my way along. I had to travel on my back; this way I could access the air provided every ten yards or so by strategically furrowed lifelines. If the access had been blocked, which I had expected, I would shove a dowel up through the earth followed by a hollow plastic reed for the required oxygen. There was only room in the tunnel for one body with no room to pass. I felt like an animal, but no less an animal than the way we were treated in the camp. If it meant freedom I would crawl on my hands and knees, beg like a dog and lick the boots of my captors. But, with regard to my dignity, that was another matter altogether. I had made a vow to never be demeaned by compromising my ethics and/ or morals even though I had been accused of the unethical treatment of animals. The animals in question were pigs that had been caught snooping in the dorms looking for Goldberg's contraband kosher corned beef. Yes, there were Jews in the camp, but they would just as soon give up a pound of flesh as they would demand one. They were highly energetic intellectually, but they had a knack for wearing an inmate down and depleting them of precious energy. Even under the most dire circumstances they bargained intensely until they had accumulated mounds of stored energy, but no group was respected more. There was something chosen about them.

I slowly pushed my body forward with the force of my feet. I got some help from my hands and forearms. My journey was uneventful for the first four hours, then I hit a snag. The Hydrocephalus Youth Group had decided to camp out near the perimeter of the field-house for the weekend. Of all places they erected their tent directly above my pathway, and I would be required to pass beneath them. Remember, my tunnel was no more than two feet below the earth's surface. It wasn't likely, but it might be possible to detect the movement of the earth if I had to struggle more than usual. I'd also needed to be particularly careful not to sneeze or cough violently.

I couldn't believe what was about to happen. The boys decided to build a campfire right above my line of direction. They hollowed out about six inches of earth, loaded the hole with twelve foil wrapped potatoes and ears of corn then covered them with charcoal. They stacked wood above the charcoal then layered the wood with bacon fat, then soaked the perimeter with lighter fluid and started the fire. Continuing now would be impossible. The depth of the fire and the heat made it too dangerous. So I decided to stop and wait it out.

Apparently this weekend was being devoted to a mysterious and secretive indoctrination, a type of preparatory to manhood, a circumcision of the mind. Dr. Hydrocephalus always said, "Raise up a child in the way he should go, and when he is old he will never depart from it." The twelve boys would be chaperoned by The Chief Executive Officer who would lead them through a series of steps, after which they would be considered men; this rite of passage was formulated to reinforce the ranks of Dr. Hydrocephalus's military youth movement, a boot camp designed to equip the boys with metaphysical mind altering psychological weapons. It was a rite we had heard about but had never witnessed. We just witnessed the results, men without chests/consciences but backbones made of steel forged in the fires of narcissism, prodigies who could bend spoons with their minds and sleep on beds of nails. Young men who, by the way, could also produce astonishing amounts of kinetic art.

The Chief Executive Officer was the second most powerful man in the cabinet, second only to the good doctor himself. He was a very muscular man and extremely handsome. He was 6 ft. 6 inches tall and weighed 240 pounds and perfectly symmetrical from head to toe. He wore his blond hair in a sharp crew cut. His exophthalmic eyes could not have been much bluer. Perhaps the most commanding thing about him, however, was his voice. Every syllable of every word, in fact, every letter of every word, was always fitly spoken and had meaning. Some men could hypnotize you with their eyes; the Chief Executive Officer could hypnotize you with his voice. When he spoke he spoke irresistible commands that were eagerly and almost anxiously followed. His sentences hung in the air like food then landed at your feet like manna. The most unusual fact about him was his tail; he actually had the tail of a reptile similar to that of an alligator's. His tail was six feet long in the relaxed state, but when he was angry and wanted to get something done which required super-human effort his tail elongated to 18 feet, three six foot sections. With his tail he could wipe out anything or anyone who stood in his path. He also had two ominous looking flesh colored horns protruding from his frontal lobe. The horns were a part of his skull. In the relaxed state when he wasn't angry they appeared to be about two inches in height, but when he got excited or angry they extended to eight inches. It was rumored that these horns were telepathic receivers with which he could read your mind. I'd seen him turn grown men into embarrassing puddles of limp emasculated clay with one nonchalant statement or question. Fortunately I had been able to avoid eye contact with him over the years, and for some strange reason he never seemed to want to pursue an encounter with me. However, one day he did cast his shadow and, either inadvertently or on purpose, he dropped me to my knees in the outer courtyard where I had been doing full squats with 600 pounds. I never knew what hit me, but one of my friends told me that the Chief Executive Officer decided to whimsically cast a giant shadow in my direction. I'd never seen it, but it was rumored that he had squatted with 1200 pounds, exactly five times his bodyweight. He had been clocked in the forty in just under three seconds. There was an eerie sense of jet propulsion about him. He regularly consumed gigantic slabs of raw beef and swilled goat's milk mixed with blood and honey. His favorite appetizer was brainstem tempura. Dessert could be any of a variety of chocolate covered vital organs. He also ate light bulbs like most men would eat pieces of fruit.

On these outings when boys were expected to become men there were a number of skills that would be tested, none of which required the use of weapons. The first and last order of business was to create a whole new person/creature, a race that would be devoted to an endless solution, the perpetuation of Utopian eugenics based on perpetual energy. We had heard about this unusual procedure in the camp, but no one had ever seen it. If you did see it you'd probably lose your capacity to exhale.

The boys would be expected to collect fireflies, as many as possible. They would gather the fireflies with nets or whatever means proved most effective then securely close them in mason jars. The fireflies possessed an enzyme called luciferase. Luciferase acts on luciferins to oxidize them and to cause bioluminescence; this is the substance that makes fireflies glow in the dark. The more fireflies the boys collected and consumed the more luminescent they would become. Rarely, but occasionally a timid young man would be repulsed at the thought of actually eating the little fellows, however, after his first taste of the juice in the abdomen he would settle down and eat the fireflies with relish. The end result of this practice was to produce boys who had become men who would look like and behave like faeries. Once the boys had become faeries they would be treated therapeutically by use of light rays; this is referred to as lucotherapy, sometimes as phototherapy. Regardless, the objective was always the same: to create angels of light who would worship the light and follow the light even if it meant being consumed by the light of absolute darkness and fallen shadows.

It had been rumored that there was a mysterious dormitory occupied by young men who had plucked their own eyes out to represent examples of what it meant to be unconditionally committed to the light of darkness. These special few had the very best privileges, and were known as Sons of Darkness. If there ever were to be a battle they said they wanted to be on the front lines to lead the charge of The Light Brigade. They alone were permitted to wear black t-shirts with the screen printed image of Alfred Lord Tennyson on the front. On the back the t-shirt read " Ours is not to make reply. Ours is not to reason why. Ours is but to do or die." These young guns, as they were often referred to, were absolutely ruthless. They had been skilled in every facet of martial arts, and it was rumored that they could see right through you even though they were blind. No, these boys were by no means suicidal, but we were convinced that they did suffer from blind ambition. Occasionally, but very very rarely, they could be seen walking around the compound without red tipped canes or seeing eye dogs. No one could hear better than them, not even the transistorized men, and they could smell a rat a mile away.

No one had ever seen Dr. Hydrocephalus, but some said he looked like a sophisticated Cyclops with enough energy contained in his gargantuan eye to light up the universe. One of the grand doctor's favorite sayings was

"Let there be light and there was light." In fact this was our wake-up call every morning; it came into our rooms over the intercom the exact moment the rays of light entered our rooms, but, before long everyone knew that the real objective was to be blinded by the light, and it was impossible to resist. Posters abounded, but the most common one could be seen almost everywhere. It depicted an obviously simple-minded boy who had been enlightened by a bolt of lightning issuing from the sun, and it said, "The entrance of thy word giveth light; it giveth understanding to the simple."

Other posters showed a young man wearing a t-shirt that had E=MC Squared emblazoned across the front with a caricature of Einstein on the back.

There was talk about a ritualistic dance each boy would perform while stripped naked. After the dance around the campfire each boy would be dressed in an onion skin suit and have a pair of colorful wings attached to his torso. He would then be required to climb the tallest tree in the forest and swing on a vine through the fire over and over and over until his wings caught on fire like an arrogant Icarus, only he didn't plunge into the Aegean Sea. With his wings on fire he would then release the rope and fly into the waiting arms of the other boys who would then douse his wings with oil and blood. This blood had been captured from a sacrificial lamb that had been provided by the chaperone, one lamb for each boy. The oil came from the sebaceous glands of a walrus. There were no scapegoats allowed in the camp; after all, this was the 22nd century and no tin can chewing sacrifice was necessary, although there generally was an element of human sacrifice even if it just meant "The Eating Of The Brain."

It must be much more obvious now why I had to escape. The older you became the more worthless you became, and sooner or later you would be cannibalized to sustain the youth movement. Everything we were commanded to do and all the rules we were compelled to obey had one objective in mind: create a superhuman race where no one was older than 30; a race of superhuman faeries, a race which had been inbred and then eventually cloned to the highest order. This was the grand design.

Women were used only to reproduce, and the pleasure of a woman's body was anathema but never entirely forsaken by the men who had been sexually euthanized and left to serve the Queen of The Midnight Sun outside the gate. If a woman became pregnant and and it had been determined that her unborn child was to be a girl, the fetus was aborted, except in some select cases. This is the selection process I referred to earlier. Some females had to be born to continue the procreative process of the superior race, but these were qualified exceptions, and they were as pure as the driven snow, virgins who were subsequently raped to death by wild bulls in a makeshift coliseum.

Our laboratories were on the cutting edge of technology. DNA mapping had become child's play. I was 29 and marked for death if I were not willing to capitulate to the pecking order of energetic free will. Sooner or later I would be brought to my arrogant knees then hung in the box as an example of a malignant narcissistic traitor, an iconoclast unwilling to submit for the greater good of the party.

After the ritual and all of the boys had become lucipetal, irresistibly attracted to bright light, they roasted a few dozen hot dogs on the open fire, dug up the potatoes and corn that had become baked by the heat of the earth, had some wine then retired for the night, but not before singing a few songs from the scout's hymnal. The accompanying music was provided for by The Chief Executive Officer; he could play six instruments and more than one at the same time. He kept perfect time with his tail, and his voice could charm the hell out of angels and turn demons into bleating fluffy lambs willing to sacrifice themselves for the good of others. The following morning the boys would be taken to a special energy chamber where they would be schooled in the theory of relativity and study the laws of thermodynamics. Graduation day would find them engaged in controlled, unemotional energy exchanges, after which they would each receive a certificate of completion, a silver, gold or brass medal, and a fifty pound tub of organic whey protein, a gross of dianabol tablets, a tub of nitrous oxide, a bucket of subatomic particles and a necklace strung with free radicals.

I was unable to confirm that a thirteenth boy, who had been caged and fattened on steroid injected wild boar meat, was removed from his cage, dipped in a vat of grease, had a sign draped around his neck that read, " I am a duck-billed platypus," then was caned senseless by the other twelve while being driven around the camp grounds until he dropped like an exhausted water buffalo. He was subsequently roasted alive on a spit then eaten. Once his bones had been picked clean his skeleton was pulverized until all that remained of him was a pile of ashes. The ashes were then gathered into an urn and transported to the Kinetic Falls where they were tossed by the handfuls into the Atomic tributary of the Enrico Fermi Lake. I later learned that the thirteenth boy always had the same distinguishing mark on the palms of his hands. It was the simian crease, a sign that would plague him from his birth. A mark that would classify him as one whose progenitors were monkeys. More often than not he would be suffering from gonadal dysgenesis and a lack of sexual maturation. His stunted caudal development was also a cause for ridicule and humiliation. That is why this kind could conveniently be sacrificed without conscience including the retarded convolutions and fissures that were often excised and pickled, stored in mason jars, then placed in the laboratory to be used as an object lesson when studying eugenics.

Once the boys had been sung to sleep I felt I could once again begin my laborious effort to escape. I was able to make it past the hot earth with little difficulty. Unfortunately my timetable had been delayed by approximately six hours, and my energy level had been unsuspectingly sapped. I was forced to go to the canteen for extra energy much earlier than I would have expected. The energy was thick with protein, vitamins, minerals, enzymes and every element necessary to create and sustain life.

This was the first time I had actually tasted processed energy; mine had always come in great abundance from the sun. Five minutes in the sun for me was the equivalent of an hour, and that is precisely why I had never run out of energy, and why I never had to take another man's. This unforeseen delay and high degree of stress had dramatically robbed me.

My cortisol levels were off the charts, but the energy from the canteen was like a mega shot of B-12 fed intravenously. I immediately felt like a free radical looking for an innocent electron to attach to.

I was moving along nicely when again something unexpected happened. I was shocked, dismayed and seized by panic as I came to a fork in the tunnel.

I knew it was a fork because of the strange turn my body was taking after my head suddenly hit solid ground. My question now was how to proceed, and, more importantly, who had been in this tunnel besides me? I had no idea how to proceed. All I knew was that somebody was on to me and wanted me dead.

Going in the wrong direction was tantamount to suicide so I decided to pray. I prayed to God but thought of my mother; she had had the greatest influence on my life, and although she had been dead for a number of years I was certain she was aware of my dilemma. I was reminded of the story of a young man who fell in love with a wicked woman. The young man loved this woman very much but he also loved his mother very much. The love the young man had for his mother made his fiancé very jealous. In fact, it made her so jealous that she told the young man that she wanted him to prove to her that he loved her more than he loved his mother. She said he could prove it by killing his mother. Furthermore, he was to cut his mother's heart out after he murdered her, and he was then to bring his mother's heart to his fiancé as physical proof of his love for her. The young man protested vociferously for days but then finally under extreme pressure and numerous threats he conceded.

The young man did as had been instructed. He killed his mother at night and cut out her heart. While running through the woods to bring his mother's heart to his fiancé he stumbled and fell. When he fell the heart flew out of his hands and disappeared into the bushes. He panicked, and while anxiously combing the area looking for his mother's heart he scraped his knees and hands and began to bleed. He finally was able to locate the heart, and when he picked it up he heard the voice of his mother speaking to him. She anxiously asked him, "Son, are you hurt! Son, did you hurt yourself! Son, are you OK?!"

This story always reminded me of the unconditional love of a mother. So I prayed to my mother until I thought I heard her voice directing me. She guided me as I resumed my journey to freedom. The story also brought to mind the relationship the great Houdini had with his mother. Erich Weiss, better known as Harry Houdini, had become the world's greatest escape artist, and I now felt myself also communicating with him. Even though Houdini had become famous for exposing spirit mediums I sensed his presence and had become inspired with new confidence. I was certain I would make a successful escape while breaking the psychological and physical chains that had bound me. However, the stress of encountering the fork in the road robbed me of additional energy, and the canteen was almost empty. A certain degree of fear was attempting to create a negative mindset even though I knew that perfect love could cast out fear and open the door to my ultimate success. The problem was that no one loved me, except my mom, and she was dead. Or was she? Furthermore, I had never met anyone who was perfect, so I would continue to rely on my self and let the id's instinctual impulses satisfy my primitive need to survive and be victorious.

I began to move forward thinking I had about four more hours to go before I reached my freedom. I couldn't imagine anything else happening which might detain me. Unfortunately I was wrong.

After two more hours of steadily moving towards my exit I came to another fork in the road. I was stunned. How could this have happened? Who had come into my tunnel? Why had they come? What did they want? So once again I was presented with the same opportunity; I prayed to my mother. Only this time she did not answer. I heard the voice of my father, a man I never trusted or respected. He was exhorting me to go to my left. I was very skeptical. I couldn't imagine him leading me in the right direction; he never had when I was young, or so, at least, I thought. Furthermore, he was to the right of far right, and I was in love with Pushkin, Pasternak, Gorky, Mayakovsky, Yevtushenko and company.

I wanted to write, and he wanted me to box. I wanted to paint, and he wanted me to wrestle. I wanted sculpt, and he wanted me to play ice hockey.

I wanted to take tap, and he wanted me to take kung fu. Unfortunately I had to do it his way until he died.

I was always very big and very strong for my age. I was also a natural athlete which didn't help when it came to my artistic inclinations; that is, as far as my dad was concerned. The last thing my dad wanted was to have a son who might join a dance troupe or become an interior designer. He almost took my head off one day when I commented that my sister's outfit presented a perfect reflection of compliments on the color wheel.

His voice now sounded very sincere and almost believable. He sounded somehow different than how I remembered him when he was alive. Maybe he actually did care about me when he smacked my head with a hand made heavy by transporting ingots, and then told me to be a man and to eat more meat and to not fill up on vegetables. How would I know? He died suddenly at work when a fork truck crushed him against a stone wall impaling him with an iron blade. They said he was in the wrong place at the wrong time trying to befriend an injured dog. What do I know? Anyway, I decided not to listen to him. I moved to the right and continued on my way. I was certain he was wrong, as wrong as when he embarrassed my older brother into joining the Special Forces. The last message we received about his patriotic zeal was that his chute didn't open, and that he apparently landed in enemy territory never to be heard from again. He got a purple star; it hangs from the mantle above the fireplace along with his picture. He has his marine hat hugged tightly under his left arm while saluting proudly with his right.

I moved in the opposite direction from which my father was directing me. Hell, you barely got 10% of the real story. Could you blame me? I recalled the words of a song recorded by 'The Who,' and I was not about to get fooled again.

I felt certain I would reach daylight in about an hour. With about fifteen minutes left to my journey I hit another fork. Only this time no one was calling me to the left or to the right. So I stopped and just listened to my beating heart. I was experiencing severe tachycardia due to the stress I was under. I could almost hear the beats echoing off the tunnel walls. Its funny how different thoughts enter your mind at times like these. All I could think about was Edgar Allen Poe's "Tell Tale Heart." Surely somebody above ground would hear my heart beating and furiously begin to dig up the ground to unearth me, and my end would be worse than my beginning. After about five minutes of deep breathing my heart rate returned to normal, and I began to relax and become much less paranoid. It was as if I now had become one with the Good Earth, my new home. It reminded me of a transdermal infusion, and I suddenly recognized that I had been born from the dust of the earth, and that someday I was bound to return here, but not now. Furthermore, I had a secret desire to roll and revel in leaves of grass, and there was no grass in sight.

I decided once again to go neither to the right nor to the left. I just meditated for a few moments, and then I thought I heard the voice of the Cheshire Cat speaking to Alice. He said, "If you don't know where you are going, any road will get you there." At that moment something intuitively told me to push myself with a steady force against the earth directly at the fork using my head like a pile driver. So I dug my heels and my hands into the earth and pushed with all of my exhausted might. Nothing happened at first, and my head was about to explode when suddenly the earth gave way. I had made the right decision. I was now moving in my original plane, the one I had dug so assiduously for years. Exhilaration filled my mind. I had outsmarted my opposition. Something told me I would conquer my fears and succeed. I would be the Great Liberator, and I would return to the camp to set the captives free. I was proud of myself and felt as if I could move mountains with or without faith.

The moment of truth arrived. I was about to exit the tunnel. I was about to become a free man, and I would lead others to freedom as well. I couldn't wait to see the sun. My canteen had been emptied of energy long ago, and

I was operating purely on intestinal fortitude, endorphins, and adrenaline to combat my oxidative stress.

I paused just long enough to offer up a prayer of thanksgiving. I then opened the earth above me and began to slowly emerge like a butterfly from his cocoon. With my body still halfway beneath the earth I saw the sun and pushed as hard as I was able and freed myself from the shackles of the tunnel. I was high with anticipation and yelled with my loudest voice as I fell on my back and beckoned the sun to fill me with my final volume of life giving energy. If I didn't get an immediate infusion of light I would die within seconds. I had seen it occur thousands of times in the camp. Men dying for just one nanosecond of infused light, a light which never came for various reasons, mostly the sinister manipulation of the light by men who had been transformed into angels of light. But this could not and certainly would not happen to me. I was free and beyond the pale of manipulation, the malevolent prestidigitation of beings who were actually once human, but who now had transformed themselves into angels of light.

But then it happened almost as fast as eternity happens in the mind of God, that immeasurable, incalculable equation producing the unsolvable conundrum of the ages, sovereignty versus free will. An eclipse of the sun was about to take place, and I would be the victim of the moon, just one more foolish dreamer, just one more misdirected lunatic with high ideals who thought it would be possible someday for all men to be free.

I prepared to take my last breath just as the moon was about to eclipse the sun, that was when Dr. Hydracephalus appeared. He didn't ridicule me. He didn't even question me. He mentioned nothing about my attempt to escape. He didn't even discuss the consequences. He just offered me an opportunity to live. He offered me the necessary energy to live. Energy which would be administered on his terms without option or alternative. I had never seen him in all of his glory before, but I knew it was him even before he spoke.

He looked like what God would look like if he were a man who had risen from the depths of hell and death, a man who had conquered the grave and had established that contradictory assertions are equally true and that man is the measure of all things. Is it any wonder, I thought, that he would always have it his way. There was something mysteriously beautiful, handsome, intriguing, astonishing, astounding, incredible, majestic, phenomenal, and irresistibly attractive about him. Maybe this is what a Greek god actually looked like in the flesh.

I was unable to respond to his offer. After his third invitation and my refusal to speak he reasoned with me by saying, "You've heard it said that energy can be changed from one form to another, but it cannot be created or destroyed. The total amount of energy and matter in the universe remains constant merely changing from one form to another. Energy is always conserved; it can't be created or destroyed. You've also heard that in all energy exchanges, if no energy enters or leaves the system, the potential energy of the state will always be less than that of the initial state. This is commonly referred to as entropy. You've been taught that entropy is a measure of disorder, and that we are devolving not evolving. Well, I am here to tell you that this is not true," he said didactically with the aplomb of a seasoned professor of philosophy.

He then took a few steps closer to me until he was close enough to touch me, then he continued, "I've already scaled The Tower of Babel, and I have created a society of one language. In my inner circle we all speak the same language, and we understand each other. We are energetic gods, and when we run we fly like Phaethon, son of the sun god, Helios, only we are not mythological, and, if we were, Zeus would be our servant. We've already launched some men well beyond the ionosphere who have yet to return, but you can bet that when they do return they will be dragging imploded black holes with them. The black holes will be filled with subatomic elementary particles and hadrons composed of quarks which we will separate and eat. Can you imagine being able to eat quarks!"

I was shaking, frightened and didn't say a word. I just stared into his big blue mesmerizing eyes. He had a full white beard down to his clavicles and long, shiny, purple-black hair to just below his shoulders. He had a rainbow robe that ran down to his robin egg blue, blue suede shoes and, of course, a golden scepter in his left hand. When he began to speak, his face and the color of his skin changed. His visage reminded me of an inconstant chameleon, a lizard related etymologically to chamomile based on the place you would expect to find them, "on the ground," khamai.

"Don't be afraid," he said kindly. " I do not want to hurt you. I want to help you make the right decision. Listen, we have had our eyes on you for years. You have great potential. You have more energy than ten men put together, and it seems to come naturally to you; somehow from within, and we are interested in that, however...." He hesitated then captured my glance with his third eye, that mysterious pineal eye that emerged from the tip of his skull like a periscope. He extended his massive hand and forearm towards me then continued, "When two systems are put in contact with each other, there will be a net exchange of energy between them unless or until they are in thermal equilibrium. That is, they are at the same temperature. So, play it smart. Give me your hand as an act of obedience. Humble yourself in the sight of god and he will lift you up to a place you may have only thought about. You can realize the unspoken dream of most men. You can occupy your own throne. I can make you co-equal. Give me your hand," he continued with a voice as inviting as any I had ever heard before.

He actually looked kind, and I could only see goodness in his eyes. I wanted to be a part of that kingdom. I wanted to see what it was like on the other side, and I was within a few seconds of taking his hand when I had the urge and good sense to close my eyes. I took one step backwards then opened my eyes and was now staring at the most beautiful creature I had ever seen. My tank was empty, and I was desperate and delirious. My brain was getting no oxygen. I'd become completely energy deprived, but I was being uncontrollably sexually aroused. A certain degree of enthusiasm was filling my mind with a libidinous song of myself and dividing my mind. I suddenly felt as if I had no rudder and was fast adrift in a sea of short division filled with radical and rather odd integers.

"I Am Thermal Equilibrium. I am the unknown fifth law of thermodynamics, and I want to be one with you. Please come, come to the mother of all mothers, then afterwards we will eat the fruit, be fruitful, multiply and fill the landscape with our love, planting explosions, land minds, that will turn the earth counterclockwise in the direction of a dynamic meditative, willingly molested and pregnant medulla oblongata," she/he said with an irresistible magnetism. "This is your fourth invitation, and there will not be another. Choose wisely, and might I remind you that "Every atom belonging to me as good belongs to you."

I wish I could say that my answer came without hesitation, but I would be lying. I had become more confused and weaker than ever. I did not want to die. I wanted to live. I also thought that I could still handle myself as a man, and perhaps, if I succumbed I would be given another chance to escape, another chance to be free and to lead others to freedom. So with all the candor and genuineness I could summons, I must admit the offer looked inviting, after all, we were talking about life and death, but to my surprise I declined the final offer. I felt as though someone was now speaking for me, a supernatural ventriloquist able to recognize the truth in absolute terms. Inwardly, however, and on my own limited creative terms I garnered comfort from the tension expressed in Yeat's poem "The Choice," which begins:

> The intellect of man is forced to choose
> Perfection of the life, or of the work,
> And if it take the second must refuse
> A heavenly mansion, raging in the dark.

Yes, I refused what might have been a life of great promise and chose death rather than compromise and become a dead man walking. For some reason I chose not to sacrifice the future on the altar of the immediate. I was prepared to die rather than trust in my limited wisdom, even though I was sure the Sun would come up tomorrow.

I was prepared to die, but to my astonishment he didn't kill me. He didn't even raise his voice. He didn't get angry, but he did begin to spin faster than anything I had ever witnessed. He had begun to transmit nerve impulses away from his central nervous system in an act of accelerated humility; he'd temporarily become centrifugal until he regained his senses and had, once again, become the dictatorial centripetal force, the need to draw all men unto him; the magnetic force that had made him King.

"Just one more thing before I set you free. You need to know that only certain living things-human beings among them-collapse the wave function of things they observe. Humans are therefore highly dangerous to other life forms which require the full diversity of uncollapsed wave functions to survive."

I didn't want to give him the benefit of a response, but I couldn't contain myself. "That may be true, but I'm no weeping angel. You can't describe me as being "Quantum locked," which means I do not exist while being looked at but can prove deadly when unobserved. We both know you can't have your cat and eat it too."

He then somewhat hastily summoned a group of faeries to strip me, hose me down, strap me down, then feed me intravenously with a gallon of cold-pressed, one thousand year old, virgin energy drawn from the fecund loins of the mystic prophets of the absolute, a gallon of postulate that had been diluted by a pernicious vial of hemlock in the guise of relativism. This exponential infusion of energy made me feel like an unleashed hungry whore in search of perpetual energy contained in the barrel of the shadow-light.

It was as if I had been changed in the twinkling of an eye, an eye that could only be viewed from within the center of a unique storm.

An obvious uncontrollable physical and emotional transformation had immediately taken place. It was just as if I had been born again, a corrupt human phagocyte. They then colored and perfumed me like Jezebel, strapped me to an ass and lead me back to the camp where they crowned me with a beautiful wreath of woven sunflowers and a dress of many colors.

I remained a prisoner in the courtyard for forty days and forty nights, a quintessential metaphysical freak of unnatural selection, a nature-boy held in suspended animation, the humiliation of faith, hope and love and all things considered impossible. After forty days my shackles were removed and I was placed in a steel, black box along with a vial of hydrocyanic acid, a small amount of radioactive substance and a strategically placed hammer, that, if activated by a single decaying atom, would shatter the vial, and I would be killed. The box was sealed tight. A fluorescent label was then emblazoned across the front of the box that read "Schrodinger's Cat."

Something

That atypical Something began to form inside of him just as it had on other occasions. It felt as if his intestines were being meaninglessly spun and twisted without obvious intention. This queer sensation seemed to begin in his stomach, but it had always originated in his head. Today's sensation brought back memories of how he'd observed cotton candy being spun, or the way Turkish Taffy was pulled and twisted on the taffy pulling machine. Yet there was nothing sweet or amusing about these convoluted feelings that temporarily possessed him and left him feeling somewhat unbalanced, fearful and emotionally obstructed. Once, when he had been forced to describe it, he likened it to a descent into an inferno of contradictory thought, or, even worse, a place where contradictory assertions were equally true.

His brain was the sole generator that dictated what his body did. Even those unidentified flying objects that occasionally struck him from the outside seemed to have somehow been attracted to his body; it was as if his body had become a helpless magnet, a conduit of uninvited psychomotor agitation.

Against these malicious onslaughts he'd almost become defenseless, at least at first, but that, over time, would change. Furthermore, what made his life even more unmanageable was the fact that some of these attacks came in the guise of wolves in sheep's clothing; these attacks required keen discernment and the ability to read between the lines, an abandoned place where frequently no space existed, except, maybe, an existential space without a precise dimension or identity.

When it came right down to it, he was one of the most trustworthy individuals, and it really wasn't that difficult to persuade him that you were a friend, someone who could also be trusted. Of course, he'd give you the shirt off his back, and he'd be anxious to give anyone the benefit of the doubt. His kindness was often misinterpreted as gullibility, and he was frequently referred to as a 'soft touch.' He was by no means naïve, but he preferred to always consider an individual's motivation. His problem was that he judged everyone's motivation based on his motivation, and his motivation had always been pure. He particularly liked what Emerson said, "Every man I meet is in some way my superior, and of that I learn from him." He hadn't an enemy in the world, but he really didn't have any close friends either.

He'd become acutely aware when something atypical spoke to him. He recognized those times when something would need to be done to preserve his sanity, otherwise, he would assuredly crossover to territory from which there would be no return. He'd witnessed a few of his friends, family and acquaintances step rather nonchalantly into that black hole and not return. Or, if they ever did return, they'd become entirely different people, and the change in character that had taken place was generally very negative. Few, if any, lost in that imploding world where the brain had been sucked dry of all its cerebral spinal fluid ever returned happier, gentler, kinder and more understanding. Based on appearances most, if not all, presented an aura that appeared angelic, and it would have taken a psychic with absolute powers to discern what would otherwise be considered a transparent evil nature, fangs designed to render one helpless while hiding behind a broad smile.

He didn't believe in malicious animal magnetism, although he did believe that a degree of merit could be ascribed to the power of positive thinking, and this is mostly how he thought about the world and the people in the world. It was rather difficult to get on his bad side. Even if a person seemed to be treating him unkindly, maliciously mean, he'd take it in stride and give the person the benefit of the doubt. He often said he believed there was a bit of good in even the worst person; you just had to look hard enough, and sure enough you'd find it.

These bouts of 'no holds barred' psychological wrestling had almost become second nature to him, and he was generally able to pin his opponent in a round or two. It didn't take him long to learn his opponent's weaknesses. He knew exactly what offensive or defensive posture to assume. He'd always emerged victorious, though sometimes he was as worn out as his opponent. It frequently took him weeks to recover, but he always did. He never looked forward to these bouts, but they did appear to make him stronger, and even though he had acquired the reputation of an unvanquished victor he secretly wished that, perhaps someday, he'd lose one of these battles and thereafter be left alone. Or, if not left alone, he'd reside in a mental state of impenetrable oblivious delirium. Here he'd be unaffected by all things extracorporeal, although he did like the world around him, and he really did like most people.

This time, when the, by now, familiar Something spoke to him, he was meditatively walking in the sand near the sea. He'd taken his shoes off and was slowly walking into the water. This was his favorite spot on the beach. This section was very quiet and out of reach of the general public. He frequently came here when he wanted to be alone; he often brought a book to read, and, of course, a pen. Sometimes he would bring a notebook. At other times, when he felt moved to write something, he'd write it in the book he had been carrying. He even thought that someday he might become a writer.

He'd never learned how to swim. He was afraid of the water because when he was four years old his father, recognizing his fear of the water, and thereby considering him a sissy, threw him into the family swimming pool. If it wasn't for his mother, who was in the pool on her raft, he'd have drowned. She didn't see him being thrown into the water, but she heard a sudden splash behind her. When she turned around, she saw her husband standing at the side of the pool laughing. She intuitively knew something was wrong. That was when she saw her son struggling beneath the water. She rushed to him, pulled him up and took him out of the water. She'd saved his life. He was certain his father, if he had wanted to, could easily have taught him how to swim, but he had no patience for a son he considered a mommy's boy.

Ever since that traumatizing event he'd never been in a swimming pool and had never gone swimming at the beach. However, he had no fear of walking into water at the beach, and sometimes he'd wade into the water to just above his ankles. It couldn't be said that he didn't like the water; he did like the water, and he had great respect for the power of the water as well as a reverential fear of the water.

Whether stream, pond, river, lake or ocean, he could sense that poetry was forever present in various bodies of water. He had learned that 71% of the earth's surface is covered by water, and that the oceans hold about 96.5% of that. "If only my father had not thrown me into that swimming pool I'd swim out as far as I could and maybe never come back," he thought as he scanned the horizon where the sky met the water. He'd grown to love novels about the sea, especially "The Old Man and The Sea," "Moby Dick" and "Lord Jim." Various poems such as "The Rhyme of The Ancient Mariner" also became some his favorites. If he could, he'd join the Navy and become a Navy Seal; if not, he'd join the Coast Guard. Maybe he'd become a longshore-man. Perhaps a tugboat operator like Mark Twain or more pragmatically, a professional fisherman.

For reasons unknown to him, ever since his father had thrown him into the pool, he'd become enamored with water and its related mysteries. He'd read of the healing properties of water. He'd learned that Bronze Age Greeks called dead bodies "The Thirsty." Parched souls ended up in a place called "the dry country." He also learned that Western philosophy begins with Thales' saying "Everything starts with water." The oldest sources of Hellenistic thought traced the generation of all life to Okeanos, the body of water encircling the globe. This river was also a god: "He from whom all gods arose." In classical antiquity, to be alive was to be in a state of watery wetness. Young people were described as "abounding in liquid."

"Don't be afraid of the water. You have nothing to be afraid of. The water can't hurt you. You can go in as far as you want to, but just don't go in over your head. Remember, you can go out as far you would like, but you must always keep your feet on the bottom. There is absolutely no reason why you shouldn't be able to enjoy the water, and you cannot possibly enjoy the water as it is meant to be enjoyed if you only go in up to your ankles. It is as safe as you would like it to be," the encouraging voice spoke kindly and confidently to him as he began to dig his toes into the wet sand.

This time, after evaluating the geography, including not only the water and the horizon, but the sand, the sea shells, the foliage, the birds and the potential of clouds holding life breaking water, he didn't feel the same as he had in the past when his assailant had come. Maybe that was because he'd learned to recognize the various types of camouflages intended to deceive him. Something about the sound usually alerted him to the psychological booby traps that had been set for him. This voice sounded kind, and the kindness echoed the truth, and the truth echoed trust. The voice seemed to be coming from the water, an unexplored depth before oxygen's existence.

"Actually, this makes a lot of sense. I really don't have anything to fear as long as I don't go in over my head. I also need to be certain to keep my feet on solid ground. What could be so difficult about that?" he thought while fantasizing about going out farther. The sound of this voice sounded different; it sounded trustworthy. There wasn't a hint of deceit in the voice. He was certain this voice was in concert with his ability and willingness. Furthermore, it was appealing to him based on his desire to overcome fear that he considered childish. It was nowhere near the sound of the voices that had encouraged him to jump off bridges, or high-rise buildings with the assurance that he could fly, nor the voices that told him he could walk on hot coals or jump into a fire and not be burned. He'd always had acute discernment when Something didn't seem quite right, and this was exactly what he wanted to hear, unconditional truth related to wisdom and bravery.

"Yeah, don't you think it is about time you test the waters? Based on what I know about you: your fear, doubt, worry, uncertainty and lack of confidence, it is about time you put all that behind you, and you take the plunge. This is not something so ridiculous as encouraging you to jump off a high-rise or to walk into a burning building. This is strictly common sense whose foundation is courage. "'The journey of 1,000 miles begins with the first step.'" The first step you will want to take is to get in slowly up to your knees. Fear not. Have I not told you to be of good courage?" the encouraging voice spoke logically.

"Of course, up to my knees. What would be the harm of that? Certainly no one had ever drowned standing in water up to their knees," he said while laughing inwardly with sophomoric confidence. All he ever wanted to be was 'one of the guys.' Average, typical, normal, friendly, fun to be with, included, agreeable, ordinary, unremarkable, and even funny sometimes, but Something must have happened to him when he was young.

When he first heard the voices, he didn't tell anyone. He kept the conversations to himself lest people thought he was crazy. He was smart enough to realize that most people never heard audible voices. Sure, they might have consciences that were pricked from time to time with thoughts that might be considered abnormal, but never audible voices that encouraged them to do bizarre things. Sure, they might even act on those psychological promptings, but it would usually result in doing or not doing something or saying or not saying something. But, it was never something like the Something that he'd hear. For example, perhaps not the best example, "Something told me to place a bet on Serendipity in the 4th race at Pimlico. Something like that generally was never seriously questioned, and often the horse would win. Frequently people had been spoken to in their dreams, and their dreams would come true. Classic examples of this could be found in the bible where God spoke to the prophets by way of dreams, and, of course, sometimes audibly, or the classic case of the dreams of Nebuchadnezzar. But, that's only God stuff if you believe in God.

He rolled his pants legs up and slowly and excitedly began to wade into the water up to his knees. He moved very methodically, one baby step at a time. When he got up to his knees he was filled with an unspeakable joy. Besides the exhilaration of his position and the touch of the water he also felt a sense of power. He felt so good about himself that he reached down into the water and began to splash with his hands. He stayed in the water for quite a while, digging his toes into the wet sand. What an exhilarating feeling as he watched some of the tiny fish swim between his legs. When he surveyed the horizon, he wished he could swim out to where the water met the sky.

He then made his way back to the shore, proud of his bold accomplishment. He prepared to head home. However, as he was about to put his shoes back on, he heard Something. It sounded like that same voice of assurance.

"Hey, cowboy, Congratulations! What an accomplishment. You sure can be proud of yourself. You did it! You took that psychologically immovable dilemma by its obstinate horns and taught it a good lesson. Now, that is what I call overcoming a paralyzing fear and pulverizing it to smithereens. But, listen, that's just the beginning. You're just getting warmed-up. The confidence that infuses you at this moment needs to be taken advantage of. Think of it like a thirsty man who comes upon a water pump. He's just about dying of thirst. So, he grabs that old handle and begins to pump, pump, pump, and pump some more, and when that water is just ready to gush out of the neck through the throat of the spigot he gives up. The water that would have quenched his thirst was one pump or two away from gushing out, but it now goes all the way back down to the bottom. So, the alternative is to either start all over or walk away defeated," Something said with the voice of trust he'd never heard before. There was also a sound of integrity in the voice, a voice he felt he could believe in, not something his dogmatic, pompous, untrustworthy father might say just to sound important.

He listened, but he wasn't certain of what might be expected of him. He'd already done much more than he could possibly have dreamed of. He was happy to head home. He thought he might even tell his dad that he'd gone in up to his knees. Although, on second thought, that would probably be a bad idea, unless, of course, he was willing to risk being ridiculed.

"Listen closely. A child can easily go in up to his knees, but you are not a child. You are a man. The last thing you would want to do is to tell your dad you only went in up to your knees. He might not laugh you to scorn to your face, but he'd find your effort meaningless. He might even applaud your efforts, but behind your back he'd think you were still a pathetic coward. What you need to do is to take your pants off and go in up to your waist," the voice said to him with absolute confidence and assurance.

He wasn't sure he had heard correctly so he got very quiet. It seemed as if Something had just read his mind. He closed his eyes and began to meditate. "If I can go in up to my knees, I should be able to go in up to my waist. I'd have my feet on solid ground, and I certainly couldn't drown if I was only in up to my waist. I'm sure the water surrounding my lower body would feel great; I could probably even safely do a few knee bends. Wow! What a sensation that might be. That would even be pretty darn close to swimming, but, but maybe I should do it tomorrow."

"Tomorrow! Tomorrow! Heck no. Don't put off until tomorrow what you can do today. I'm sure you've heard that before. Seize the day. Don't wait for your ship to come in; go out and meet it. Either move or be moved. Today is the tomorrow you were thinking about yesterday. Just do it," Something said again with assurance.

Something startled him, and he opened his eyes to look around. Quite a way down from him he thought he saw a beautiful girl frolicking in the water. She sure appeared to be having fun. His first thought was to get dressed and to head for home, and that is exactly what he began to do until Something spoke to him.

"Jack, don't leave. Don't go home. I know you haven't had much luck with girls in the past, but this is now. This is all the more reason why you should remove your pants and get into that water right up to your waist. I can categorically guarantee you that when she sees you in the water she will move in your direction. Furthermore, all that weightlifting you've secretly been doing has really begun to pay off. No one has ever questioned your intelligence; you're a brilliant young man whose mind any woman would find attractive, but now look at your pecs and biceps, and your six-pack. Are you kidding me!"

"But I'm afraid," he said.

"Afraid! Afraid of what! "'You can discover what your enemy fears most by observing the means he uses to frighten you.'" "You have absolutely nothing to be afraid of. The only thing you should be afraid of is the way you will feel tomorrow morning when you wake-up and realize what a fool you have been," Something said loudly with a hint of irritation in its voice.

"But, what about my father. What if he"

"Your father! Your father! What about your father? You've got to stop trying to please your father. You've got to stop trying to prove to your father that you are a man. You already are a man. But, if you still think you have something to prove to him then a better opportunity will never come your way. Success is staring you right in the face. Your future is at stake. You damn well better believe that you have the chance of a lifetime to prove to yourself, your father, that beautiful girl, and anyone else, that you are indeed a man," the voice sounded rather angrily.

"But you don't know my father. My father.

"Stop it, Jack. Stop the bullshit about your father," the voice abruptly interrupted him then continued. "I know all about your father. I probably know more about your father than you do, and if he was here this very minute, he'd be encouraging you to get into that water with boldness. Why in God's name do you think he threw you into that swimming pool? Do you think he wanted to see you drown? I don't think so. Now, get your shit together, Jack. Just do as I say. Take your pants off and get into that water and do it now. No more fear. No more doubt. No more fraidy cat stuff, and remember what one of your favorite authors, Ray Bradbury, said, "'Go to the edge of the cliff and jump off. Build your wings on the way down,'"OK? OK!"

Holy-Cow! Something about the voice began to sound very familiar. It reminded him of a voice he had always wanted to hear. It was a voice that exhibited tough love; it wasn't the least bit demeaning. This was a voice that had no ulterior motive. It may have sounded a bit like drill instructor boot camp stuff; but it was for his own good. All this voice really wanted was to support and encourage him to do what was best for himself, not what was best for the voice. At least, it sounded that way.

So, he quickly took off his pants, and, surprisingly enough, his underwear, and headed towards the water, naked and unafraid. He wasn't sure if would be able to go in up to his waist, but he knew he could go in up to his knees and maybe up to mid-thigh. He began to slowly and confidently wade in the water.

"Very good, Jack. You're doing just great. Keep moving. Once you get into that water up to your waist you will have conquered your biggest fear. You will have achieved a confidence level you've never known before, and it will be exhilarating. In fact, Jack, you will find that when you get in up to your waist you will want to go in even deeper."

Jack continued to move into the water up to his waist. He felt as if he was becoming one with the water. His feet had been securely planted into the sand below the water; he felt comfortable, confident and in control. He double-flexed his biceps then waived to the girl down on the beach. She didn't see him, but he didn't care.

"Jack, Jackie boy, you are incredible. You have come so far along, today. Who would have ever thought you'd have had the courage to conquer unfounded fear. The shackles of fear have been broken and are now floating out to sea, the sea of forgetfulness. There exists a careless buoyancy in your newly found spirit that is destined to lift you to heights of confidence heretofore unknown," the supportive voice said enthusiastically.

This was the sound of Something Jack was becoming familiar with and almost expecting. It was the kind of support he always wanted and needed. The water was becoming active, not at all turbulent, but more active. He thought it best to return to dry land, but then Something spoke with the familiar voice of assurance, compelling him to keep his eyes on the western horizon where the sky met the water.

"Jack, this is no time to go back or to even think about it. This is your opportunity. This is your time. You are about to grab that brass ring you have always thought about, but never had the courage to reach out for, let alone to grab. Jack, as ridiculous as this sounds; you don't need to worry about not being able to swim, because if you really wanted to you could walk on water. Now, let's get back to moving to higher ground. Don't go in only up to your chest. Go in up to your neck," Something said to him. "Up to your neck!"

"Up to my neck!" Jack exclaimed.

"That's right, Jack. Right up to your neck! Not an inch lower than your Adam's apple."

The Butterfly Effect

When he decided to stick his two cents into the discussion he often ended-up sticking his foot into his mouth, or so it seemed. This phenomenon appeared to happen on a somewhat regular basis. It wasn't that he didn't know what he was talking about. He was smart enough. It was just that he didn't know when to merely listen instead of offering his opinion on almost every subject. He knew a lot about a lot of things, but he didn't know a lot about everything. He was a pleasant enough fellow, and he was friendly. He was even well liked, but he had a knack for bullying his way into places where his head ought not to have gone, but once he got his two horns into the carcass he had a difficult time surrendering the lacerated body. Did his positive attributes outweigh the negative? Yes, they most certainly did, but it wasn't necessarily by a wide margin.

I'd only known him for a short time before it dawned on me that he'd been hiding behind an opaque countenance that was masking his true identity. He wasn't an intentional liar by any means. In fact, he was truthful to a fault, but even when the truth was more than enough he seemed determined to add a rather officious layer or two to the facts to make them incontestable dogmatic diatribes, needless layers of clothing. It was as if he had become a fully clothed emperor who was afraid to take his clothes off when he went to bed like everyone else lest, for some unknown reason, he be ridiculed, not realizing, of course, that he was already naked, and that no one went to bed fully dressed. Based on his intelligence the pomp and circumstance were totally uncalled for and absolutely unnecessary. Was he a malignant narcissist? Yeah, to a degree, but he still had a way of humiliating people into liking him.

One other very interesting thing about him was that he never seemed to get angry. He very seldom raised his voice when discussing any controversial subjects. He would make an ideal debate team leader. He was a wise bulldog, but he wasn't an hungry bulldog, and he held onto his position with locked jaws that would seldom surrender the meat of the matter. He was willing to share but only after he got his fair share first. I'm not saying that you always only got leftovers after all was said and done, but you rarely were served first. Your opportunity to take a big bite out of life, if you were lucky, would come in the form of an appetizer.

If you were to ask him to list his shortcomings you'd come away with a blank piece of paper. After which, of course, he would laugh then ask you to list yours. Furthermore, when it did appear as if he'd, once again, put his foot into his mouth, he'd deftly remove the shoe and place it into your mouth. Interestingly enough, when this phenomenon occurred he'd add smartly, "If the shoes fits wear it." More often than not you'd find the shoe to be the perfect size.

An iconoclast? Well, he did seem to attack certain established traditions and could often be seen on the outside looking in. A Peeping Tom? Maybe, and maybe that is why he usually kept the blinds closed. I couldn't necessarily say that he had a suspicious nature, but he was guarded just enough to know when to back off. He'd told me that he had developed an internal gyroscope that alerted him to his potential to act violently. He'd only developed this learned response when he recognized that the genie in the bottle was actually a devil.

One day I treated him to lunch. Of course, he showed-up wearing his typical Nebraska Corn-husker football cap. He loved the Corn-huskers and just about anything else about Nebraska, especially the corn. He once told me that there are over 3,500 different uses for corn products. When he was young he liked to play "Hide-N-Seek" in the corn fields. Sometimes those corn stalks could grow ten feet tall. If you ever got lost in a field you'd think you were in a maze, and you might think you'd never get out. He said, "You could actually die out there and no one would ever know it." He'd won more than one corn eating contest and had the medals to prove it. I'd never eaten lunch, breakfast or dinner with him when he didn't bring either a newspaper, a magazine or a book. Today, he brought a book. He'd make the best Trivial Pursuit partner of anyone I'd ever met.

During lunch we were talking about time and matter plus chance and the multiplier effect of some sovereign force living outside of the known universe. We were behaving as if we were much smarter than we actually were, and we knew it, and we laughed almost continuously. During one of our bouts of boffo laughter, I asked him how far out on a limb he thought he could go before falling off into an abyss where men had been advised to "Keep their hands full and their minds empty." Of course, he asked me if the abyss had a bottom, and if I might be implying that he was about to hit bottom. I laughed, took a drink of my coffee then asked him what he thought. Of course, he asked me why I had a tendency to answer a question with a question, but he already knew that answer.

"OK, Crick, I realize that in your world the abyss has no bottom because you typically think in terms of infinity. I really didn't need to ask you. I could have told you, but I just wanted to hold your feet to the fire and give you a chance to unfurl the web you have woven yourself into," he said smugly with a twisted smirk he'd conveniently turned into a thrust and parry.

"Hold on, mister. This is not a man caught in a web you see before you. I'm the man who spins the web that encloses my naive victims, fools who act before they think. Most men I know do not ask, seek, and knock; they just barge right in to immediately gratify their wants by classifying them as needs. They've never faced a dilemma that they could not solve by just violently grabbing the horns. These macho creatures think that by going around the horns they would be considered cowards, men without backbones. These problem solvers don't rely on logic to solve their issues; they rely on pure emotion. However, they often destroy themselves in the process, and find themselves permanently attached to the horns or impaled," I answered smartly with a rather confident air he'd seen before.

He didn't respond as quickly as he generally did. In fact, he was actually thinking before responding. This was a good thing, but I'm sure he would soon come at me with both barrels blazing, in good fun, of course. Before he did answer I added, "Are your feet getting hot?"

"Holding one's feet to the fire" is not the same as giving someone a hotfoot. A hotfoot usually comes as a surprise; it's typically a prank. "Holding one's feet to the fire" is a deliberate act designed to force someone to respond to a situation they have created. It might be in response to a promise an individual has made. The expectation being that he will now be required to "shit or get off the pot." So, when I mentioned it, as it referred to your present position, I wasn't necessarily expecting you to give me an explanation as to why you believe the way you do. I was merely planting a seed to see if you might try to rationalize your way out of the conundrum," he answered confidently.

"Someone guilty of rationalization is generally employing a defense mechanism in which they unconsciously find plausible explanations to justify unreasonable or intolerable behavior or feelings thereby to conceal true motivations. Have I been guilty of this? Sure, I have, but I am not defensively indignant. Nor do I use misrepresentation, self-righteousness or storytelling. I do not suffer from a lack of self-awareness. Neither do I suffer from an inability to accept ignoble parts of my self or guilt. Furthermore, I would hardly refer to my position as a conundrum. The puzzle was not solved by me but for me," I responded in faith.

"So, come clean, and don't hide behind a mirror. Be your typically transparent self, and let me know just how far out you think you can go or are willing to go before the limb breaks?" I continued politely.

"You know one of the things I like about us? I like the fact that whenever we don't want to respond directly to a question posed to expose our ignorance we choose to use non-sequiturs. We're both really great at it, but I think you're far better at it than I am. You have a real knack for going around the horns as if the horns never existed or taking weird segues down roads less traveled. For example; If I said I think you are intentionally constructing a maze to hide your real intentions. What do you suppose you would say? Go ahead, answer," he said with congeniality while spearing a strawberry.

"What do you take me for? A minotaur?" I answered without the least amount of hesitation. "And, oh by the way, who has been holding onto Ariadne's shiny thread?"

"Why, me! Of course. And you are about to die," he said with the most serious look of the afternoon. "Prepare to meet your maker."

"How many times do I have to tell you that since I have been born twice that I will only die once, but those who have only been born once will certainly die twice?" I asked him as I steadied the carcass. "Furthermore, when you find and kill the minotaur you will have discovered that your creativity can then be released. If you are unwilling to be transparent, aren't willing to expose your true nature, you will never achieve success in its purest form. In a creative journey you must find your way out of the labyrinth, and you should strive to never break a promise made to another or one you have made to yourself, especially after you have slain the minotaur and have emerged victorious."

"I agree that true success, as posed by Confucius, begins with integrity and manifests itself with honesty, and I honestly believe that you believe what you believe with all of your heart. For 'out of the heart proceed the issues of life.' I also believe that in my former life I was a kangaroo," he answered while deftly sticking his middle finger into the evolutionary hole in the dike.

"Wait a minute. Let's just suppose this was a story that someone was writing. Don't you think they'd say, "What a crock of bullshit!" I asked while contemplating literary suicide.

"Of course, they would, but there is a hell of lot more bullshit available out there that is passing itself off as writing compared to this. The individual I feel sorry for is the reader, but at least this isn't a romance novel where the closest thing to a sexual encounter would be something like this, "Oh my! She looked at his handsome body in the high school year book and got goosebumps accompanied by a mysterious wet discharge between her virgin legs. He was wearing the high school football team's black and gold sweater with a gigantic X in the upper left hand corner.

The next day he asked her if he could hold her hand on the way to biology class, and the next week they got married and had their first baby, a little boy they named Stanley Pashkowski. They went to confession every Saturday night, and he never failed to tell the priest that he frequently wore a rubber. For that heinous sin he got his typical 10 Our Fathers and 10 Hail Mary's. They lived happily ever after and made a vow that they would make love every Saturday evening, before confession, of course, until either one, or both of them, died."

"So what should we think about all this malarkey regarding serious thinking? What do you think?" I asked. "By the way, that previous paragraph got me about as emotionally fired-up as if I had just seen a pair of skirts on a 56 Chevy."

"If people thought more seriously about thinking seriously they might want to read something like this conversation if they could find it in a book. But, why would anybody want to think when they could have others think for them?" He answered. "Besides which, porno gets right to the point before you even get to the second page, and everybody that I know is in a such hurry nowadays. This is not the time to think. This definitely is not the time for all men to come to the aid of their party. It is the time for all men to unabashedly and unashamedly get their blow-up balloon dolls out of the closet. Why waste your precious time on foreplay? That requires thinking and a certain amount of patience and understanding. Do you get my point? Do you now have an idea as to what I'm thinking? Or do I need to think twice about what I have been thinking while hiding between the paragraphs like some Peeping Tom lecherously waiting patiently to see some naked similes and metaphors dancing in the moonlight?" he asked right before he began to lick his plate with his trombone tongue.

"I thought that is what you might have thought about serious thinking. I personally am not not so sure what to think. I guess if I thought really hard about it I might think otherwise, but I'm not sure if I want to think that hard about serious thinking. I think we both should leave that up to those serious minded thinkers you can find on the campus of some liberal arts college; they're the real certified, bonafide thinkers. Don't you think?" I asked right before I stuck a fork in the emerging conundrum of beef patiently laying on my plate just begging to be eaten by an enlightened vegetarian tree hugger who had just wrapped his arms around a Redwood.

He didn't answer very quickly. He must have been thinking, so I thought of another question I might consider asking him a little later. I wondered what he might think about the serious Greek thinkers, in particular the great philosophers and also the great Greek tragedies. He'd already revealed to me the significant family problems he had been facing, and how he felt that his life was being orchestrated by an influence beyond his control. I think he may have considered himself to be a pawn in the hands of the gods of Mt. Olympus.

"Well, yeah. At least I think so because they always seem to be asking people to learn how to think for themselves. Whatever that means. I think it might have something to do with their liberal arts minded narcissistic professors.

What could two bibliophiles like ourselves have to offer? Remember, if you've never been gorged through to the bone and watched the bacon seep through the cracks you wouldn't understand what it means to eat regurgitated mush.

So what do you think it means?" he asked me while he lowered the landing gear on his approach to the fiery terminal occupied by travelers who had lost their luggage prior to boarding.

"Well, if you were to ask me, I'd say it would be pretty difficult not to think for yourself. Unless, of course, you were the recipient of a brain transplant. I mean, even if your thinking processes were somehow being dictated by an outside force, you'd still be the one doing the thinking. At least this is what I think. So I guess, and I must qualify my answer, that it is not possible for one person to actually think for another. What do you think?" I asked while considering the metabolic potential of muscle compared to fat and the consequent epidemic of obesity. I was about to ask him a true or false question about the Krebs cycle as it relates to glycolysis and fat burning, but I didn't. I didn't want to waste my energy and my chance to throw a Change-Up.

"I think your point is well taken. However, what about mob mentality? How would you evaluate the acts of individuals thinking for themselves when it comes to this phenomenon? While not exactly the same, it does appear as if the mob, as a whole, is thinking as if it were the sum of its parts. In fact, it would seem as if one man's mind, the ring leader, is actually thinking for more than one man. Not only is one man thinking for another man; it would appear as if he is thinking for more than one man at the same time. To take it even one step farther, think about the act of brainwashing. If you could brainwash one man at a time you might soon be able to brainwash an entire nation. Of course, when one speaks in terms of brainwashing most people think of Germany's propaganda minister, Joseph Goebbels, and rightly so. Goebbels said many interesting things. Here's a profound one: "It would not be impossible to prove with sufficient repetition and a psychological understanding of the people concerned that a square is in fact a circle. They are mere words, and words can be molded until they clothe ideas and disguise." Do you think these people were thinking for themselves?" he asked.

"Obviously not. These individuals are more than likely suffering from "existential frustration." These mindless individuals have been unable to find any meaning in their lives. They are haunted by the experience of their inner emptiness, a void within themselves. According to Viktor Frankl they have been caught in that situation which he referred to as the "existential vacuum." Something had to fill that vacuum of meaninglessness. It was as if their minds had become empty vessels in search of meaning, and along came this Pied Piper who could delude them into believing that he had the answer. So he simply poured a believable lie into their empty minds that gave their lives meaning. Voila!" I answered wisely. "Isn't that what you're looking for? And isn't that why you've joined me for lunch?" I asked.

"Not exactly, but it sure is close. The only difference is that I want to empty someone's mind. I want to empty every vestige of contrary thought that exists in a mind that appears to have been brainwashed by certain societal mores, and especially as it relates to sex, marriage, extra marital affairs, murder and divorce," he answered with an invitation to understanding. "As the twig is bent so the tree's inclined."

"Sounds to me as if you would like to be the creator of a generation of individuals whose minds arrive empty at birth, a blank slate, if you will. Or what is commonly referred to as Tabula rasa. Without built-in mental content these minds could be molded to suit the creator's purposes. In this case, or state of mind, all knowledge comes from experience or perception, or nurture as opposed to nature. Isn't that what you are proposing?" I continued and asked, then added. "Unfortunately, you weren't there at the beginning, and you need to deal with minds that have been born with and furthermore subsequently filled with a certain degree of knowledge. Teachers and books, remember? Furthermore, I might add that I've never met a sexaholic."

"Neither have I, but, well, yes. I guess I have been left with the monumental task of a potter who must nurture helpless, though rebellious, clay into various forms of absolute obedience. So, I guess if my hands are full and my mind is empty I can go out on the limb as far I'd care to because I wouldn't be held responsible for my behavior. Therefore, it stands to reason that killing her could never be held against me. To put it another way I'd be incapable of hitting bottom, so the consequences of my behavior would have no bearing on an act of omission. Why? Because I'd obviously be in a free-fall with no bottom in sight. How could I possibly be held accountable for my actions if they were beyond my control. Time plus matter plus chance would have neither a beginning nor an end, and I'd be in a state of continuous unaccountability. We're talking here about the perfect crime," he answered with his typical bravado.

He held my gaze with omniscience that widened his brown eyes as if they had become mesmerizing saucers ascending gently on innocent ground. "And, don't forget about the gravity of books. There's always been a certain intellectual gravitational pull that keeps our feet firmly planted to the earth while our imaginations soar among a multitude of metaphorical galaxies. Some words, of which, when put together in sentences can take on metaphysical powers. They can actually be considered to possess a supernatural quality. Nathaniel Hawthorne said, "'Words-so innocent and powerless as they are, as standing in a dictionary, how potent for good and evil they become, in the hands of one who knows how to combine them,'" he added nonchalantly while polishing off his almond croissant.

"But, wait," I said while picking at my salad. "Someone besides you would be bound to know about it. Nothing is ever performed in a perfect vacuum. I know you've heard about the "Butterfly Effect," and that somehow nothing happens anywhere that is ever totally isolated from other events. You will never get away with it. And, if you did get away with it, you'd never get away with it."

"While that is true, it doesn't necessarily mean that another human being is involved or affected by such an event. It could just be another butterfly whose flight is disturbed by some mysterious emotional wavelength traveling at the speed of light across an ocean or a continent based on the flapping wings of another butterfly a continent away," he answered while stabbing small pieces of melon with a plastic toothpick.

"Yeah, but not murder, because, obviously another person is involved besides the murderer. Even suicide, when you think about it in those terms, involves more than one person. So, I don't see how you can get away with it. Unless, it is a story, of course. Say, like some Greek tragedy," I answered logically though being wrapped in an emotional shroud of concern. At first he seemed unmoved, but then he answered almost angrily.

"Get away with what? Murder? Who said anything about murder? I think you, of all people, know that it is possible to commit murder without killing someone," he answered. "One of the very best ways, if not the best way, to kill somebody is with the proper use of words. Is not "The pen mightier than the sword?" Have you not heard that "'The basic tool for the manipulation of reality is the manipulation of words? If you can control the meaning of words, you can control the people who must use the words.'"

"You're talking about dead men or women walking. Those who are leading lives of quiet desperation. Those, who, if they had a choice would prefer to be dead. Unless, of course, someone, anyone, came along with just the right words of genuine encouragement, compassion and support. Isn't that right?" I asked.

"Yes, but I'm also talking about putting them out of their misery without them, or anyone else, knowing about it. And that includes the innocent murderer," he answered. "Can you think of anyone who was so hopelessly miserable that they wouldn't welcome the opportunity to be kindly put out of their misery? Mind you, please, that I am not talking about someone who is terminally ill and in constant pain. That, as they say, goes without saying."

"Highly unlikely because in chaos theory, the butterfly effect is the sensitive dependence on initial conditions in which a small change in one state of a deterministic nonlinear system can result in large differences in a later state. Lorenz's metaphorical example stated that the flapping wings of a butterfly can potentially influence the time, formation and exact path taken by a hurricane.

I'd find it very hard to believe that humans, on some level, would be unaffected by a hurricane let alone murder, even the so-called "perfect murder," I answered while squeezing my stubborn grape tomato with my fork. The skin of the tomato broke open violently and squirted some tomato juice into his eyes, forcing him to run to the men's room to wash out the acidic discharge. While rinsing the acid from his eyes he took a hard look into the mirror and focused solely on his eyes and thought about his wife.

His wonderful wife had once been the "apple of his eye," but now she had become an insidious causative agent that was slowly rotting his bones and causing a disintegration of his common sense. He was also experiencing bizarre flights of imagination. He'd recently become fascinated with criminology and law. He told me that he had been watching hours upon hours of "CSI" "Forensic Evidence" and "Law and Order." He often referred to the perpetrators of crimes as outrageously stupid idiots.

When he returned I asked him if his eyes were OK. He said his eyes were fine, but he did question the connection between physical sight and perception. He did say that he agreed that "Beauty is in the eye of the beholder," but he added that some beholders were blind and had a tendency to lie to themselves in light of the obvious truth.

I added that I thought there was truth to what he said, but that perhaps those who he thought might be lying to themselves had been blessed with the privilege of "seeing through their eyes rather than with their eyes."

He didn't respond then added that we didn't know enough about chaos theory and the butterfly effect to continue an intelligent conversation. He said we should probably talk about the ten books listed on the New York Times best seller list, all, of which he had ordered and read. To describe him as a voracious reader would not do justice to his love of literature and his capacity for reading. If he could he would read in his sleep. He had a gold key- chain with the following inscription, "To gain glory by means of books you must not only possess them but know them; their lodging must be in your brain and not on the bookshelf." I'd never heard that quote. He said it was by Charles Isaac Elton. I'd never heard of him. He was a walking thesaurus and had memorized thousands of famous quotes, poems, song lyrics, etc.

"Besides, if I killed her, I'd then have to kill you, and I can't imagine performing two perfect crimes. Furthermore, butterflies are free. Aren't they? And isn't there enough chaos in the world without having to blame innocent butterflies, most which live to the ripe old age of two to six weeks?" he asked while stirring his tea and honey. "By the way, did you know on average an ear of corn has 800 kernels in 16 rows, and that corn will always have an even number of rows?"

"Well, no. I didn't know that about corn, but I do know that it is an important biofuel. The next time I eat an ear of corn I am going to count the rows. By the way, speaking of trivia. Did you know that some butterflies can be poisonous?" I asked smartly.

"Who doesn't know that!" he responded arrogantly. "Some butterflies such as the Monarch and Pipevine Swallow Tail eat poisonous plants as caterpillars and are poisonous themselves as adult butterflies. Birds learn not to eat them. However no butterflies are so poisonous that they kill people or large animals, but there is an African moth whose caterpillar fluids are very poisonous. The N'gwa or 'Kaa caterpillar's entrails have been used by Bushmen to poison the tips of arrows. When shot by one of these arrows an antelope can be killed in short order."

He then continued to discuss the issue he was having with his wife. She was considerably younger than him and teaching full-time. Lately, that is, for the past six months, she'd been rather cold towards him, and she told him more than once a day that he was always doing things wrong. She began to consider him somewhat of a dunce, and he was far from that; everyone knew that about him, and if you didn't believe him you'd only have to ask him. Yet, as I already mentioned; he was nothing short of one of the most brilliant men I'd ever met, and we were friends. I told him that something else was on her mind. Not only was it not him, but it probably was another man or even perhaps another woman.

"You may be right. In fact, you are right, because I saw the two of them together the other evening. They were in the library hiding behind six large stacks of books. He had his hand up her skirt while she was pretending to be reading one of his novels. He's a second rate novelist; I've read everything he's ever written. Dime novel, trailer trash, unimaginative, intellectually innocuous, and about as exciting as a eating a bologna sandwich on white bread or stepping into a lukewarm hot tub," he said with disdain while squeezing the honey into his tea from the plastic bear-shaped bottle. "His palliatives are without the courage or intestinal fortitude to deal with life at its core. If you aren't already in a nursing home he puts you there, where you can be spoon-fed on soft food, his pablum meant for children; sentences, paragraphs, and chapters that require absolutely no mastication."

"I really don't know what she sees in him. He's at least ten years younger than her. Of course, he's quite handsome and has plenty of money, but his writing stinks. I wouldn't recommend it, but if you ever do read one of his books be prepared to detoxify your system of the putrefaction that would have invaded your literary senses. My god! What could have gotten into her? I can honestly say that if she was having an affair with Tolstoy or Dostoevsky, all would be forgiven. But this guy! God forbid! I would be the first one to throw one of his books on the fire, then I'd yell, "Fahrenheit 451! Fahrenheit 451! Burn, baby! Burn!"

We had a lot in common. We both had become classic enablers, and, furthermore, we did things around the house that were better left to women, or at least tasks that a woman should perform occasionally, but we had entered that same trap common to brilliant men, not necessarily men of low self esteem, but men who believed that keeping the peace often became more important than offering proof of being a man. However, of course, just like in any marriage certain types of assumptive behaviors are unacceptable, and, depending upon the man, the consequences could be disastrous.

"Kill my wife! Hell, I'd rather kill myself," I said. "I didn't know what love was until I met her. I still haven't come down from the ceiling. As corny as it sounds, I'd take a bullet for her."

"Corny. Couldn't you have chosen a less corny word? Haven't I reminded you more than once of what Mark Twain said about choosing the right word? Don't just remember what he said, but practice what he said: "The difference between the almost-right word and the right word is really a large matter-it's the difference between the lightning bug and the lightning.""

We left the restaurant. We shook hands and embraced as we departed for our respective cars. His parting words were from Ecclesiastes, "'Of making many books there is no end, and much study is a weariness to the flesh.'"

When they found her body in the corn field she'd been carrying an over-sized book-bag loaded with more than one dozen hardback books. The book-bag had been strapped to her back and seemed to have weighed her down. She was dead, and it appeared as if she had died from natural causes; exhaustion, dehydration and acute atrial fibrillation that must have caused her already weakened heart to skip one beat too many.

The bizarre nature of her death made no sense. The assumptions were many, but for some unknown reason a mysterious force must have compelled her to travel through almost 200 yards of neck high corn. There was some speculation that she may have been headed for a neighboring barn where the authorities found a few empty bottles of champagne, some plastic cups and a queen size mattress located in the hayloft.

When her body was discovered the only curiosity, besides the burdensome book-bag, was the Monarch butterflies they found twisted in her golden hair.

The Trunk

he insipid, lifeless, asphalt pavement stretched its hot tail of steamy black indifference beyond the horizon like a tasteless tongue whose oval shaped clusters of cells had been scorched dry, parched and without a voice. Of course the road had purpose beyond which it had no meaning, but its intentions were obvious. And the wind, the kind wind had given up its longed for comforting breeze, preferring to rest between the scarps and faults of rocks, ominous formations of our imaginations conjuring up shade, a place to hide from death in the valley, some poisonous snake you'd not think twice about handling with your bare hands if it could provide respite, deliverance from uncertainty, the albatross that often imposes a stranglehold on hope. We'd always been told that the shortest distance between two points was a straight line, and we were determined to never deviate, unless, of course, some unfamiliar lust should raise its alluring head and burn pockets of regret indelibly into our flesh, scarred cheeks knifed with the crescent moon's beam in an alley with a stranger you had things in common with, hidden things.

Fear crippled our wills that soon might be broken by something greater than ourselves, a pile-driving higher power capable of dividing and conquering the proud head of malignant narcissism. We'd been looking desperately for a bridge to nowhere as long as the plunge would find us braver than we could have ever expected. We never wanted to be accused of standing on some stormy bank while casting hopeful eyes. It had always been "an eye for an eye, and a tooth for a tooth." An enemy to whom you showed mercy could still prove to be a vengeful enemy. We had made a vow to only open the trunk in the presence of each other.

"Can contradictory assertions be equally true?" he once asked me when he saw me struggling with the monkey on my back. He had a confident knack for paving the way when others had given up before even one attempt. Yet, at the same time, he often dressed in colorful conundrums. Our paths had crossed at the international dateline heading in opposite directions. You might say we just banged into each other for no apparent reason, other than, of course, to edify one another and to bring the best out of each other. In spite of our diverse differences, we had found that "iron sharpens iron." We were always agreeably disagreeable even if we suspected that the other might be attempting to suppress the truth. We seemed to have a pretty good grip on the truth; that is, truth as we had come to know it in all of its slippery forms.

We couldn't taste a thing because the nerves lining this black tongue had become a deadened sorrowful monotony. But this would not stop us from going down into the mouth in search of the median fold that connects the tongue to the floor of the mouth. For, after all, when we began this trip we had a determined destination, and we brimmed with confidence. We were being driven by a philosophical metaphysically mechanical lust for life, and we wouldn't stop until we had arrived at the end of the rainbow where a pot full of dreams would await us, besides, of course, the honey on a stick that would open our eyes to sights we'd previously only heard about. I once said to him, "You will see it when you believe it." You might say an Upper Room thought.

The journey now, however, was about to become a nightmare, a grotesque stain etched as if by a permutation on our consciences, a linear deviation from one's higher power, but not necessarily the highest power. This trip seemed to have been eviscerated of hope because we couldn't stay inside the stalled car, neither could we tolerate the blazing sun that had forsaken mercy, preferring to torture the landscape with justice in the guise of a god sitting on a throne of ice bathed by purified water. Soon finding just one drop of water would be the equivalent of discovering the pearl of great price inside this oyster of doom.

"How many times have I had to tell you to grab the dilemma by the horns and bring the headstrong bull to his knees!" This time it was the cattle prod in my voice that provoked him when I witnessed his avoidance-approach manner of trying to solve a problem. I told him in no uncertain terms to man-up. "Treat that dilemma as a cathartic opportunity even if it means grabbing it by its vulnerable nuts and driving it to its knees. Have no mercy, but don't kill it. Don't be afraid to release into consciousness those repressed ideas, feelings, wishes and memories."

If we chose to walk we'd soon be on our knees crawling through the desert, two dehydrated blisters, until we'd fall spent, exhausted, helpless, and hopeless. We'd then be left for dead beneath a sky of famished buzzards, predators without fighting spirits, cowards who would only fight among themselves over the flesh of the dead carcass. Yet to remain inside would prove just as deadly. We couldn't even listen to the radio. So we reluctantly got out and lifted the hood of the car to see what ailment had caused us to prematurely ejaculate hope. Not because it couldn't be repaired, but because we hadn't the necessary tools to complete the job, and neither of the two of us were the least bit mechanically inclined. Even if we possessed the tools we'd look like two baboons sharing a left-handed money-wrench. But that didn't stop us from looking at the engine with the curiosity of two mechanical neophytes, supposing that we could twist or turn a knob or a screw or beat against certain exposed vital organs with a hammer. Perhaps these appropriately administered shocks might cause a sudden rhythmic exchange of beats acting in the guise of a mysteriously implanted pacemaker designed to restore homeostasis.

"Turn it over. See what happens," he said, sounding just like a seasoned grease monkey who could never get the dirt out from beneath his nails, a real man and with the callouses to prove it. No such luck. Not the remotest sound of life by the turn of a screw.

"Shit!" he said. "I knew I shouldn't have listened to you and taken the road less traveled. So much for your bright idea about living on the razor's edge. So much for grabbing the bull by its horns. Why couldn't we remain in Egypt where we had all the leeks, garlic and meat we'd ever need? Promise land, my ass!"

I didn't try to defend myself, but it hadn't taken much persuasion to convince him that he had no future where he'd previously hitched his little red wagon. Yes, that is correct; it wasn't hitched to a star. Besides, he was the one who carried around a dog-eared copy of "Mice and Men" in his back pocket. He'd always made it sound as if there were no boundaries, and if they existed they'd certainly be lax. Yet, if you got too close those boundaries would become impermeable. One thing he could never be legitimately accused of was inappropriate self-disclosure. I often wondered if he thought I could see through doors. He carried himself around town like a samurai warrior, but if the truth be known, he was a closet worshiper of Marcus Cicero who said, "If you have a garden and a library, you have everything you need." If the man had been 5 ft. 6" tall he would have been considered a giant.

At least we knew that we needed more than just a simple jump. We needed an internist. So we did what we frequently did best; we laughed in the face of adversity. We both always wanted to be actors and would often look for opportunities to act out certain well known scenes from movies we liked. So, after that failed attempt, he threw the wrench and screwdriver down and said, "We don't need no stinking badges."

That done, we feigned serious geometrical faces and made theoretical comments about life and death, artificial intelligence, the presumption of predestination and free will, and, of course, the man in the moon and its consistency. We agreed that there was something paradoxical about the mute pavement that was intended to lead us into an inner sanctum of life, not a plastic bag into which we would stick our hermetically sealed heads and inhale death. Neither one of us, in spite of what he said, would ever return even if we had to feed on the same slop as our fellow swines. We weren't too proud to beg, but we certainly considered it below us. Casting our pearls before swine, however, was never out of the question.

"Keep Out. Road Closed. Dead End. Danger: High Voltage." Meaningless phrases to daredevils high on adventure and home grown drugs. Point to the sky and stick your swollen, vascular, bloody vein out and pull the moon out of its rhythmic circadian orbit. Stick a shunt into its aged head of cheese and drain it of all its romantic poetry, verse by sugary verse, until it becomes an unintelligible shriveled, flaccid orb that can neither speak nor understand speech, neither figures of speech.

"Why do you lapse into such exaggerated states of dysphoria? You have nothing to be depressed about. Maybe you should get your head out of that Taber's Medical Dictionary. I can categorically guarantee you that neither Ben Casey nor Dr. Kildare went to medical school; one of our side effects will always be death. In the mean time, however, you bloated bag of famous sayings and quotes remember what Lao-Tzu said, 'If you never assume importance, you never lose it.'"

"Hell! If that's not the pot calling the kettle black, then I'll be a monkey's uncle. If you had the opportunity to become an existential metaphysically empowered prince with the cyclonic powers to rip the flowering buds of wheat heads off in Kansas you'd probably rape the corn instead just to be different," I replied while considering the remote possibility of a good Samaritan sauntering by on a donkey laden down with far too much treasure to fit between the eye of a needle. "Maybe you don't remember your Hippocratic oath." He hated trite phrases, and I'd drop them out of nowhere. He really hated "Caught red-handed," "Dead as a doornail," "Dead give away," and most especially "Gentle as a lamb." He was a real corker.

In every direction we saw the same behemoth stretching out before us: nothing. Nothing but distances multiplied by despair capable of slicing off either your ears or your nose, or a blindness designed to detach your retinas without the consequent hot red poker. There would be nothing to taste if you could taste, and your skin would slowly slough off like the exoskeleton of certain arthropods. When we saw the magnitude of nothingness before us we couldn't think of anything that could be done, at least by the two of us. Nothing. We still had at least that much common sense. So we danced deliriously between two headstones before agreeing to reluctantly open the trunk. The asphalt python had been squeezing our guts out, killing us slowly with masochistic methodical exhalations. We had agreed that death did not become us.

"Wait. It would be far too premature. It would be similar to opening Pandora's Box before we gave providence the opportunity to send the good Samaritan," he said while sticking his thumb out like a hopeful hitchhiker. "Remember when you once told me that I would see it when I believed it? Well, maybe this is the time you might have been referring to."

I remained silent then kicked one of the tires. I then went to the rear of the car and very deliberately pounded the trunk mercilessly with both fists. I raised my closed fists to the sky, but I didn't scream. I just focused on the sun, the fiery orb of life and death, a cancer-hungry malignant petty potentate, the dictator who rules the horoscope, the germinator of hope, the despot of despair. "How do I hate thee. Let me count the ways." I then slammed my blistered, melting plastic fists against the trunk violently and cursed myself inwardly. Neither would this have been the first time I'd considered suicide. Who hasn't? Well, maybe not, but it might be because you don't need to worry about what's inside your trunk. Maybe you're one of the transparent lucky ones.

He came to me and tried to console me. He hugged me but said nothing. "Maybe we should try to go back to the beginning," I said while looking forlornly into his understanding green eyes.

"I don't think so. Remember what you once told me when I was about to break into a million pieces of shattered self worth? You said, 'The significant problems we face cannot be solved at the same level of thinking we were at when we created them.' You then asked me to guess who might have said that. Of course, I didn't know. You told me it was Einstein. Yeah, Einstein. The same man you said who never wore socks."

The signs of life had disappeared except for the buzzards, and even they were losing altitude. I wasn't sure what both of us were thinking, exactly, besides the possibility of dying in the desert while playing out our antagonistic parts in this absurd drama.

This was no tragi-comedy. We were living a surreal life in the theater of the absurd, only we weren't waiting for Godot; he was waiting for us. So we decided to wait before opening the trunk. We agreed to give the future an opportunity to show-up loaded down with a cornucopia of promises, or just one.

While contemplating the significance of my tendency to behave in an exaggerated manner to offset my perceived liabilities that were motivated by feelings of inferiority, guilt and anxiety, I couldn't help but consider the supernatural, the metaphysical, the existential nature of the trunk's contents, the biological blow-back that might represent deliverance. Hell, I'm sure we weren't the only ones guilty of guilt. Yet, at the same time, or on the other hand, there could be an issue of blood guiltiness. Not necessarily an issue of bloodshed, although that familiar damned spot seemed to be gaining preeminence.

We didn't say much for quite awhile. We just took short walks up and down the pavement. He occasionally walked into the parched desert and dug below the surface. It was hard to imagine that one might find some living creature in this barren geography, but after one long walk he said he saw a scorpion. I guess anything was possible. So I went out and when I came back I told him I had seen a King Snake.

"King Snake, my ass. If you'd have seen a King Snake your screams would have brought down a heavenly deluge of holy water or some hail, fire and brimstone. Who are you kidding? Do you remember the last time you saw your shadow? Maybe you forgot, but I didn't. You were leaning on the lamp post beneath the streetlight right in front of your house. You couldn't move. You were frightened stiff. Your mom had to call 911. When the paramedics arrived you could have gone home, but you chose instead to go to the behavior ward. So, this is no time for an alienation of the spirits," he said with the two-edged sword that often exited his mouth when he was irritated, frustrated or both.

I didn't reply back negatively, but I knew he had not seen a scorpion. He'd probably seen a Jerusalem Beetle. He may have been hallucinating. Our water was gone, and we didn't know it at the time, but we'd both been independently thinking about arbitrarily opening the trunk. It seemed a little early for hallucinations based on dehydration, but we were burning up, and the mind has been known to play tricks on physically and emotionally weakened vessels. What I'd actually seen was a desert locust, which, had I not known better, could have been much more foreboding than some harmless snake.

Evening was approaching. The curtain in the sky was slowly closing. It wasn't coming from left to right, nor right to left, but was slowly descending. The stagehands were waiting in the wings. All they had to do was move the car, then we'd head for our dressing rooms. Here, behind closed doors, we'd remove our grease paint and change our clothes. Our personalities wouldn't change much, but there would be changes. However, it wasn't over just yet. We still had parts to play and songs to sing. If lucky we'd have a curtain call. Maybe roses and chocolate backstage.

"Hey, will you look at that sun. It seems as if it is hardly moving. It is almost as if it would have preferred to stick around to watch us suffer," he said as he sat on the punch drunk trunk that had since cooled down and recovered. I was sitting on the hood.

"I wonder if the moon will be any kinder to us?" I asked nonchalantly.

"Probably not, and there probably won't be any stars, either," he said with forlorn resolve.

I didn't want to succumb to the blanket of despair that had been slowly wrapping us like two hungry sucklings being held in the cruel arms of uncertainty. "Maybe tomorrow we will look in the sky and see a cloud the size of a man's fist," I offered hopefully. "Furthermore, haven't I told you more than once that "Only that which is invisible is essential.""

"There probably won't be a tomorrow. Today is the tomorrow you were thinking about, yesterday. I think we should open the trunk before we turn in for the night. It just might give us a sense of closure and put to an end our dichotomous thinking and the fear of being discovered. In fact, at this point, I don't even care if the whole world knows what we've been trying to hide. Otherwise, I don't think I will be able to sleep very peacefully. I can't see any harm in opening the trunk, especially as this is about as far as we're going," he said with a sense of carefree abandon. "It might be our salvation," he added, then blessed himself. "Maybe the atonement we've heard and read about is based on fact, an absolute truth. Maybe The Pearl of Great Price has eluded us, and it will have taken this desert experience to open our eyes," he continued.

"O Captain! My Captain! Give me the keys. Our fearful trip is done." he added while extending his transparent hand, a sensitive phantom limb with one thousand tender nerves running through it with light giving electricity, a kind hand, though just as able to shock with violent voltage and jealous rage.

"I understand how you feel. I feel the same way, but I think it best that we get through the night. Opening the trunk won't help either one of us sleep better. I think you realize that there is probably a lot more guilt in that trunk than either one of us could handle without some help from an outside party. The delusional coping mechanisms we employed in the past that enabled us to navigate emotionally stressful situations in order to maintain internal consistency while adjusting to our environment won't work in this negatively charged atmosphere. If I felt otherwise I'd open the trunk myself," I added sincerely while holding tightly onto the keys with my left hand in my pocket, but, of course, I had to get the last word in, or so I thought. "Tomorrow, and tomorrow, and tomorrow. Creeps in this petty pace from day to day to the last syllable of recorded time. And all our yesterdays have lighted fools the way to dusty death, and so on and so forth, and so forth and so on, for we, two idiots, are full of sound and fury signifying nothing."

"I swear," I thought to myself as I watched his plastic affect begin to melt into a mindless puddle hopelessness. "If we can get out of this foxhole alive I'll turn over a new leaf and join the Peace Corps, or I may even go one giant step forward and never look back. Maybe it's time for integrity to part the Red Sea and my opportunity to go right on through to the other side."

"OK. I see no need to discuss the matter any further, and I certainly don't want to argue. I guess we can wait until tomorrow; I'm just not as certain as you are that there will be a tomorrow. So, I will not impose my will upon you because, as you once reminded me, "'Forces beyond your control can take away everything you possess except one thing, your freedom to choose how you will respond to the situation,'" he said with an obvious visceral sense of freedom.

"Yes, between stimulus and response we have the ability to choose. You have chosen wisely. I'd have done the same thing, and it certainly isn't anything we'd argue about. In fact, we don't ever seem to argue, except occasionally over little things. Sure, we hash things out as we ought to, but we don't argue. Neither one of us needs to be right at the expense of the other. In honor we prefer one another. Isn't that correct?" I asked sympathetically while fingering the keys.

I was sure that if I appealed to his nobler motives he would see things from my point of view. Neither one of us ever intentionally employed distancing techniques to maintain psychological distance from and lack of emotional involvement with each other. We were "all in" as they say when playing Texas Holdem. At the same time, however, I thought it might be best to protect myself from, what might have been, a subtle attempt at projection on his part. Hell, I know I've done it from time to time, and sometimes even inadvertently. Who hasn't employed this defense mechanism in which intolerable feelings, impulses, thoughts, or other traits are ascribed to other people in order to deny that they are part of one's self.

"Yeah, you're right, and another thing I like about our situation is that neither one of us ever employs defense mechanisms, those self-protective patterns of emotional reactions that guard against conscious awareness of anxiety-inducing, internally conflicting, stressful or otherwise unpleasant scenarios. I also like the fact that the oneupmanship games we play are meant to edify one another, not to establish any type of personal intellectual or emotional hierarchy," he said in his typical subtle passive-aggressive way.

"Yes, best friend, you speak the truth," I said as I slowly pulled my hand out of my pocket after having released the keys. "And remember that each of us can say categorically without equivocation, 'I celebrate myself, and sing myself, and what I assume you shall assume, for every atom belonging to me as good belongs to you.'"

"So be it," he said. "But before we turn-in I'd like to add something for you to consider."

"Sure, be my guest, but don't let the cat out of the bag," I answered with the thrust of a hat pin while anticipating his salvo.

"'Live as if you were living already for the second time and as if you had acted the first time as wrongly as you are about to act now.'" This was his favorite Viktor Frankl quote.

When I heard that I didn't hesitate. I pulled the keys out of my pocket, and I handed them to him and said, "Remember, when we open the trunk, whether it is now or tomorrow, the contents will not speak for themselves. We will be required to speak on behalf of the contents."

How are things in general?

Whenever someone asked me how things were in general, I wasn't sure how to respond. I assumed they weren't sincerely interested in how I really felt. It shouldn't have come as a surprise. These were friends who were often far more interested in how they were doing rather than how I, or anyone else was doing. They certainly were nice enough, but they'd never been willing to go much deeper than a kind "Hello, how are things in general?" Furthermore, it was often obvious that they had something more important to discuss; an issue that revolved around what they were experiencing. It may have been an issue pertaining to their health, their finances, their marriage, their children; something they thought you might be willing to listen to, perhaps even give them advice, but not typically. They just needed someone to talk to, sometimes desperately.

Even though I was carrying a heavy load, I knew it was a burden they would not be willing to share. It's hard to find someone who is willing to share your burden, someone who is apt to place their head in the wooden crosspiece fastened over the necks of two animals attached to a plow or cart they are to pull together. I don't think it would be considered far-fetched to bear one another's burdens and so fulfill the love of Christ, even if you weren't a Christian. What would that have to do with it? Sure, you can bring religion into the picture if you want to and quote bible verses like "Come unto Me, all you who labor and are heavy laden, and I will give you rest. Take My yoke upon you and learn from Me, for I am gentle and lowly in heart, and you will find rest for your souls. For My yoke is easy and My burden is light." Of course, this is all well and good, but where does this leave you if you need someone with flesh on the bone, someone whose eyes you can look into and see compassion and maybe even get some sound advice?

Don't misunderstand, frequently self-discovery hurts; sometimes for the better, especially when we are willing to take a hard look in the mirror of truth, and we find that not only is it not the good Samaritan who is staring back at us, but that it is a religious hypocrite or sacrilegious priest afraid to be defiled by someone he deems less sacred than himself. "Judge not, lest you be judged." At least that's what I've always said. Furthermore, no burden of proof would be required to support the truth; the burden would speak for itself. If I sound judgmental, forgive me; I don't mean to be. *I believe we should always be aware of anything that puts us in the place of a superior person.*

I wouldn't find fault, necessarily. However, it sure would be refreshing to be able to share your burdens with another person, other than a psychologist at $150.00 per Fifty-Five Minute session. You'd always need at least five minutes to clear the air, make another appointment and then make out the check. Don't get me wrong. I don't necessarily find fault with psychologists. They can be helpful. They certainly seem to know how to dig up the dirt without getting their hands dirty, but sometimes their advice, based on the uncovered dirt, can leave one feeling dirtier than when you first sat down on the couch. I've often wondered how many skeletons are banging into one another in their respective closets, a dark place behind closed doors where many funny things can happen, some of which would be very enlightening, embarrassing or even incriminating, especially if observed through a keyhole by some uninterested third party who had just been passing by and heard suspicious noises.

"Can these bones live?" Probably, but what about the clanging skeletons? Do they possess some esoteric language based on psychological gobbledygook drawn from psychiatric journals whose foundation is dream interpretation? Or are these clanging bones, as diverse as they are, speaking Noam

Chomsky's "Universal Grammar?" On the other hand, maybe these bones only begin to clang together when they hear a bell ringing? All I'm saying is that occasionally supernatural intervention takes place when least expected and sometimes not. Regardless, we should never lose hope and always be ready to give hope even if it appears as if we may be hanging all alone in a closet on an abandoned steel hanger.

Anyway, regarding these bony extrusions I'd often just walk away after I'd told them that things in general were "OK." If they really wanted to know the truth, they might have noticed that my kyphotic posture was an obvious indication that I was being mercilessly worn down by my burden. If they knew me as well as they thought they did, they would have recognized that my posture was neither post-traumatic nor congenital. I had obviously been carrying a burden around that had become progressively heavier and heavier. Things in general were bad and getting worse. I guess what I expected was that they would act sincerely, and ask me how things were going more specifically, you know, get yoked-up.

Things in general can be OK, especially considering that you're not confined to a wheelchair or had recently been diagnosed with "stage four" cancer. Even an inquiry that was more specific in nature could easily be sloughed off as no big deal based on the inquirer's diagnosis and response. I mean, some of your friends might consider your problem no worse than the burden they have been carrying around. They might even say something like, "Hell, if you think you've got a problem, wait till you hear about what happened to me. You'll probably thank your lucky stars that you haven't been walking around in my shoes."

I guess it's true that most people spend about 90% of their time thinking about themselves. So, while they may truly want to know how things are in general with you, what they really want to do is to tell you how things are more specifically with them. They must think that their shoes are a lot less comfortable than yours. Hell, besides which, we all know that "One size does not fit all" when it comes to shoes; some poor people don't even own a pair of shoes let alone a pair that don't fit. How would you like to spend your entire life walking barefoot across a globe paved with hot tar, blacktop that has been baking in the sun from here to eternity? Tell me, whose steel mill working, Pollock/Hunky father hasn't been heard saying to his thankless son, "I don't want to hear no more complaining about your worn-out shoes when there are people in the world who don't have no shoes at all and in some cases no feet. Now stick some fresh cardboard into your shoes and get to school. You're going to get an education if it kills me so your kids won't have to put no cardboard into their shoes."

"Hey, Joe, thanks for asking. Things in general are, OK, but let me be a little more specific about how things really are. Do you have the time to listen? If so, I'd like to tell you about what just happened to my grandson. It's extremely important, almost urgent. I think I am going to need more than just your advice. Would that be OK?" I asked politely and very hopefully. I recognized, of course, that Joe was carrying his briefcase, something that had almost become a permanent part of him, or at least a type of phantom extension. Joe and I had been friends since high school, and Joe, when he wasn't occupied with business, had been known to take an occasional interest in human beings, other than defendants, of course.

I'd never had a burden as heavy as this one in my whole life, but I didn't want to trouble anyone else with it. In fact, I knew I couldn't burden another person; I needed someone to speak to who could provide some professional advice. Joe just happened to be one of my friends, maybe not my best friend, but a friend, nevertheless. He knew the same thing that everyone knows: friends are hard to come by, and good friends are about as rare as a four-leaf clover. He'd always been a good listener; he needed to be; his profession depended on it.

"Actually, Art, I'm on my way to the courthouse. I'm running a little late. I've been working on my summation since late last night. How about if we get together some other time? I just thought I'd say, "Hi" since I haven't seen you for a month or so. I'll give you a call in about a week, then we can have a long chat. You don't mind, do you?" Joe asked with kind assurance. His 6 ft. 6 Inch frame was impressive. I'm sure his stature contributed to his success in the court room. He certainly could be intimidating. He also had an extremely effective way of articulating euphemistic realities that softened jurors' hearts by causing them to reevaluate the facts, a way to make a felony appear to be more like a misdemeanor based, believe it or not, on words rather than evidence. Besides his ability to harness language, he could captivate his audience by using demonstrative evidence and turn death at the hands of an incompetent surgeon into a "therapeutic misadventure."

"Oh, OK. I'll talk to you later, but I don't think what I need to share with you can wait for more than a day or two. Call me at your convenience. I'll be anxiously waiting. Maybe we can get together for lunch," I answered as I extended my hand for a friendly handshake. Joe had no idea that I had come down town hoping to run into him.

I took a particular note of Joe's limp-wristed shake, an act that could hardly be considered a shake; I felt as if I had just grasped a handful of play dough, a soft lump of clammy emotionless clay that left me feeling oddly unappreciated; inconvenient might be a better description, or perhaps eviscerated of hope, at least for the moment. Hell, he barely made eye contact. He was usually in a hurry, but today he seemed especially anxious.

I watched Joe's lean basketball frame mount the steps of the courthouse then disappear into the hungry marble mouth of the monolith of truth. Before I moved on, I took a long look at my abandoned hand and thought that maybe what my grandson had done had been done unintentionally; after all, I'd been subjected to the same kinds of temptations, and, even though I'd not succumbed to most of them, I certainly could identify with my grandson's motives and actions. I recognized that there was a dark side to every man; a kind of dark side of the moon not visible to others, but a side, if not subjected to a good conscience would eventually become fermented, and, in some cases, begin to smell so odious that it wouldn't even attract a rat. On the other hand, the admonition to cut off your right hand if it causes you to sin, seems rather harsh, to say the least. It didn't take me more than a few times to learn to keep my hand out of the cookie jar. At that precise moment, I did not wish Joe any harm, but I would have liked nothing more than an opportunity to jam both of my hands into an inviting cookie jar, get caught by the authorities, go to trial, be defended by him, be convicted, then locked-up.

Disappointed, I dragged my fragmented mind to the park on emotionally buckled legs. I meandered aimlessly for a while before I came to my favorite bench, not too far from the water. I often came to the park; it had always been the most peaceful place for me, a place where I could observe some of the wonders of nature, a refuge where I could meditate and become creative. I'd often bring a book. Occasionally I'd write or sketch. Sometimes I prayed, but I just loved to feed the pigeons. Sometimes they would eat the food right out of my hand. Besides the pigeons I'd made a few other friends in the park. One guy was a pigeon expert. He knew just about everything there was to know about pigeons, and he liked to share his knowledge with anyone who might be willing to listen.

I was surprised to learn that 32 pigeons have been decorated with the Dickin Medal for war contributions, including Commando, G.I. Joe, Paddy, and William Of Orange. Cheri Ami, a homing pigeon in World Wat I, was awarded The Croix De Guerre Medal with a palm Oak Leaf Cluster for her service in Verdun and for delivering the message that saved the lost Battalion of the 77th infantry Division in the Battle of the Argonne, October 1918.

A grand ceremony was held in Buckingham Palace to commemorate a platoon of pigeons that braved the battlefields of Normandy to deliver vital plans to the Allied forces on the fringes of Germany. Three of the actual birds that received the medals are on show in the London Military Museum so that well-wishers can pay their respects. These were just some of the facts this energetic young man shared with me about pigeons.

That somber evening, when I wasn't feeding the pigeons, I spent most of my time staring out across the lake at the windows of the county jail. My thoughts drifted from the windows of the jail to the stones that formed the walls of the jail, an ornate landmark built a hundred years earlier, a place designed to protect society from evil doers. While studying the walls and windows I thought mostly about my grandson.

"Hey, grandpa, after we leave McDonald's do you think we can go to the park? Maybe we can take some food to feed the pigeons. I like it when they eat right out of my hand. Maybe we can pick-up a loaf of bread and toss it on the water for the ducks. Do you think that would be OK, grandpa?" I love you, grandpa. You're the best grandpa in the whole wide world. Would that be OK?" his grandson asked him in his special kind of grandson way.

"Hey, grandpa, look. This is the biggest fish I've ever caught. Do you think dad will believe us if we throw it back in? I wish we would have brought the camera. Grandpa, I love to go fishing with you. You're the best. Boy, am I ever lucky to have a grandpa like you," his grandson said enthusiastically while removing the hook from the fish's mouth.

"Hey, grandpa. Holy cow! What do you think about that.? This is the first time I've hit for the cycle. Single, double, triple and home run in the same game. Gee, grandpa, if it wasn't for you, I wouldn't even be playing baseball. You're the one who taught me how to hit and field. Dad was always on the road, or too busy, and even when he was home he didn't seem to be listening to me when I spoke, but you were always there for me. You're my hero, grandpa. I love you, "his grandson said after his final game for the high school team.

"Hey, grandpa, guess what? I've been accepted by your alma mater. The past two years of junior college really paid off. Now, thanks to you, I'm getting that scholarship we've been praying for. Once summer is over, I'll be heading to New England. If it's the last thing I do I'll make you proud of me. I hope I grow up to become as tenderhearted and as kind as you are. You're not only the greatest grandpa in the world, but you're also one of the wisest. I will never forget the many things you've taught me, especially how to be attentive in the presence one person or many. You'll never have to worry about me doing my best, and I will always remember what you said about doing your best, "Being the best is not as important as doing your best," his grandson said after he showed him the letter.

As loving thoughts of my grandson began to occupy my mind, I'd become oblivious to my surroundings. Suddenly the stream of my loving conscious thoughts was unconsciously rudely interrupted. The wonder of the sky, now a solvable equation, seemed to have disappeared into the geometric mouth of a black hole; a gravitational collapse had taken place; the proverbial "point of no return" had become a reality, and even though the event horizon is not a material surface but rather merely a mathematically defined demarcation boundary, it apparently had been crossed. I'd never been so consumed with the vicissitudes of life, especially those that seemed cruel and unfair. The "What Ifs" had me firmly in their irrevocably changeless grasp.

The disarticulated limbs of parched trees had lost their leaves; they limped away painfully then disappeared beyond the horizon on lifeless pitiful trunks. The fresh water lake, once full of life, was now empty; it had become a dry mouth full of frog skeletons and fish fossils. Nothing and no one were dancing; the music had been crushed beneath the heavy feet of sorrow; lead weighed down the belly. No discernible language existed except for some bizarre incoherent babble and an occasional squeal.

My forlorn thoughts seemed to have become incarcerated, and the key was hanging on the belt of an unknown inquisitor whose position was to never ask questions. This keeper of the keys trudged up and down the halls like a deaf mute consigned to his own prison; he dragged his left foot behind him, and if, and when, he did speak, he muttered words that were not discernible. I needed someone to ask me some questions. I needed desperately to be engaged.

I don't think people know how important it is to ask questions. Asking questions is generally how discussions begin, but most people aren't prepared to listen, so they don't ask questions, at least meaningful ones, that is. Asking questions should then be followed by listening intently, not necessarily to give a response, but to listen actively with one's heart and soul. Not like a priest, or anything like that, but sincerely. I'd always been known as a good listener, but all I could hear at this moment was the sound of my tears.

Suddenly from behind me a pigeon landed softly on my left shoulder. What a pleasant way to be startled out of my depressed melancholic stupor. When I turned to my left to study this beautiful creature, one gently landed on my right shoulder. Thereafter I was besieged by numerous other pigeons, a few on my lap, many on the bench to my left and right, but mostly at my feet. They surrounded me. It was as if they were sharing my burden. They temporarily comforted me. My joy was being restored, and sense of hope began to fill my mind; a renewal of my spirit was taking place, then.

Then for some strange reason I had a vision of Burt Lancaster who played Robert Stroud in "The Birdman of Alcatraz." Burt was feeding the pigeons.

The Lumberjack

The remains, having disintegrated to the point of almost being uniden-tifiable, could be found sealed in a bell jar. The bell jar was floating in a familiar cesspool on the outskirts of the little Greek village that had once become a famous tourist trap; the trap has since lost some of its allure due to an innocuous smell that seems to have come, and continues to come daily, out of nowhere. The smell wasn't necessarily of the worst kind; for example a maggot breeding dumpster or mounds of discarded sanitary napkins being drip-dried in the sun. Unlike many odors, this odor wouldn't necessarily make one sick, although it could, but it definitely had a negative effect on one's appetite. It was particularly evident in the local restaurants, and try as they might these small business owners could not eliminate the odor. More than one of these restaurants had to close their doors after decades of success. It wasn't as if these owners didn't try to find and then eliminate the smell. They tried everything, including gutting the interior and fumigating every square inch, especially the kitchen, a potential haven for bacteria. No smell is without substance, visible or otherwise, and probably could be captured under the right conditions, but one wouldn't want it to be captured by a slab of beef or a shank of lamb.

A great deal of scrubbing on one's hands and knees was being employed using various kinds of bleach and disinfectants. Perhaps the problem was the nature of the smell; it was so subtle that when you thought it had been eliminated it seemed to mysteriously hang in the air, but not everybody could smell it. Some people had absolutely no idea that a smell even existed.

They just seemed to go along their merry old way as if the people who objected to the smell were crazy. But, the smell, nevertheless, was real and caused a great deal of consternation among the more sensitive villagers. At first, most tourists had no problem with what they referred to as the 'purported' smell, until one prominent woman wrote a letter to the editor. She used a lot of big words in her letter and also peppered it with medical jargon. She wasn't from the village, but she owned a condominium there as her summer home. She said that unless an individual had been afflicted with anosmia, a loss of sense of smell, the smell was undeniable. She went on and on about olfactory this and olfactory that, and how important the sense of smell was. She accused one restaurant owner of claiming that she must have been suffering from a bad case of parosmia, a perverted sense of smell whereby odors that are considered agreeable are assumed to be offensive, and disagreeable odors may be found pleasant. The straw that broke the camel's back was when a garbage man accused her of suffering from an extreme case of kakosmia, the perception of bad odors where none existed. Such a preposterous accusation from a man who obviously couldn't tell the difference between a dinner fork, fish fork, salad fork, desert fork, oyster fork, or even the difference between a fondue fork and tuning fork, almost left her in a permanent state of apoplexia.

The next thing you knew, after the infamous letter to the editor had been published, people began to walk about town, more so than ever, in groups, while sniffing uncharacteristically, especially in the family owned restaurants. Street vendors were not nearly as adversely affected. Neither were the dogs, and as long as the feral cats continued to bat dead mice around like their most favored toys the streets were somewhat safer.

The villagers became obsessed with the smell, and couldn't resist talking about it. The innocuous odor was so subtle that if you weren't thinking about it, it probably didn't really smell all that bad. However, before long it became the topic of every conversation. In spite of the subtle nature of the smell, denying it would cause a great deal of suspicion. The pressure to admit that an odd smell existed caused people who could not recognize the smell to deny themselves and agree that there indeed was a smell coming from somewhere. After being badgered they'd confidently confess by saying something like, "By jove. I do believe you are correct, and I can certainly smell it. Is there anything that can be done about it before it overwhelms us? My God! Why, we've all read about the Black Plague, and I wouldn't put it past those in control, you know who I mean, because in the end we'll be in danger of losing our mortal souls as they relate to tithes, offerings, and even penance money. We may very well find ourselves blindfolded then stretched out on the Bed of Procrustes. Some will be made bigger. Some will be made smaller, but they will have one thing in common; they will be forced to believe and to tell a lie about the true nature of the mysterious smell."

Typically a smell, a foul odor, or other odiferous anomaly requires an origin. If you can get to the origin of the smell you should be able to eliminate it. The problem with this smell was that no place of origin seemed to exist. It just was. Of course, exterminators and other scientific experts had been hired to determine the nature of the smell and its origin. After considerable amounts of money had been spent on these experts the result was inconclusive, to say the least. It was also embarrassing. Eventually the locals became accustomed to the smell, but revenues from the tourist trade had dropped to an all time low. When an ignorant tourist happened to visit they'd almost immediately ask about the odd though subtle smell. The poor locals tried to pass it off as some unique odor that was indigenous to their delightful village, and, of course, that response made it even more obvious. Since no natural source of the smell had been uncovered the villagers began to question the odor of certain individuals, especially those who were suffering from various kinds of inflammation that would produce exudation, or what might more commonly be known as the pathological oozing of fluids. Suspicions began to abound, and even the closest of friends, when in each other's presence, felt an almost uncontrollable urge to smell. Shaking hands had become a rare gesture. The sell of certain aromatic specialty soaps took an exponential jump in volume as did perfume and cologne, and, as did, of course, anti-inflammatories. Bathing two or three times a day had become common, but far less common had become the act of bathing together. No one seemed above suspicion, and the nature of certain relationships had dramatically changed. Trust was at a premium, and enemies seemed to have become those of one's very own household.

Friendship had taken on a new meaning, and the saying "A man who has one true friend has more than his share," had never been truer. However, one funny thing did take place one Sunday afternoon in the park. Two young men, who had been the butt of many a denigrating joke, came into the park together holding hands, and each had a clothespin on his nose, pinching his nostrils tightly closed.

No one could have imagined that the charred remains of the unidentified body stuffed into a bell jar floating in the cesspool had anything to do with this mysterious smell. The lid of the bell jar had not merely been sealed tight; it had been hermetically sealed to protect the contents from the filthy, putrefying, odious, excrement that kept it afloat. The only feature that could distinguish the bell jar from its environment might be the shiny brass lid. Otherwise, it seemed to be a part of the effluvium, the mire, the expelled waste matter, the dung unfit for flies, the diseased excrement, the infectious excreta of dying bodies, the indigestible residues and bacteria of the walking dead, and other almost unimaginable filth and carrion; e.g. the decaying flesh of dead animals, slaughtered slit throats of the dangling carcass, others maliciously hacked, butchered and chopped or sawn asunder, and others, of course, by natural death or the humane act of hunting with shotgun, buckshot, bear trap, bow and arrow, knives, dynamite caps, pungi-sticks, poison, etc. Why would anyone want to protect death from the death surrounding it?

One day, just like that, out of nowhere, similar to the bizarre invisible elephant in the room that was flooding the atmosphere with silent, but not so deadly, flatulence, along came a lumberjack. He moved with a steady gait, one deliberate and powerful step at a time. He wasn't in a hurry. There was something casual about him that invited confidence among the observers. It may have been his face; he appeared to be smiling, almost laughing. Occasionally he whistled. His lumberjack leather logger boots came to just below his knees, the point at which his wranglers had been tucked in and dressed neatly. His checkered black and red flannel shirt had also been neatly tucked into his wrangler jeans and was secured by a thick cherry-red, leather belt that sported a brass buckle in the shape of a wolf's head. His shirt was opened about half way down revealing a massive chest covered with thick red hair. His full beard was also red, but his hair was blond and came down to his shoulders. He wasn't wearing his black hat; it was in his back pocket. His bronze skin displayed two high shiny cheekbones. His protruding blue eyes sparkled. He was six feet eight inches tall and weighed 314 pounds. It would be very difficult to find an ounce of fat on him. His features weren't necessarily different from a number of other lumberjacks who had passed through the village over the years, but the one characteristic that distinguished him from all the others, besides his massive body, was the size and shape of his nose.

This lumberjack's nose was unique from the perspective that it would be considered incongruous compared to the rest of his face. It was sharp, streamlined on each side of the bridge, not round at all. The nostrils appeared to have been tightly pulled where they attached to the portion of the face just above the extremities of the lips. The tip of the nose was slightly square, but not exactly square, and when viewed from the front the nose appeared like a triangle, except for the tip. There was also a subtle shine to the nose compared to the rest of his ruddy tight leathery skin. His nose was not one of those big ones that drew attention and that made it difficult to talk to a person without focusing on his nose, especially those carbuncular bulbous ones that invited the opportunity to practice hypnotic eye contact. Neither was it so small that it might draw attention as if a marble had been planted in the middle of his face. Thank God it wasn't one of those pig noses that seemed to be staring at you from two dark cavernous flared nostrils. No, the uniqueness of this nose did not necessarily draw and hold one's attention, but it was different in a beautiful way. None of the villagers knew that he had a reputation for possessing the ability to smell better than any dog known to mankind. He'd not been invited to the village because of his ability to smell; he was just passing through. He was looking for someone important who may have gotten lost.

When he got about halfway into the village the smell he had detected outside the camp had become much more obvious, but he gave no indication that the smell existed. He just sauntered casually into the nearest restaurant for a bite to eat while carrying his huge ax across his shoulder. The ax occasionally produced a blinding glint based on the angle of the sun. Sometime later it was discovered by one of the scouts that he occasionally used the reflection of the sun off the blade as an instrument to start fires or to blind his enemies, of which he had but a few. It didn't take more than about five minutes alone with him to determine that he was powerfully nice. Peace seemed to run in his blood as naturally as war seemed to run in the blood of other men.

Once inside the first restaurant he detected a slightly more pungent smell than he'd noticed on the outside, but he, once again, gave no indication that anything was unusual. He ate heartily while feasting on steak, potatoes and various types of squash. He also engaged in some small talk with a few of the patrons, including the waitress. He spent the next seven days visiting the various restaurants in the village, eating heartily and making many friends among the locals. When he wasn't in a restaurant eating he could be found in the library. And, if he wasn't in the library he was in an art gallery, and if he wasn't in either of these two places he could be found in the woods. He preferred to sleep in the wild, either in a tent or in a tree shack; the length of his stay depended on how long he'd decided to stay in one place, which typically wasn't for more than a week or two. He'd never intended to become a drifter. He knew that someday he would become the past, the present and the future all wrapped up in one, and that he would live everywhere but be in the same place at the same time while living elsewhere. Furthermore, no one would ever be as powerful.

It appeared as if he would be staying in this little village somewhat longer than he had expected. It was the mysterious though somewhat familiar smell; the smell in the air had convinced him that he was in the right place. It had been a number of months, this searching, searching that had consumed him. It was just as if he had been searching for himself, and he'd been looking so hard and so long that he'd even begun to look in places where no human could possibly have been hiding, like under rocks, big and small. He'd looked in brooks and streams, wading waist deep; she certainly might be there. He looked in lakes and rivers and often swam to the bottom, or as close to the bottom as his breath would allow him. He looked into the hollow of fallen trees and up live trees. Some trees were filled with bees and some had provided him with honey. He looked in caves. He looked in barns, corrals and shelters. He'd even begun to look to the sky for her presence. He thought for sure he'd find her there silhouetted against the blue backdrop. At night he studied the moon, the stars and imaginary planets; during the day he looked to the sun, searching the beams for a hint of her body. He studied the billowy bodies of the clouds as well as the soles of their feet moving casually across the face of the sky, sometimes black, some times blue, and sometimes black and blue. He'd occasionally get frustrated, but never depressed, and perseverance came as naturally to him as fatigue to sluggards possessed by the entitlement gene. Nothing, no matter how fowl, how putrid, how disgusting, how acrid, how abominably preposterous, how embarrassingly ridiculous could distract or discourage him from his purpose, his holy grail, his quest. He'd never considered himself to be in any way substitutionary, but he was selfless.

One day he had climbed to the top of the highest mountain in the world, and when he finally made it to the top his head was in the clouds, but she wasn't there, so he looked down into the valley, and he could have sworn he saw her there. She was scantily clad in a flowing robe, a diaphanous robe of many colors, and she was dancing among gray shadows like an inspired rainbow.

There was a certain innocence about her that was common and endearing to those who knew her, and even strangers who'd seen her for the first time were impressed with her transparent innocence. Furthermore, there wasn't a man who wouldn't desire to be found in her presence, even sitting at her feet while hanging on to her every word, or somehow serving her by providing her something to eat or drink, most especially her beloved cupcakes, crumpets, chiffon pie, dainty demitasses and honey-sweetened elderberry tea. Her preferred location to be attended to was beneath an angulating Weeping Willow tree that cast a perfect shadow across a pond of swans she loved to feed by hand. She was a fairy princess in a make believe world who'd been known to flit like a butterfly from flower to flower without a care in the world, attaching herself to no one until she met the lumberjack. She'd found herself irresistibly attracted to his sublime humility. He most assuredly could have had any woman he wanted. If they didn't come willingly, he certainly could have taken them by force, and no man nor animal could have prevented him.

From the mountain top that day dark shadows seemed to be converging upon her; they didn't embrace her, but they seemed to be holding her down against her will. He could tell because she was struggling to free herself from their arms, gray arms that looked like sticks with long pointy fingers typically belonging to witches. She'd lost her voice long ago among weeds disguised as flowers while trying to set a hummingbird free, so she couldn't scream. And if she could have screamed even the sun, the moon and the stars would have answered her cry, and every living creature big or small would have come to her rescue. With teeth bared and instruments drawn and with every metaphysical exponential power unleashed they would save her, and if it meant sacrificing their lives so that she might live, so be it!

It appeared as if she might be seriously harmed or even killed. So he quickly charged down the mountain like a sure-footed, fleet-footed bull, but when he got there she wasn't there, and neither were the dark shadows. He began to beat the air with his fists, punching into submission the frustration and the pain of once again having been left alone with hope intangibly etched into his mind and heart. He threw powerful lefts and rights and combinations, lightning fast razor sharp jabs, uppercuts, bolo punches; he even threw kidney punches and rabbit punches. He relentlessly pounded the body until he broke every rib of his opponent. He crushed his stubborn skull with the thunder in his right hook and knocked him to the ground. He then fell to his knees and beat his helpless opponent into the earth with his pile-driving iron fists. He ended the onslaught by head-butting him into bloody submission and finally to his death. And then...

And then the wind began to blow like an angry zephyr tearing the heads of flowers off and tossing them willy-nilly into the spineless atmosphere. The wind was so powerful that it knocked him off his feet and forced him to roll across the valley floor like a bundle of tumbleweed, and when he was able to get up it knocked him down over and over again until he was finally able to take refuge in the cleft of a rock, but not before his face had been lacerated. The lacerations from the wind ran deep like inflicted whip strokes delivered at the hand of a sadistic centurion, and he began to bleed and mourn like a wounded animal. He'd been certain that she would be found caught in the wind tangled by some deceitful voices promising redemption, and that he would unravel her, but she wasn't in the wind. The wind stopped suddenly, and an eerie calm ensued causing him to slowly leave the refuge of the rock. A shadow had passed over him.

Thereafter it began to rain, and he thought he saw her in the rain, but what he saw were tears dripping from imaginary bloodshot eyes, cascades of sorrow flowing from an imaginary face, twisted shadows merging into roughly braided strands composed of ghostly flesh, drooping jowls, screaming mouth, melting ears, imploding nose. His imagination continued to run wild, and sometimes he could swear that he actually saw her, or at least a vision of her either to his left or his right, some lovely vision that raised his hopes then quickly and rudely eluded him, dashing with an extreme sense of discomfiture those same hopes against the rocks, and sometimes blood oozed out instead of honey.

In spite of all the failed attempts to find her he knew someday he would be successful. It was just a matter of time, and as long as his smell held out he would be successful. Occasionally he allowed himself to think the worst; that he would find her, but that she would remain nothing more than a memory, or, God forbid, that she had died, been buried in some unmarked grave, or that her beautiful body had been cremated and her ashes had been sealed in an urn or a floating bell jar. And just maybe, just maybe her heavenly body would be gently washed to and fro endlessly and forever on the crest of a sea that looked like the billowy undulations of the unseen sounds of a rhapsody in blue. That night he slept on a familiar foreign shore, but in his dream all the trees of the field were clapping their hands while mercy and justice kissed the bride.

It wasn't just another casual Saturday in the village. People were meandering through the quaint shops while others were having breakfast or an early lunch at one of the outdoor cafes. The smell was definitely blowing in the wind, but so was the smell of 10,000 roses and various flowers being carried into the village in donkey drawn carts. This was the festival of "Dancing Flowers" that the town's people had been planning for, and they couldn't afford to let the smell drive the tourists away. They'd already lost far too much money, and the village would soon become a slum unless something could be done about the smell; not just the smell, but it's source.

He'd already had his breakfast in the woods. His favorite place to eat was anywhere he could build a fire and cook his own food, usually bacon and eggs along with some fried bread and black coffee. This was festival Saturday, and an art show was being held in the town's most famous art gallery. The event was attracting quite a few visitors, mostly tourists who'd either disregarded the smell in the air or had been informed that it was nothing to be alarmed about, just some temporary aberration that had something to do with a sanitation alert being orchestrated to train a group of new sanitation workers, some of whom had been hired in spite of their lack of experience with olfactory challenges. No garbage could be found. Even dainty tissue paper and cotton balls were being incinerated immediately, and the streets were continuously being hosed down.

When he entered the village he was struck by the number of people gathering outside a particular art gallery. This was one studio/gallery he hadn't visited yet. He'd meant to visit, but the day that he had planned to visit the shop had closed early. He'd looked in the window and thought the gallery looked particularly attractive and very inviting. Something about the interior seemed almost familiar to him, and when he tried to open the door, just for the heck of it, the obviously closed front door, he detected a smell that also seemed familiar. The odor seemed to be coming through the key hole. No obvious vapor was exiting the keyhole, but when he bent down to take a whiff the invisible vapor gently blew against his face. He had an impulse to sneak in, but he didn't. If he had wanted to he could have walked right in.

The next day the gallery was sponsoring an open-house, and he would be sure to attend. When the door was opened the people who had been standing outside began to slowly filter in. They were greeted by the hostess, not the owner, and they were offered cheese, caviar, crackers, baguettes, and wine.

This gallery was by no means small. There were four rooms, and each wall of the four rooms displayed paintings of various artists who offered different mediums and styles. The styles included Realism, Painterly, Impressionism, Expressionism//Fauvism, Abstraction, and Abstract. He was acquainted with each of these styles, but there was one style on display that he was unfamiliar with. That style was Photorealism. Photorealism creates an illusion of reality through paint so that the result looks more like a large, sharply focused photo than anything else. Photorealism is a style which often seems more real than reality with detail down to the last grain of sand or wrinkle on someone's face. Where nothing is left out nothing is too insignificant or unimportant not to be included in the painting, even an imaginative odor might exist within the canvas, blood and sinew, mind, body, soul and spirit. Studying this last offering might bring up the ghost of Dorian Gray, and one might experience a supernatural transference of feeling that could capture one's logic and squeeze it between the arms of an emotional vice being turned by the relentless hands of time. Life and/or death, or life hereafter, a glimpse of heaven or the smell of hell almost brought him to his knees. It was just as if he was about to fall face down before Madonna and Child while anxiously awaiting the wafer's miraculous reconciliatory transubstantiation. He had her photograph.

That day while closely examining every painting on every wall in all four rooms, he didn't just look closely and thoughtfully at the paintings, he put himself inside the heart and soul of each artist. No detail escaped his acute examination. He counted every finger, toe and eyelash. He traced each painter's signature and probed every nuance the human eye was capable of discerning. It was as if each painting had been placed beneath the micro-scope of his intuitive mind, but not just his sight. He could hear the sound of each painting, the taste of each painting, the smell of each painting. A few paintings captured his imagination and transported him into a surrealistic realm where neither a beginning nor an ending existed; he was standing on the cusp just outside the gates without an invitation, and scaling them would be impossible. The smell he had been hoping for was not present. Nevertheless, some unborn child of promise ministered to his perseverance and told him he was closer than he had ever been to the absolute truth of unconditional love, and that he would find the key to the door without a handle, and it would open easily based solely on his command. A myriad scent of indistinguishable blossoms filled the air, but for the first time since he had entered the village he knew intuitively that he had come for an express purpose, and that it wasn't only about her; it was about everyone.

He'd completed his artistic tour and had become a nonplussed voyeur who'd been blinded by star clusters dancing dangerously close to the perimeter of an inviting black hole. He actually was about to leave when he spotted an odd door labeled "The Elbow Room." Below the sign in very small letters he read: "This is neither an entrance nor an exit. Enter and exit at your own risk, but know that you are neither coming nor going." He stood just outside the door for about ten minutes and watched people enter and people exit. Before entering the people had knocked on the door, and he heard three knocks on the door right before three others had either exited or entered. Each individual had either entered or exited alone; there were no partners. People continued to come and go, one at a time. The knock on the door was specific; it wasn't just three, four or more knocks. It was the familiar sound of: dut-duttadutdut-dutdut, "A shave and a haircut, two bits." He'd often used the same playful knock when visiting her.

There appeared to be nothing unusual about those who had been entering the room, but those who exited seemed to be much lighter on their feet than when they had entered, and they had very broad smiles gracing their angelic faces. Some were laughing, but every single one held a dainty pink silk handkerchief to their nose that they alternately smelled then gently wiped their brow and face with. It was a delicate move that caused one to think of a kind of royalty. In fact, the lumberjack had specifically witnessed one memorable unsavory and uncouth looking man enter the room, only to emerge some time later looking like a dandy. Apparently an invitation to enter or exit was not required since no one was entering or exiting, so he decided to try his luck to see if he could get in or out, come or go, or perhaps be held in purgatorial limbo.

He knocked on the door using the rhythmic beat, but nothing happened. So he tried again. Still no response, so he tried a third time, only this time he knocked a little louder. A peep hole about four inches high and six inches wide was suddenly opened. He was able to look into the room, but what greeted him was a pair of eyes beyond which he could see nothing; the eyes were familiar. The eyes then disappeared and a nose appeared; the nose was also familiar. At first the nose did nothing, then it began to sniff very deliberately while taking rather long inhalations followed by exhalations that took place through the mouth. The exhalations were directed through the peep hole by a delicately lip-sticked beautiful mouth that was exceptionally inviting and very alluring; the mouth looked familiar. The lips of the mouth were so inviting that his first impulse was to kiss them. The more he studied the lips the more familiar they became, and the smell, the odor exiting the mouth was also very familiar and very distinct. He recognized it almost immediately. The mouth, the lips and the smell had become irresistible and drew him as close to the opening as possible. He was absolutely certain, categorically, unequivocally, unambiguously, convinced beyond the shadow of a doubt, that he was about to be reunited with his dream. A momentary conviction witnessed to his spirit, but the same supernatural power that had always sustained him and had brought victory assured him that he would, once again, get the crown even if he had to make the ultimate sacrifice.

As if mesmerized and without further thought he placed his hungry mouth to the peep hole and struggled to embrace the inviting lips. Within seconds he'd been hooked by the tongue as if he were an ignorant fish that had taken the bait. He'd immediately become lasciviously intoxicated, lost in an imaginary world of lust he'd mistaken for love. His head began to swim in a sea of memories, and the bizarre smell that had invaded the village invaded his mind; it began to consume him like an insidious viral infection that was torching his organs, a type of internal cremation process. His skin began to tingle, and the most exciting sensations he'd ever experienced began to flood his mind. He'd been hallucinogenically transmogrified then transported to another dimension of false perceptions unrelated to the reality of the situation. His hallucinations were primarily related to the olfactory, but visual and auditory delusions had also taken up temporary residence in his divided mind. Physically his blood-brain-barrier was safe from intruders that might cause damage, but psychologically an exponential explosion of deranged thought patterns were leaving him crippled with no capacity to think straight. In spite of what was happening to his body he somehow remained glued to the lips until he suffered an emotionally violent reaction that flat-lined him just as if he'd been torn into two distinct and unrecognizable hemispheres at the hand of a demented ax murderer, an autocratic administrator of seizures. He collapsed, but he was not dead, although he might have easily been mistaken for a colossal vegetable.

The people who seemed to control the mysterious Elbow Room apparently had something to hide. Maintaining the status quo of this tiny village was of paramount importance, and apparently the smell that had suddenly subtly invaded the village had a lot to do with gaining then maintaining total control.

The owner was a kind, compassionate, considerate, philanthropic sort who hadn't an enemy in the world. He was an ear, nose and throat specialist who frequently treated his patients gratis, except for an occasional offer to barter his services for fruits, vegetables and loads of flowers, and sundry kinds of titillating perfumes and powders of diverse fragrances. The best way to describe his body odor was "inviting." One thing he knew that most people didn't know was that the sense of smell is one's most powerful sense. He knew that the lumberjack's sense of smell was 10,000 times more sensitive than any of his other senses, and that the recognition of smells is immediate. He also knew that most people were ignorant of the fact that other senses like touch and taste must travel through the body via neurons and the spinal cord before reaching the brain, whereas the olfactory response is immediate, extending directly to the brain. The nose is the only place where one's central nervous system is directly exposed to the environment. The lumberjack had come a little too close to the truth for comfort. He was a kind and gentle sort, but he'd become just a bit too inquisitive. Once over a cup of coffee the doctor had implied that the lumberjack would be better off if he kept his nose out of other people's business. His reply had been that everyone's business was his business, and that he was in the people business.

The door was slowly and cautiously opened. His huge limp body sprawled out on the floor seemed to stretch for miles. Although his eyes had not been reamed out by a hot white poker, and his hair had not been shorn, he resembled a modern day Samson, a man who had met his doom, his Delilah.

His massive size produced a sense of incredulity and awe in his observers who just stood there for a few minutes looking at him. He was then laboriously dragged into the Elbow Room by these four strong admirers. Once in place he was immediately stripped of every ounce of clothing. His body was then meticulously whitewashed including his beard and hair.

That night, while the men attended to his body, a subtle wind had begun to blow through the village. The wind was carrying the previously rather innocuous smell on its invisible back and shoulders then depositing it like a blanket over the village. It was suddenly as if the village had been tented in an attempt to treat termites, only it was the invisible smell that had invaded the village and had tented it. The subtle smell began to intensify and rather quickly. Before long it had become so foul that people had begun to choke violently. Many had begun to vomit. Some seemed to have lost their ability to hear, and some appeared to have gone blind. All had suddenly become afflicted with an unfamiliar pox.

The smell had invaded every home and every building. There was no escaping the smell. Some people had passed out, and some had become suddenly so sick that they were lying on makeshift deathbeds. It wasn't the plague, but it was like the plague. It wasn't the Death Angel, but it was like the Death Angel.

The Elbow Room, while not hermetically sealed, was pretty well air-tight, and the four men had no idea what was happening outside. They were too busy with the task at hand. Two of the men needed to stand securely on stools in order to lift him up; a rather arduous task that made the four of them appear quite clumsy.

They were able to get a linen loin cloth to cover his private parts and sandals for his feet. They stuck a bright and shining Morning Star in his right hand and a golden scepter in his left hand. They secured these items in place with a type of stickum. They placed a brilliant signet ring on his ring finger. They draped him with a rainbow robe of many colors and placed a crown of jewels on his head. He was then lifted up and onto a beautiful piece of cedar from Lebanon, only this time his torso, hands and feet were secured to the cedar by chains. Holes had been drilled into the cedar to accommodate the fastening of his arms at the wrist, his torso at the waist, and his feet at the ankles. His head was not secured, and it hung down forlornly; it was tilted slightly to the right; the magnificently adorned crown was secure.

Before exiting the entrance for the night, the men, as they had been instructed, lifted him upright, leaned him against the wall then nailed the cedar securely to the wall directly into the studs. This was the most difficult task, because the cedar was to be six feet off the floor, not an inch higher or lower. This space on this wall had apparently been left blank. It had been surrounded by numerous existential abstractions that upon close examination appeared to be screaming faces and tortured bodies. If you closed your eyes and held your breath you could swear the screams were real. Now that the empty space, the mysterious vacuum, had been filled, all eyes thereafter would appear to be focused on the solemn lumberjack, whose burden had been supernaturally lifted by sovereign predetermination.

Their task having been completed the men took one last look upon him. He looked helpless, hopeless and worthless, a pathetic excuse for a man, especially one who had seemingly appeared all-powerful. One of the men said, "This man looks more like a ghost than a man." Another said, "Well, if he isn't a ghost now he'll surely be a ghost by morning." Another said, "Why didn't he just leave well enough alone? What made him think he could get away with it?" And finally another said, "What a waste of what might have been. All he had to do was go along with the program and keep his nose clean."

That night a young man throwing smooth stones into a familiar cesspool struck a floating bell jar that upon impact seemed to explode into infinity. Closed channels of communication hidden in constellations were divided by the insertion of a finger and out gushed vowels and consonants. Paragraphs dropped down from swollen clouds, and flowering sonnets sprung forth twisting the tails of shooting comets driving them onward and upward to the infinite edge of the horizon, a land where you could live forever because every brother was the son of humility, and men were without excuse.

Closed wombs in dark places lost their stitching and out came bursts of light that opened the eyes of the blind, and the recollection of the past was a distant memory lost in the lake of forgetfulness. The lap band of implicit indifference and discrimination that had been slowly and methodically squeezing the globe at the equator snapped; its intended division designed to breed enemies coalesced into brotherhood. In some places where man had never set foot trees could be seen, and on the trees were leaves that looked like humans, and all the trees of the field were clapping their hands. The moon stood still for eighteen minutes then disappeared behind a star that illuminated the sky as if it had become the sun, and above all there was a kind voice that had become continuously articulate and smelled like a rose.

These are but a few of the miraculous things that happened that night shortly after midnight when the lumberjack laid his ax to the root of the tree of narcissistic wickedness.

Hitting Pay-dirt

The very moment, the instant, the nanosecond he began to dig into the seamy layers of convoluted flesh, the spiral tubing noodles of history, they had the distinct impression that he may have struck pay-dirt. It wasn't just a gut feeling accompanied by empirical evidence manifesting itself as cold-hard facts. No, it was much more serious. They had concrete evidence supported by eye witnesses. The proof wasn't in the pudding, it was in the brain's convolutions. Memories seemed to have become particles of differing sizes that could be seen rising into the air like tangible bubbles. This was no illusion; nothing could have been more serious. It could be likened to the first ship not falling off the edge of the earth into an unknown abyss.

It was so very serious, in fact, that not a word was being spoken in this holy chamber. This was an "Oh, My God" moment that could convert sinners without a word having been spoken. The proverbial paradigm shift, the 180 degree about face, for some, was so difficult to accept that they removed their scrubs and turned in their resignations rather than take the road less traveled. Had they deemed this a sacrilegious undertaking they should not have volunteered to participate to begin with. What did they expect, some trephination spinning old time religion? The viewing chamber was full, and some jockeying had even taken place for front row seats.

The seat of reason had not been catapulted into this arena against its will, and it didn't just get in by the seat of its pants. It came willingly, but it had been dressed in skepticism. Its presence did not represent a reversal of the White Coat syndrome, but there were some subtle signs of high blood pressure and tachycardia. There was also, as might be expected, some camouflaged ridicule.

The stainless-steel autoclaved instrument had been heated to the point of being white hot. The delicate insertion of manmade fire, the thermocautery, was like entering a slab of room temperature butter. It was painless, and there wasn't a bit of smoke.

The probing began cautiously, at first, requiring the patience of a saint. This precise invasive procedure was the entrance into an unknown blue cheese cave of mental fermentation that had hieroglyphic origins. Presumably the aging process had been completed, but when the astonishing facts began to appear as rainbow blips on the monitor's screen, the tool was moved along at a much faster pace. This wasn't a race, but it was now seemingly being treated as one. A fair amount of hand wringing was taking place, and some jaws were locked and loaded. Brain plasticity could almost be heard. Looks of astonishment lead to more astonishing looks that crucified heliocentric thinking; all roads apparently did not lead to Rome.

The oxygen in the room was becoming scarce, but it had not yet become obvious. The iconic Nobel Peace Prize winning surgeon had been overcome with the potential discovery of a new world that lie hidden just beyond the lost horizon. He could not refrain the belly laughter ascending his diaphragm. It was now making its way joyfully up his throat. It came somewhat muffled from behind his mask the moment he'd struck pay-dirt. He had to admonish his assistants, mostly interns and students, from doing the twist, after they'd heard him laugh. They'd been filled with a spirit of boundless joy, and one of them said, "Gotta dance!" Their heads appeared to have become swollen, and the only way they could survive would be to have their biological voices shunted to relieve the pressure between the dura matter and the skull. It was almost as if the apple had landed squarely on their inquisitive contemplative heads. Gravity was everywhere.

Dr. Abraham Abrahamson had somehow been able to enter the dark side of the moon where everywhere you looked, all you could see were strands of Angel Hair wrapped around the medulla oblongata. This lower portion of the brain stem seemed to be the seat of depression that had been driving the inhabitants of the institution to the inviting point of suicide. Other psychologically mystifying forms of aberrant behavior had also been noted. No causative agents, real or imagined, could be uncovered that might reveal an etiology. Activity overruled somnambulant behavior only when the residents were in deep dream states. In that realm they were dancers, marathoners, sculptors, painters, preachers, teachers, world-wide travelers, and other hyperactive manics. This fine establishment was not intended to be a morgue, but something had sabotaged the community's good intentions, and the resort-style safe place had been making headlines like, "Thorazine Shuffle Has A Whole New Meaning At "Treasure Oaks."

This home, and other homes like it, had become pharmacology laboratories, and Dr. Abrahamson had made up his mind to explore cutting edge options, alternatives to shot-gun prescriptions, prescriptions that induced and perpetuated hallucinations, delusions and illusions of the mind. The collective neurotransmitters that had become unwired would now be made whole; the mentally challenged would become victorious. Schizophrenic stigmata be damned! One day, while lecturing a group of psychiatrists on bi-polar disorders, he removed his designer scrubs and revealed a t-shirt he'd designed. The t-shirt featured Rodin's thinker with the following byline; "The Two Shall Become One."

So, after a consensus among those still standing, Dr. Abrahamson agreed to excise the brain. This procedure certainly wasn't new. Numerous brains had been excised from cadavers, but this procedure would be different, because the patient was alive, and once the brain had been removed, he would still be alive, and, furthermore, would be required to answer questions presented to him. Is it any wonder that at least one surgeon smuggled-in a straitjacket?

There would always be "Doubting Thomas's" who, even though they can plainly see would still prefer not to believe.

Dr. Abrahamson deftly removed the cranium, the portion of the skull that encloses the brain, then carefully set the bloody cranium aside. The exposed brain was now in plain sight and waiting to be removed. A sense of drama and anticipation had descended upon the attendees. To those in attendance old enough to remember it reminded them of the first lunar landing. Was Dr. Abrahamson an illusionist? No, but there was something magical about his posture. He had a certain of knack of being able to perform the most difficult tasks while making them look so easy. A more sophisticated word that might best describe his surgical performances would be aplomb.

Dr. Abrahamson made the necessary incisions then carefully removed the brain. He had anticipated some resistance, but none had been presented. The brain came willingly then was swaddled in soft raiment and placed into a wicker basket. Dr. Abrahamson then removed his gloves and disappeared behind a curtain along with the basket holding the brain.

A high degree of murmuring began to run through the auditorium. No one knew what to expect next. Fidgeting became common and consternation possessed all in attendance. All in attendance seemed to be awaiting the return of Moses, an ordinary man with pockets full of miracles.

While behind the curtain Dr. Abrahamson approached a makeshift brazen laver and washed his hands thoroughly up to his elbows. His assistants had also washed themselves thoroughly. While these washings were taking place, the patient's body had been removed from the operating table and was now sitting comfortably in a leather recliner. He had been clothed in what appeared to be a foreign dress code, including combat boots. The man had come voluntarily from nowhere. He said he was aware of the risks the study presented, and he said that if he died, he wanted to die with his boots on. This unusual man simply said that he had lost his one and only love years ago, and that his luck had also run out, besides, he really needed the money. He'd experienced more than his fair share of hard knocks; some had come as rabbit punches disguised as acts of kindness. He was vulnerable, gullible and clinically depressed. Somehow, his name had appeared at the top of the list. The questionnaire he'd completed showed a high degree of comprehension. He appeared to be an exceptional communicator.

When Dr. Abrahamson appeared from behind the curtain, he was holding the brain by its brainstem in his gloved right hand. He was holding a magnificent Faberge egg in left hand; Dr. Abrahamson was lefthanded. He was tall, dark and handsome.

"Ladies and gentlemen, as promised, we will now begin the process of passing the brain around for observation and the right to question the patient. You are to address this patient simply as, Joe. Remember, no questions are considered off limits. Nothing is considered too personal. Try to ask open-ended questions as opposed to those requiring a simple yes or no response. Let's try to get inside this man's head," Dr. Abrahamson said with a sense of enthusiastic expectation. "We are about to rewrite history, so exercise wisdom," he added.

He was about to pass Joe's brain to the first intern, but the anxious look on the intern's glowing face gave him cause, so he waited then said, "Remember, use your pen to touch the appropriate synapse before asking your question. Also, please keep in mind that synapses are susceptible to fatigue, offer a resistance to the passage of impulses, and are markedly susceptible to the effects of oxygen deficiency. Pay close attention to Joe's facial features and body language when presenting your questions and especially when he responds. Our intention is not to cause any spasmodic muscular twitching due to a neurological disorder. If neurospasm appears obvious, reframe your question. Don't forget. We are basically dealing with neurons, nerve cells, that represent the structural and functional unit of the nervous system. We are very fragile beings subject to whim and fancy, slings and arrows of outrageous fortune, and often uninvited neurological interlopers camouflaged as friends."

Dr. Abraham Abrahamson placed the brain on a silver platter then passed it on to the intern who was now calmly sitting in the front row; the frenetic enthusiasm that previously possessed him had abated, so it seemed. The brain was rather slippery, so one had to be especially careful lest it slip off the plate onto the floor and become contaminated.

The young man balanced the plate on his lap, careful to control the slightest movement of the brain. Before beginning his examination, he carefully put on his sanitized latex gloves. He looked sympathetically at Joe before inserting his pen into the convoluted gooey mass. He had determined, based on his personal experience with a slight speech impediment, that he would insert his pen into the left hemisphere of the brain at the posterior end of the inferior frontal gyrus. This area, referred to as Broca's area, contains the motor speech area responsible for movements of tongue, lips, and vocal cords. As soon as the pen contacted this part of the brain, Joe simultaneously crossed his arms and legs. He appeared to have mumbled something.

"Hey, Joe. My name is Jeremiah. I could have sworn you just said something, but I couldn't understand it. So, I'd just like to ask you a few questions. Are you OK with that?" the young man asked politely.

Joe said something that sounded like a "Yes."

"Actually Joe, I have two questions I'd like to ask you before I pass your brain along to the next intern. I was wondering where you come from. You know, I mean originally. What part of the country, city, etc. are you from? "the intern asked while carefully watching Joe's body language.

Joe answered the question, but his answer wasn't very clear. It wasn't gobbledygook, but it wasn't discernible. When he recognized the intern couldn't understand him, he got a little frustrated and kept trying to spit out the answer. He seemed tongue-tied.

"Joe, I'm afraid I didn't get that. I thought I could make out a P and what sounded like a long I, and what might be interpreted as an urge; like an urge to do something. Am I close?" the intern asked while carefully keeping his pen on the Broca's hot spot.

"Piiiiiitsitsssssbrrr," Joe answered again.

"Sorry, Joe. I still didn't get that," the intern answered. "Let's move on to something else. Joe, what is your nationality? Dr. Abrahamson didn't give us your last name, so, we are at a disadvantage from that standpoint. You have a rather imposing body, and sharp skin tone. You had a rather handsome face while on the operating table, but your face has become quite flaccid and lacks shape. I can barely make out where your eyes are located. We still can't be sure where you may have come from. You know. Your origin. Were you born in America? Maybe you're a foreigner. Maybe that's why we can't understand you. What is your nationality, Joe? Knowing your nationality can help us understand you. Maybe you're just a little nervous. This happens to a lot of people when facing a crowd of curious questioners. This obviously has nothing to do with your intelligence. I mean, you're not a retard or anything," The intern continued with inquisitive kindness while applying a little more pressure to Broca's area with his pen.

"Piiiiitsitsssbrrr," Joe answered angrily while uncrossing his arms and legs. He slammed his right fist into his left palm, made a growling sound then stood up. He then began to move on his very wobbly knees towards the steps that descended the stage. "Piiiiiitssss, Piiiiiitsssss, Piiiiiitsssbrrr, gggg-gggg," Joe said rather angrily while continuing one wobbly step at a time.

That was when Dr. Abrahamson made a move towards Joe and told him to stop. Joe didn't stop because Dr. Abrahamson was addressing him directly, rather than directing his voice to the brain resting on the silver platter.

"Dr. Abrahamson, here, here! Talk directly to the brain. Talk directly to Joe's brain," the frightened intern yelled. He quickly stood up the moment he saw Joe approaching the steps. He wanted to pass the brain back to Dr.

Abrahamson, but, in his spontaneity, the brain slipped off the plate and landed in the lap of a beautiful Ukrainian female intern who was in her final year. She was an aspiring psychiatrist, and she was the only one in the room who knew Joe personally. Joe's name was not Joe; it was Vladimir.

The female intern's name was Natasha. She knew where Joe was from. She also knew his last name. She knew almost everything there was to know about him. They'd met at an underground meeting of anonymous revolutionary poets in the Ukraine; these meetings took place at the height of the pogroms. Generally, all that was known about the other poets were their first names. When they got up to read, they would identify themselves like this, "Hi, my name is Boris, and I'm a poet." These underground poets had formed what might be considered a secret society, a society that had developed a unique language. Natasha and Vladimir had adopted it as a love language that had sealed them inseparably. They had quickly become conjoined twins whose hearts had become one. When Natasha exhaled Vladimir inhaled. She could hardly contain herself while waiting to get her hands on Joe's brain.

Natasha and Vladimir had produced volumes of romantic poetry reminiscent of the Browning's, but they were rudely separated when the society collapsed under the hand of a jealous group of non-fiction writers. These writers had been politically bathed in an alphabet of propaganda, and they lathered themselves with libelous potions prepared beforehand by the party. There was no escaping them, especially if you had a voice-box and weren't afraid of losing your tongue. It was a dangerous time to be a poetic purveyor of truth.

Vladimir's and Natasha's life seemed to have been permanently unwritten. They weren't expunged, but they had become expurgated, just as if they were two previously banned books appearing to be human. They'd been labeled as metaphors and were required to wear red bandanas in public. They were humiliated but didn't care as long as they were together. One cold winter night their bungalow was invaded by armed guards. At 4:00 AM a blunt dissection was employed, and they were rudely separated. There was nowhere to run except in the direction of freedom, and run they did when the sun changed its clothes between shifts, and the ice melted.

They hadn't seen each other for years, and they never thought they'd ever see each other again. This bizarre encounter was, obviously, the making of a Ripley's Believe or Not Story, but it was true. Sure, it begs the imagination, but sometimes all we have is our imagination.

Natasha was carefully holding onto the brain that had suddenly been dropped into her lap. She'd refused the silver platter that had been extended to her. She was cuddling the brain similar perhaps to how one would cuddle a child or something so priceless, that, if dropped, would represent disaster to the object and the holder.

"Put your gloves on!" Dr. Abraham Abrahamson yelled from the stage. He had been startled by the events, but he was an adventurous sort, and did not object to what was taking place with Joe's brain. He knew the Ukrainian intern very well. They'd shared some poetic interests, though he did prefer Yevtushenko to her Mayakovsky, who "consciously stood on the throat of his own song." Dr. Abrahamson had always felt Natasha could be trusted, and he trusted her now at this most historic moment. He wasn't sure what she might do with Joe's brain, but he knew she would do the right thing. She would exercise her left-brained intuitive skills and appropriately handle the brain as well as the excited group, whose ophthalmic eyes were inquisitively molesting her.

Joe, by this time, had been directed back to his chair by Dr. Abrahamson's confident and commanding voice; his command had been directed towards the brain, rather than to Joe's body. Two off-duty policemen, who had been hired to witness the event, came out from behind the curtain; they'd been positioned in the wings of the stage. They'd been told to protect the brain at all costs. They accompanied Joe back to his chair and saw to it that he was made comfortable. They couldn't help but take a quick peak into Joe's bloody shell. What they saw made them nauseous. They'd been struck dumb and sent to the infirmary.

Natasha began to carefully examine Joe's brain that was now resting comfortably in her lap. The areas she examined looked very familiar to her. She could almost recognize sections of the brain that appeared like memories. The sulci, or fissures of the brain, looked inviting. The gyri, especially the superior temporal, didn't look convoluted at all; they appeared to be friendly, family-like, but it was what lied in-between that really mattered most to her at that defining moment. She'd learned the hard way that sometimes what comes between two people can bind them together, making their bond even stronger, like a synapse or the space between the junction of two neurons in a neural pathway.

Natasha felt as if all eyes were on her, and they were. The group of surprised, delighted and somewhat frightened interns, along with Dr. Abrahamson, were expecting her to do something. Joe didn't know what to expect. She didn't act. She grew quietly contemplative until she heard a bevy of voices almost shouting, "Will you please stick your pen into that brain! Can't you please do something! That brain must be shared, so please put your mind to it and do something or pass Joe's brain along!"

When Natasha finally stuck her pen into Joe's brain, she did so very gingerly. She had put her gloves on. She entered Wernicke's area, as might have been expected. Wernicke's area is in the temporal lobe on the left side of the brain and is responsible for the comprehension of speech. With pen in place she began to speak to Joe in an unknown language. Dr. Abrahamson and all in attendance were confused because it appeared as if Joe was compre-hending the language. They didn't know what in the hell was going on. Almost at the sound of the first word out of her mouth, Joe jumped for joy, but he remained in his seat. He didn't know what was happening. All he knew was that only one other person in the world spoke that language. The two off-duty policeman had been replaced by two Russian Wolfhounds.

Natasha continued to speak to Joe in this foreign tongue, and he began to respond

In the same unknown language. The room was soon in a frenzy. No one knew what to expect next, so they all began to call for the brain. "What in the living hell is going on here? Is this some kind of a conspiracy or something? Give up that brain, and give it up now," one mad intern said menacingly. "If you know what's good for you, you will pass the brain around. What are you? Who are you? Are you some kind of Svengali of something!" Then others chimed in with loud threatenings, "Mad Magician! Mad physician! Witch Doctor! Brain Scrambler! Frankenstein!!!"

Natasha stayed calm as she continued to communication with Vladimir. While examining Vladimir's brain, she discovered things about him that she never knew. He was an even a more exceptional human being than she had previously thought. She also discovered more than one benign mass of unpublished poetry. She also discovered a small section of his seat of consciousness, thought, memory, reason, judgment and emotion that had been subject to numerous unsuccessful attempts of brainwashing. She was delighted when she found her name hidden among the cerebrospinal fluid. "This really can't be happening," she said to herself. "Although, she continued, "Vladimir, on many occasions, believed and prayed with faithful certitude that a miracle would happen, and it often did. Why not today? Why not, today!"

The anxious crowd began to angrily move towards her. It appeared as if they might be out for blood. Mob mentality was about to take control of reason. A few of the interns had scalpels drawn and ready, that is when Dr. Abraham Abrahamson stepped in.

"Stand back, men!" he yelled. The mad men didn't seem to listen. "Stand back, I say!"

"Stand down!" he yelled again while motioning for the wolfhounds. The crowd stopped when they saw the wolfhounds front and center. Vladimir was silent, but he desperately wanted Joe's brain that was resting in Natasha's lap. The wolfhounds moved to either side of Joe and were kissing his hands. Vladimir had once said, "You can't call yourself a poet if you aren't a lover of animals."

"Natasha! Natasha, you must release Joe's brain. His brain must be shared. I don't understand what just happened, but I genuinely don't care. You probably have a good explanation for it, but I will hear you out later. For now, just pass Joe's brain around, and do not hinder history in the making due to some emotional connection to this brain," Dr. Abrahamson said sternly then somewhat kinder.

"OK. OK. I will gladly pass the brain around but let me first take off my gloves," she answered calmly and compliantly, but, once she got her gloves off, to the astonishment of all in attendance, she quickly entered her bare finger into Joe's hippocampus. This was bound to be the straw that would break the camel's back. If her action contaminated the project she would pay a great price that would find her in an isolated cell with unpadded walls.

The hippocampus is a small organ located within the brain's medial temporal lobe and forms an important part of the limbic system, the region that regulates emotions. The hippocampus is associated mainly with memory, particularly long-term memory. Natasha was attempting to restore Joe's memory. She'd recognized him when he was rolled into the operating room. At first, she thought she might be hallucinating, but when she got up real close, she knew it was Vladimir, and she was especially certain when she saw the unusual scar on his neck that resembled a hammer and sickle. She was present when the sickle had struck.

"Hey, what are you doing in his hippocampus? Hey! Hey! What in God's name do you suppose you are doing?! Turn over that brain just as you have been instructed to or risk becoming a memory. Besides which, that's the last place you want to be. Trust me. If I were you, I'd navigate out of there," came the voice of an excited intern who was sitting two rows behind Natasha anxiously waiting his turn with Joe's brain. His voice startled her, but she didn't respond; she just kept her naked finger on the hippocampus while lightly stimulating the tissue. She could tell by Vladimir's body language that she was getting through. Other voices joined in the chorus, and it got rather loud, so she waded in a little further until she was sure she had hit the sweet spot. Joe immediately jumped up from his chair, made a strange sound and began to dance. The sound Joe made was a joyful one, and it was only recognizable to Natasha, otherwise it was an unintelligible growl.

Two team member neuroscientists, not exactly casual observers, were immediately on the alert and rushed to Joe's sides. They got him to relax then put him back in his proper place. Each man couldn't help but look into the empty space once occupied by Joe's brain. They quickly lost control of their senses, ran behind the curtain, and violently vomited. Unable to speak, they were comforted, counseled briefly, then sent home by cab.

Dr. Abraham Abrahamson, who had been anxiously watching the aberrant behavior of

Natasha and the angry crowd, finally intervened and asked Natasha to take her finger out of Joe's brain. Initially, he had become apoplectic and speechless. It was as if he had been waiting for an existential conclusion to a sovereign intervention that would quell the mindless behavior of everyone in attendance.

Dr. Abrahamson suggested she may have overstepped her bounds, and that her unusual behavior might have compromised her professionalism and potential for advancement. "This matter is quite serious. So, do as you have been told, Natasha. Please, and thank you very much," Dr. Abrahamson said autocratically but with the voice of understanding.

Natasha complied. She removed her finger from Joe's brain, but only after she was confident that she had made contact with Vladimir's long- term memory. This brief encounter, and hopefully eventual reunion, reminded her of the times she spent with her father on the beach hunting for hidden treasure; those moments when they would joyfully hit pay-dirt.

The Fossil

The moon, deprived of oxygen, blacked out, fell from the sky and hit the concrete with a thud; cheese was everywhere. That was the night he left the party; that same night the stars were ashamed to be seen up close, and astronomers had become dumbfounded by the irregular alignment of the planets. It really wasn't much of a party; it was more like a gathering of eggheads whipped together to produce an intellectual soufflé.

That night, Guy would go into the woods to find the fossil that had been mentioned by Johnny Fox, the same professor he'd sat under during "The Resistance," a time of brash uncertainty based on contradictory assertions held to be equally true, and that man is the measure of all things as proposed by Protagoras, the long-winded, loquacious philosopher who debated with Socrates about, among other things, virtue. Protagoras of Abdera is considered the greatest of the Sophists of ancient Greece and the first to promote the philosophy of subjectivism, arguing that the interpretation of reality is relative to the individual. Guy often quoted him, but he also believed absolutism, the acceptance of a belief in absolute principles in political, philosophical, ethical or theological matters, played an important role in certain interpretations.

Guy's behavior could only be described as foolish as well as impetuous, even presumptuous. A few of his friends tried to talk him out of it, but he would have nothing to do with that. When they said it was so dark that you could hardly see your hand in front of your face, he held his hand up to his face and laughed. Humor certainly wasn't one of his strong suits. He rarely laughed, and rarer still was his ability to make others laugh, but in spite of his generally serious nature, he did attract people and they loved to be in his presence. He didn't know he wouldn't be going out alone that night, and that it wouldn't be a laughing matter.

On that same auspicious night, his best friend, Stuart, said, "Guy, you are, once again, acting based on sentences that have become convoluted paragraphs, that have become chapters in absurd novels that make no sense. Whatever happened to your acquisition of language capacity? Before you head out into utter darkness where the likelihood of your finding that fossil is about as likely as walking on water, dissect the statements that have been made, diagram each sentence and see if the logical conclusion is that you risk your life just to prove a point or to satisfy some curiosity based on the absurdity that you can categorically establish a universal absolute. I'd hate to see your properly punctuated life become a run-on sentence. Furthermore, if that fossil is out there somewhere it will still be out there in the morning. Wouldn't it be a lot easier to find a fossil in the sunlight rather than in a blue moon's half shadow?"

Stuart was a professor of English literature and had published two marginally successful novels. He met Guy while they were attending a creative writing workshop being taught by Johnny Fox. Fox had a unique way of incorporating the metaphysical into classic Russian literature. He occasionally conducted seances at his home in the backyard around a blazing fire pit, where he would also read from the works of Russia's iconic poets. His favorite was Vladimir Mayakovsky. He'd spent one of his summer vacations in Moscow where he'd participated in an archeological dig. He also engaged in bouts of revelry that included vodka, caviar and Russian rye bread dipped in borscht. He'd spent a few weeks sleeping in a tent in the Black Forest, where he claimed to have chased a black bear up a tree. Fox was famous for his imagination. He had a framed picture on his desk of himself along with Yuri Geller; they were toasting at a spoon bending event held at the home of Alexander Pushkin. Fox liked to inform his new students that Pushkin was the Black father of Russian Literature. Pushkin's great grandfather was an African slave, Abram Petrovich Gannibal, who later became a general to Peter the Great.

Stuart and Guy were the best of friends. They'd frequently play chess or board games; their favorites were Scrabble and Trivial Pursuit. They were also sports enthusiasts and had frequently gone to sporting events, baseball, football and basketball. Almost every Thursday night they'd meet to shoot pool at a local pool hall/saloon. When they played Nine Ball, they would put .50 cents on the five and a dollar on the Nine. They were equally good. Coincidentally, they'd both learned how to skillfully control the cue ball with proper English.

Early on, Stuart recognized that Guy had a way with words that tended to mesmerize the listener. When he spoke, regardless of the subject matter, he had a command of words that might lead one to believe his head, that is, his brain had become a thesaurus; not a copy of the Encyclopedia Britannica, because he didn't know something about everything; it was just that even when he spoke about a subject he knew little or nothing about he sounded somehow brilliant. He also had a peculiar way of asking questions, a way that made the person he was talking to seem smarter and more important than they were. He would have made a great diplomat.

Stuart could not figure out why Guy had not become a successful writer, or why he'd never even tried. He owned the English language as if it were an indentured servant, and his imagination was a constellation of electrical impulses, synaptic transmissions that were multi-directional. Besides all of this, he possessed wisdom reminiscent of Solomon. His decision making, up to this point in his life, had almost been flawless. He'd been defined by some of his friends as a modern-day sage, a type of Confucius. When Wisdom came to town and cried out loudly in the middle of the street or in an alley, he'd go out to meet her. Furthermore, he'd never lost an argument because he never argued, and winning had never become that important to him, especially if it meant one of his friends would have been the loser. Win-Win was his favorite way to end a discussion when two opposing views emerged. He was a man's man who loved to spend time with those who may have been considered of a lower estate. He didn't go to church on Sunday; he'd go to the bowery and spend hours volunteering at the "Soup Kitchen." Good works were very important to him. He was very familiar with the bible, and he often quoted it. He believed servitude should be exalted, and he would often quote, "'Faith without works is dead,'" or other verses that would support his position.

Once while they were sitting on their favorite park bench, they began to discuss words, not specific words, just words in general. These two bibliophiles had no preferences; be the word big or small; size did not matter. It was only that which was inside that mattered, and not just the definition; neither synonyms, nor antonyms, nor homonyms mattered. Guy said, "If a person loves words and takes pleasure in words-their sounds, their shapes, their colors, their texture, their taste, and their multiple shades of meaning-he could enjoy any conversation at any time with any person anywhere, because that person would delight in watching the other person's lips forming words that exited his mouth like delightful dainties, seeds of mercy blossoming forgiveness, wisdom married to knowledge giving birth to understanding, words of love conquering hate, or blue collar language that would give off sparks, some welder's unspoken fiery autobiography, or girders forged in a blast furnace that became the solid underpinnings of an architectural fountainhead displaying the reality of one's uncompromising imagination, or exponential degrees of determination that would smile in the face of adversity and laugh with the resonating power of humility." That was the same day Stuart got at least one answer as to why Guy had not seriously tried his hand at writing. When asked, he quoted Hemingway, who said about writing, "There is nothing to writing. All you do is sit down at a typewriter and bleed."

Guy loved few things more than to be put in the position of having to respond to questions, some which may have been attempts to trip him up, questions designed to place him between a rock and a hard place, a place that might force him to compromise or be crushed by presumption. How to survive a Socratic interrogation was a method of survival Guy had learned to employ at a very early age. His father, a prosecuting attorney, had a lot to do with his ability to ask questions without becoming argumentative or arrogant.

There was also something mighty about Guy. He possessed power of speech and action, frequently subtle, but mighty in its nature. In a room full of dignitaries, ambassadors, consultants, generals, presidents and CEO's, his presence caused the room to stand still and the conversations to cease. Sometimes when he spoke, even when he whispered, it was as if his voice had become distant thunder that suddenly had entered the room, but it was never frightening, and it wasn't ever loudly abrasive. It could be mesmerizing. When most people think of power they think in terms of atomics, fission, fusion, explosive power, or rank, or money, or muscular strength, but most don't think in terms of oratorical power. Yet, there are few things more powerful than the ability to control people with words. Few people give much thought to the biblical power resident in The Word whereby the world was supposedly spoken into existence. To the finite mind this kind of power is incomprehensible; furthermore, to the majority it is considered "Something out of nothing" nonsense, The Prime Mover argument, but without a leg to stand on. Guy did not necessarily believe that "might makes right." Just because someone was mighty, did not mean that they might not be mighty wrong. Guy knew precisely "How to Win Friends and Influence People," without ever having read the book of the same name.

Stuart would prefer spending time with Guy to any other person in his company of friends, except for his wife; she was his best friend. Stuart's wife had graduated with a degree in library science. She spent numerous hours in the library, but she never worked there. She had a library of her own, and the shelves were filled. Above the tallest and widest book shelf she had a framed quote from Desiderius Erasmus, "When I get a little money, I buy books; and if there is any left, I buy food and clothes." Before she met Stuart, she'd been a High Society call-girl who accompanied millionaires, and only millionaires, to operas, plays, political affairs, art gallery grand openings, and a variety of blue- blooded soirees. She was stunning, intelligent and spoke four languages. She'd spent most her life on Cloud Nine, luxuriating with her lascivious friends in a land that time forgot, a visceral land where books had taken on flesh. Stuart had brought her down to earth, but he didn't do it on his own.

Guy and Stuart had developed a relationship like Jonathan and David; they were that close. They had something most men dream about, a friend who would willingly lay down his life for his friend. This aspect of their friendship had never been tested, but there had been occasions when their friendship required standing up for one another, even to the point, on a few occasions, of needing to fight. Of course, they were pacifists at heart but believed the biblical proverb, "A friend loveth at all times, and a brother is made for adversity." Typically, however, the defensive postures they took were usually over various intellectual subject matters. Guy and Stuart were almost always on the same page even when they appeared to be disagreeing with one another. They expressed civility of speech of the highest order. They mirrored one another without the slightest hint of envy or jealousy. Iron sharpened iron in their presence. When they met for the first time it was if their encounter mirrored something Carl Jung once said, "The meeting of two personalities is like the contact of two chemical substances: if there is any reaction, both are transformed." They only differed on one point to the extent that compromise was not possible; it was almost as if they were as far apart as the east is from the west. This dissimilarity was not based upon proximity; space had nothing to do with it.

That night at the party Stuart coincidentally commented that sincerity meant that the appearance and the reality were identical. He said one need not call on anyone to back up his word. One's word ought to be sufficient. Whether people believe us or not is a matter of indifference. He didn't dismiss the etymological justification for the common story that the word sincere means "without wax." (sin cerae). He did, however, point out from the Latin sincerus, the following definitions, "whole, clean, pure, uninjured, unmixed," and of those figuratively "sound, genuine, pure, true, candid, truthful." He said the ground or root sense of the word seems to be "that which is not falsified." "Free from pretense or falsehood."

Stuart had an uncanny way of rallying a heretofore dull party into some-thing exciting by either asking for opinions or by making categorical decla-rations. His charisma was contagious, but he sincerely never wanted to be the center of attention. He'd rather spend hours on his knees in his garden where he'd experience the mystery of creation and coexistence and maybe disappear back into his mother's womb. In his garden he became a humble seed planter. He would water and fertilize, but he knew he could not be responsible for the increase. Sure, he could pull a rabbit out of a hat to the delight of mesmerized on-lookers, but nothing could compare to a shoot breaking the earth's surface that he had played a minor part in. Stuart wasn't an "only" son, and he didn't behave like an "only" son, but he was treated like an "only" son. He wasn't born with a silver spoon in his mouth. He was born with a pen in his mouth. Stuart had black, naturally curly hair and a lot of it. He wore glasses and looked like Clark Kent. He was a natural born athlete, and he lettered in four sports. He'd spent hours in the free weight room while listening to books on tape. He was a Harvard man, and he graduated with honors, but not until a little later in his life, did he question why Harvard changed its original motto adopted in 1692 from "Truth (Veritas) for Christ (Christo) and the Church (Ecclesiae) to merely "Veritas."

All the guests at the party related stories about how they had been deceived by an individual, at one time or another, who came across as the sincerest person they'd ever met. Many of them had lost large sums of money to incredibly sincere con men. Others, especially the women, had lost something more important than money. This became a very lively discussion among the gregarious guests, and some of the stories were almost frightening. A few guests seemed reluctant to share their stories, but when they did, they were able to open-up and discharge their pain. The word "devil" was not used but someone did remark that these pseudo sincere individuals were like wolves in sheep's clothing. Their power was in the way they used words to manipulate people into believing that these demi-gods, these petty potentates, spoke directly on behalf of God, and in most cases, they were asking people to give, but their appeal was largely to people who wanted give, only to get. No one understood better than these parasites that a degree of larceny resides in the hearts of all men. They would hypnotize, mesmerize and paralyze, if need be, to seduce reason. They took great pleasure in "washing the brain."

At one point, of course, televangelists were mentioned. These were the worst of men, bottom feeders who preyed on anyone, but most especially seniors with physical afflictions. One patron of the arts mentioned her admiration for Burt Lancaster who played Elmer Gantry, the charlatan preacher/evangelist in the novel of the same name written by Sinclair Lewis. The name Sinclair lead to a discussion of Upton Sinclair's novel, "The Jungle." And it was no surprise that everyone agreed that all that seemed to matter was the bottom line. Lawyers, stock brokers, used car salesmen, physicians, and politicians particularly received the brunt of the conversation. These types were being depicted as malignant narcissists and sociopaths, men devoid of conscience, morally bankrupt men whose motive, agenda and behavior were always ulterior. Were they silver-tongued orators? Of course, they were, but they also had the Midas touch, and they knew just where to touch friends, neighbors, relatives, co-workers, and especially hungry strangers looking for inside information, or a short cut. To them, life was a game played with shaved dice or marked cards. They'd learned early on that it was much easier to pick-pocket a man's mind than his pocket.

One after the other of the guests castigated individuals who had been praised and elevated to positions of great power, wealth, and respect, but who had secretly been conning the public, and who were eventually exposed and humiliated. "I can't believe that these brilliant people actually thought they could get away with wholesale larceny," one wealthy entrepreneur offered. "One would be compelled to believe that these people wake-up every morning with the same immoral objective: rape, pillage and plunder people, not only of their money, but of their self-worth, self-esteem and self-respect."

Guy hadn't spoken up, neither did he add anything to the conversation. He had just been listening attentively with great interest. Then one of the female guests looked at him and said, "Guy we haven't heard from you. You are one of the sincerest individuals I've ever met. Is there anything you'd like to add about sincerity?" All eyes were now on Guy who had been relaxing on the love seat. Guy had an uncanny way of becoming one with any piece of furniture he chose to either sit or lie on

"Yeah, Guy. Come on, let's hear some of your thoughts on this subject. There isn't a person in this room who doesn't absolutely admire and respect your transparent sincerity," the tallest guest at the party said enthusiastically with a sincere double-jointed intellectual kowtow.

Guy hesitated then stood up, walked to the china cabinet and brought forth a specific fine classic china dinner plate. This plate had not been in plain sight; it never was, and even though it was in Stuart's home, Stuart had never seen it. Of course, Stuart and his wife were surprised, but neither said a word.

They just looked at each other with looks of amusement and surprise. After all, this was Guy who never lacked for those mysterious shades of gray.

Guy acknowledged Stuart's and his wife's surprised looks, then returned to the love seat with the dinner plate in his hands. "I agree with Stuart; I usually do, and what I would like to add, especially after all the stories about the pain inflicted by con men, in no way is intended as a contradiction. Wisdom and keen discernment are invaluable when trying to determine whether a person is sincere; unfortunately, we are unable to see into a person's heart for "'Out of the heart proceed the issues of life. The heart is deceitful and desperately wicked above all things. Who can know it?'"

"As was previously pointed out by Stuart, according to folk history, the English word sincere comes from two Latin words: sine (without) and cera (wax). In the ancient times there were many fine pottery makers in the Roman world, and it turned out to be a lucrative business. The pottery would be formed, then placed into an oven to cure. The well-respected potter would inspect his pottery after firing, and if any cracks were found, the vessel would be discarded, and he would start over. Naturally, this would increase the overall price and value of fine pottery. Given the same situation, other less reputable potters would take the blemished vessel and rub wax into the crack, perhaps melting it somewhat, then paint over the imperfection and sell it as if it were pristine. These individuals could sell their pottery for cheaper prices, thus undercutting the sincere pottery makers. This prompted the honorable pottery makers to hang a sign over the entrance to their stores: "Sincerus," Meaning this store has pottery without wax. Whether true or not this analogy represents an excellent way to examine one's sincerity. Don't we all want to be considered individuals who are "Without wax?" Guy then carefully examined the front and the back of the plate for a few minutes. He was smiling broadly, but he didn't speak.

The dinner plate Guy was holding was no ordinary dinner plate. It was ornate and appeared to be quite expensive. The intricate design and complex patterns presented a magnificence rarely seen in dinner ware which would normally not be considered works of art. From the center of the plate a tree seemed to be emerging. The leaves of the tree appeared to be climbing out of the plate, and each leaf, there were too many to count, was different, but the more conscientiously one studied the leaves their asymmetry seemed to coalesce, making something seemingly so different appear to be either alike or at least similar. No colors were left to the imagination, and the tree had become a bearer of a variety of fruit. While the trunk of the tree wasn't entirely visible, if you stared diligently into the center of the plate, it seemed as if you were looking directly down into the trunk, where there seemed to be neither a beginning nor an ending but rather an infinity of filamentous connections called dendrites that resembled tens of thousands of little trees.

On the back of the plate a convolution of roots was apparently supporting the tree. If one studied the roots long and hard enough one could see the image of a naked man, but if you didn't concentrate, and if you took your eyes off the man for a split second, you would lose him in the roots. The roots looked like a bed of snakes. It was difficult to distinguish between the man, the roots and the snakes. Just when you thought you had a clear picture of the naked man he'd disappear among the roots like a snake. Frustration would quickly set in and almost drive the examiner crazy. You might as well attempt to distinguish between the 100 trillion neurological connections where neuron meets neuron inside the human brain.

All the dinner guests were impressed with Guy's story about the history of the word "sincere." One woman quipped that she thought his explanation of the word's origin was appropriate and accurate. She wondered why the etymological justification for this common story had been dismissed. Her response generated a lively response among the guests. A handsome male model said maybe someday they'd find a fossil that verified the story. "I've gone fossil hunting a few times, but all I ever came-up with were some Indian head arrows and a Grecian urn," he said somewhat disappointedly. "I hope

Guy has more luck fossil hunting than I've had. However, Guy, even if you don't find that special fossil you are looking for, remember what Keats said, "'Beauty is truth, truth beauty, that is all you know on earth, and all you need to know.'"

Stuart got up from his seat and went to Guy, who was comfortably sitting back on the love seat. He asked him for the plate. He examined the plate thoroughly then handed the plate to the person closest to him. He asked each person to examine the plate for any obvious imperfections and then to pass it on to the next person.

The ornate plate made the rounds. It passed from one pair of forensic hands to the other. The inquisitors were thorough in their examination of the plate, to the point of being laborious, as well as to the consternation of the other impatient guests who couldn't wait to get their hands on the mysterious plate.

Once the plate had made the rounds Stuart asked that the plate be returned to him. He then asked if anyone had seen any imperfections. Everyone proclaimed that no imperfections had been seen, and they all agreed that they had never seen such a mysteriously beautiful dinner plate. Stuart then returned the plate to Guy and offered, "It appears as if this plate is without wax."

Guy took the plate from Stuart. He stood up and walked slowly across the room. He stood motionless for a while then handed the plate to the person closest to him. He said, "Please look at this plate, but don't look for any imperfections in the plate; you've already determined there are none. When you look at the plate this time, examine it as if you are examining yourself. Be sincere. Look deep inside for any cracks that may have been hidden by your deceitful behavior. Look for that wax you may have applied to hide something from everyone but yourself, that counterfeit moment when you passed yourself off as authentic. Before the night is over most of us will probably agree that Stuart's topic of sincerity will have produced an exhilarating and mutually beneficial discussion. Others may have wished for a topic less emotionally invasive with far less exposure, something more humorous and far less serious, something that might generate some belly laughs, rather than an emotionally moving catharsis designed to loosen then eliminate constipated thought, thoughts that previously would have transgressed trust. This night, your rapt and sure attention will be required. Think of it this way, "'The secret of popular writing is to never put more on a given page than the common reader can lap off with no strain on his habitually slack attention.'" "You may consider this night to be a book, and the previous quote by Ezra Pound will be matched by another of his when he said, "'No man understands a deep book until he has seen and lived at least part of its contents.'" "Tonight, we may be courting history while writing on the tablets of our hearts a book that will live forever as a classic."

When the first dinner guest got the plate for the second time, he acted as if he had just been handed a hot potato. He looked at every person in the room, focusing carefully on each face while holding the plate in his lap. He then began to carefully examine the plate even more carefully than he had the first go around. The plate seemed to have become a hot plate that if not passed soon enough would scald the holder, causing 3rd degree burns in the subconscious that just might lead to memory loss or a form of intentional amnesia. However, as hot as the plate might have become while in one's hands it wasn't that easy to pass on. It was as if the inanimate had become animate and capable of communicating. More than one guest became so emotionally moved that they were brought to tears. One very prominent guest, a hedge fund manager, raised his voice to such a high pitch that he scared the other guests. Yet, when he was asked to pass the plate along, he refused to release it. "Take this plate from me! Take this plate from me! Please, won't someone take this plate from me!" he yelled. Eventually the plate was forced from his hands, and he was able to relax. He had become bathed in sweat. It took him twelve minutes to cool down. He looked as if he had aged 18 years. The psychologically induced metamorphosis had apparently caused a regression similar to an onslaught of repressed thoughts; the butterfly doesn't die; he just loses his wings and is forced to crawl on his belly until he turns into a sybaritic drone who mates with the queen; afterwards, his endophallus is ripped from his abdomen and he dies shortly thereafter.

Guy had instructed the guests that they could only pass the plate along if they had agreed that, by doing so, they were acknowledging that they'd been insincere at one time or another, perhaps even some time this evening. Guy had also made it perfectly clear that no guest would be required to relate the nature of his or her insincerity before passing the plate along, assuming, of course, they'd been insincere at least once in their life, but they would certainly be given the opportunity to share their feelings if they chose to do so. He also suggested that each guest hold onto the plate for at least five minutes before passing it along. He'd also made it clear that the plate was not to be confused with truth serum, one of several hypnotic drugs supposedly having the effect of causing a person on questioning to talk freely without inhibition. Neither was this plate to be likened to a bugbear, an imaginary creature evoked to frighten children into good behavior. He did, imply, however, that personal Copernican shifts might take place that one had no control over. On the other hand, he also implied that resistance to heliocentric thinking might be employed to substantiate ones' cave dweller mindset; not that that mindset would necessarily be considered wrong.

So, that was the beginning of one of the most interesting evenings that might lead to forgone conclusions that were neither forgone, nor conclusions. Occasionally the atmosphere at the party took on the air of an AA meeting, an emotional strip search. On more than one occasion a catharsis, that emotional experience of relief from tension and anxiety as the result of releasing into consciousness repressed ideas, feelings, wishes, and memories, took place. It was at such moments that Guy's power of facilitation became obvious. Something voluntarily mysterious took place in the minds and hearts of the guests during these moments of intimate sharing.

"I suppose the roots of the tree depicted on the plate can be linked to someone's ancestry," the historian said with Salt Lake City, Utah assurance.

No one spoke to his assumption. None of the guests looked at one another, as if to agree or disagree with the historian's assumption, but each eventually looked at Guy.

Guy said nothing. The plate had been returned to him, and he was holding it in his lap. Guy carefully looked at each guest, sure to make eye contact. He then got up and went to the linen closet. He opened the closet and removed a soft cotton cloth that resembled a fleece. He returned to his seat and began to lovingly polish the plate with thoughtful deliberation.

"I absolutely love this plate It is almost as if there is something tectonic about it. What I mean is, when you hold it in your hands it becomes an indescribable moving experience. The movement takes place beneath the surface of the earth just like the subconscious moves beneath the conscious mind. Most of the time it is dormant, then occasionally it erupts, revealing threatening emotional fissures that suck the life out of us and bring us down to where 3rd degree fire had been discovered by the ugliest god of all gods, Vulcan. The earth, our mind, quakes then opens and sends invitations more powerful than black holes that cannot be refused. There appears to be no escape, yet you still climb walls. You get the rock near the top of the hill, then it rolls right back down, and you start all over again. Futility establishes insurmountable barriers, mountainous mental geographies that cannot be scaled alone or together. Your neurotransmitters are compromised, convoluted, twisted and bound like a series of Gordian knots. But then a fossil, once held in the powerful grip of Alexander the Great, is found. This fossil gives you hope because many who have gone before you and have survived the relentless onslaught of false hope find faith among the ruins; faith that there is something greater than yourself, not the arrogant nobility of Ozymandias whose broken body speaks a truth that during his lifetime eluded him, "'My name is Ozymandias, king of kings: look on my works, ye mighty, and despair.'"

"Furthermore," Guy continued. "You are encouraged by incontrovertible truth; for some, an absolute they have arrived at and prospered from based on their sincerity and integrity," Guy said joyfully. "I'm certain I would not be accused of a contradictory assertion if I echoed Walt Whitman, "'I celebrate myself, I sing myself, and what I assume you shall assume, for every atom belonging to me as good belongs to you,'" he continued. "Neither, I'm certain, would I be accused of overcoming anticipatory anxiety with paradoxical intention. My intentions would be obvious, and my advice, should you desire it, would be advice rendered by Viktor Frankl, "'Live as if you were living already for the second time and as if you had acted the first time as wrongly as you are about to act now.'"

No one responded. It was as if Guy, himself, had just tied them to the bed of Procrustes. He wanted to stretch their imaginations, not their bodies, without harming them. He had no desire to disarticulate their thinking or to rudely rupture their thought processes. Neither did he desire to place them beneath the Sword of Damocles where the fear of decapitation might force false confessions, but he did want to free them from self-imposed gravitational pulls that held them immovably in a vice situated between their ears.

Guy continued, "It is as if this plate possesses metaphysical properties, and a transference of feeling takes place between a therapist and his patient. When clutched to your chest it is almost as if it has life, and, to a degree, can give life. If you were to hold this plate up to your ear, you would hear the Tower of Babel being translated into an ocean of its original language, a language understood by all who came within its hearing. Dare I say, "the voice of God?" Embodied cognition is inherent in this plate just as our thoughts are rooted in the physical. We think about abstract concepts such as time and space in terms of physical metaphors; in turn, physical sensations can affect our thoughts and beliefs. This plate is all about time, and it brings to light this statement by Albert Einstein, "The distinction between past, present, and future is only an illusion, even if a stubborn one.'" Wow, don't you just love this plate," he asked with a smile that gave a pink sound to his words as if a daughter had just been born. His broad smile was contagious. All the guests felt encouraged and motivated to cultivate gardens of integrity that would feed society with faith, hope and love. Everything had become momentarily lighter and quieter; the sound of silence had set in, but it soon grew too loud for an acoustically average audience more familiar and comfortable with innocuous ear tickling.

"The life of the flesh isn't in the blood; it is in the plate," Guy said dogmatically though kindly. Then he added, "It is as if this plate has the supernatural power to grant absolution," he continued.

Stuart, particularly, took umbrage to Guy's reference to Leviticus, but he didn't say anything. The subtle sound of murmuring also seemed to travel around the table from guest to guest, but no one spoke up. It was like a desert scene where the same old food was being offered day after day, after day, and everyone was wearing forty-year old clothing that appeared to never grow old.

"Guy, I'm sorry to say, but your obsession with the plate is confusing and almost amusing. That plate is nothing more than a plate, a piece of glass. It may be ornate and more beautiful than our own dinner plates that have been set before us, nevertheless, it is nothing more than a plate. What do you suppose would happen if I took that plate from you and smashed it to pieces? Would you be heartbroken? Would you cry like a baby? Would your blood pressure suddenly escalate? Would you have a sudden heart attack or stroke? Or would you just gather the broken pieces and throw them in the garbage can? Knowing you, and how much you love the plate, you would gather the pieces and attempt to glue them back together attempting to restore your perception of perfection. Or, perhaps, some sympathetic souls might come by and attempt to put you back together as if you were Humpty Dumpty, and that you were the one who had taken a humiliating hard fall," the bond trader said in an arrogant and rather demeaning fashion to the astonishment of everyone present. "Guy, my poor deluded Guy, you are acting as if this plate in the first cause, a cause which I don't think you even believe in."

The shocked guests were breathless as they watched Guy, while awaiting his reply. This bond trader was a kind of outsider. He'd only been invited as a guest of another guest who knew Stuart's wife. He was on the heavy side, about 240 pounds at 5ft. 6 inches. He was bald because he liked to keep his perfectly round head shaved. He always sported a nice even tan. He wore green tinted contacts that favored his piercing eyes. He liked to brag about the fact that he'd never worn a coat and tie on his way to the top. He preferred pastel polos to go with his khaki pants and his Martin Dingman Crocodile Arlo leather shoes. He had more than one pair, but his favorite was the Mauri-2209 Hornback Wonder Blue & Caribbean Blue Baby Croc Dress Shoe that retailed for $1200.00.

After a few minutes, a long few minutes, Guy responded. "Jacob, I noticed that when the plate was passed the second time, you didn't examine it. You just quickly passed it to your neighbor.

Why was that? Was there something about the plate that didn't agree with you, or did you just consider the whole idea to be foolish, and meant only to entertain? Perhaps you were hiding something, something from yourself and others. I couldn't say, but I found your behavior to be very interesting. Did the passing of the plate frighten you? Or should I ask, did the presence of the plate inhibit, then prohibit you from attending your own "white funeral?"

Jacob hesitated then said, "Scare me? Something to hide? No, and not necessarily foolish. I've seen these kinds of games played before. I guess they can be fun in a way, but I certainly don't take them seriously. Neither do I intend to attend my White Funeral, and if I did it would be more like a smorgasbord, and I'd have been the chef, who, once again, would feed his flock with a quintessentially gourmet endless last meal."

"I understand, and I certainly am not questioning your integrity; neither am I questioning your bravery but, would you then mind if I placed the plate in your lap again for about five minutes? You wouldn't object to that, would you?" Guy asked.

Jacob did not respond. He just looked at the other anxious guests before agreeing to Guy's proposal. "OK, go ahead. Let me have the presumptuous plate, if it will make you happy, but don't assume you are about to witness any sign of obvious discomfort. I've never been an intentional trouble-maker. I don't think I've ever had an obsessive or unhealthy preoccupation or attachment to anything, including an inheritance. Sure, I've listened to voices other than my own, and one occasion of weakness changed the trajectory of my life forever. I opened-up Pandora's Box and reaped the whirlwind, but hoping against hope, I gathered strength from my grandfather and never looked back. Now, give me that ornamental piece of glass and stand back."

"OK, here's the plate," Guy said as he moved towards Jacob, but I don't want you to avoid looking deep into the plate. I want you to promise to diligently observe the intricacy of the plate and to examine the roots. Furthermore, when you find yourself in the cave remember what Soren Kierkegaard said about life, "'Life can only be understood backwards, but it must be lived forwards.:'" Be open. Be transparent. Do not rationalize. Do not project. Do not repress. Do not regress. Do not employ displacement. Do not sublimate. Do not employ denial. Be sincere. Look for the man, and "'it shall follow as the day the night......'"

Jacob welcomed the plate. He had agreed to become as transparent as an open book. He fixed his gaze on the plate, front and back. Into the third minute of the agreed five-minute interlude he began to sweat profusely and to shake almost uncontrollably. His face was slowly becoming more and more ashen by the second. He feigned normalcy, but everyone could see that he was in a dire emotional and physical strait. Something bad was about to happen if no one interceded. Stuart moved towards him, but he was restrained by Guy. Jacob's shiny bald head was awash in bubbles of sweat, and his underarms had become two leaking dikes. He could speak all right, but his throat was slowly closing; a peculiar type of dumbness was overtaking him.

Jacob managed to stand-up while holding the plate tightly in his unsteady hands. He appeared transfixed by the plate. He attempted to speak but he couldn't. Into the fourth minute his throat opened, and he could be heard choking out the following confession, "I didn't mean it. I really had no intention. I was just following orders. I couldn't have been more wrong, even though I may have been sincerely wrong. Am I the only person who ever stretched the truth? I just wanted to protect my inheritance and receive a blessing from my clients. Oh, my God, my God. Who will deliver me from the body of this death? I'm sorry. I didn't intend for anyone to get hurt, let alone to suffer intolerably forever the pangs of outrageous fortune. How was I supposed to know the gun was loaded? I could swear the light was green. I can't imagine anyone not being tempted by insider trading and a guaranteed opportunity to quadruple their investment. How was I to know the stock would go down, and that my clients would receive margin calls that might bankrupt them? Occasionally my suggested shorts would go long, and my longs would go short, and my clients might lose their total investment. My job was to keep them safe and to make them as much money as was possible, and I offered them the same ladder of opportunity I'd had," he offered with a squirming voice laced with guilt that caused his skin to squirm and his brother's angry face to appear before him. His five minutes was up, but he could not let go.

"Oh! Oh! Oh! Who has been left alive that might forgive me? "'Out. Out. Damned spot.'" "'Oh, that pang where more than madness lies. That worm that will not sleep and never dies,'"

He continued grievously while barely able to remain standing.

"What about the starving impetuous young man, the gullible hunter, you deceived then abandoned in the Black Forest? What about that savory young man? Do you want to talk about him, and the hidden scars that have become scar tissue hardened to the point of indelible memories that can never be erased? Perhaps he survived the unethical animal onslaught, perhaps not. His young innocent bones may have been picked clean then scattered among the other ruins. Maybe they have become fossils. Do you suppose we should go look together beneath the unturned rocks of youthful exuberance, the gullibility of the innocent, those uncontrollable urges, to find them? Maybe what we will find is a pound of flesh. Dare say we gather the twisted roots and yank the truth out of the dry ground breeding lilacs in April?" Guy prodded effectively

"No! No! Please don't go in April!" Jacob begged lamentably. He'd fallen to his knees, but he clutched the plate to his chest. He then extended the plate as an offering to anyone willing to grab it. "Here! Here! Won't someone please take this plate from me?" he begged. No one responded. It was as if every guest had become a statue. A stranger suddenly appeared who seemed to be willing to take the plate, but before he could hand off the plate, Jacob fell to the ground. He began to convulse and foam at the mouth, while still holding tightly onto the plate. He seemed to be protecting it. The moment he involuntarily released the plate his convulsions ceased, he lost consciousness, and the stranger disappeared.

Panic seized the guests. Someone screamed, "Call 911!"

"No! Don't call 911. I will attend to him," Guy said firmly. "Stuart, please get the plate and be careful. See that it has not been harmed."

Guy, using his paramedic background, quickly assessed Jacob. He determined that Jacob had suffered a mild cardiac event. He had lost consciousness and wasn't breathing normally, but it wasn't anything major. Guy performed CPR, and Jacob was revived and returned to normal in less than 15 minutes.

He didn't realize that he had come as close to the "event horizon" as was possible without being sucked into a black hole of nothingness where he would spend an eternity as a number.

The party resumed as if nothing significant had just happened. Jacob, of course, was flabbergasted, but he didn't say much when questioned, except to ask for the plate again so he could examine the roots. "It wasn't the tree that dug deeply into my subconscious; it was the roots. I'm very curious about these roots. There's a hell of a lot more to be said about this tree and its roots than meets the eye. I don't ever remember feeling so unconditionally blessed, detoxified by the two-edged blade of truth. I don't think I will have much more to contribute for the rest of the evening, but I am now content to listen with the acute sense of hearing found among men trapped in corners with no apparent avenue of escape. Here, in the company of other men searching for meaning I hear Viktor Frankl "'When we are no longer able to change a situation, we are challenged to change ourselves.'" "Wait, wait! Let me add one more very important thing. This plate's roots have the power to change your name."

"Well, I suppose they could be roots attached to someone's ancestral tree, but, on the other hand, maybe they aren't attached to the tree on the opposite side of the plate. Maybe those roots are just searching for a tree to attach to. For all we know, maybe those roots have been cut off from their family tree, or perhaps there is no family tree. Those roots may very well be orphans suffering from a crippling sense of alienation, a sense of not belonging, the fearful sense of estrangement," One of the female guests, a psychology professor, quipped nonchalantly, attempting to break the silence and to open the floor for further discussion while addressing the initial question posed by the historian.

As the other guests pondered the remarks by the historian and the professor, Guy continued to methodically and gently polish the plate. He maintained his silence and listened intently, looking only at the plate. The more he polished the plate the more he appeared to be transfixed and profoundly contemplative. From the look on his face it was as if he and the plate were becoming one, or that he had found himself up a tree and standing nonchalantly on a branch while staring down into the valley of the world's kingdoms, kingdoms rooted in search of the truth, though anxiously denying it when meeting it face to face.

"That may be true, of course, but not very likely. Yes, there is a line of demarcation, and it is hidden from our view, but I don't think the artist was intentionally trying to hide the truth. We can't see the connection necessarily, but I don't think any other conclusion can be drawn other than that the tree is directly related to the roots. Evidence to the contrary doesn't support any other conclusion," a young prosecutor, sporting a closely groomed beard, added as if he had just completed his summation.

"Maybe an ax was taken to the tree, and all that remain are the roots. Furthermore, maybe the tree is slowly dying. Sure, it certainly looks robust, but in the sense that it has been separated from its roots it may be a tree doomed to die. Maybe another plate exists that can tell us more about this abundantly flourishing mysterious tree. Take a real hard look at those roots before you presume that they belong to the tree. Look closely at their convoluted strangulated patterns. I'd say they seem to be stretching down and out, and there can be no foregone conclusion regarding their genealogy. This may very well be the artist's attempt to portray the Gap Theory. Guy would appreciate this; the roots look like uprooted, dangling participles in search of a subject," the professor of paleontology said, smiled demurely, then sipped her dry martini.

"Speculation about the roots is intriguing. To me, they appear to be clutching. I think the roots are in great pain because they have been separated from the tree they gave birth to like a parent who has been shunned by a child. Although, on the other hand, it may be the arrogant child who has chosen to disobey its parents, and the parents have disowned the child. Rare, yes.

Unlikely, yes. However, when it comes to genealogies and birthrights it still happens. We can make a case for either one or the other, but there are no facts to conclusively support either of the two. Furthermore, there may be a missing link if the roots have been rooted and grounded in the truth, like the notorious root out of dry ground described by Isaiah," the rabbi said.

This reference to Isaiah caused Jacob's heart to bang like a drum, but no one heard it. His heart then skipped a beat, and everyone heard it. It came from the dark side of the moon's jealous, fratricidal language. It was a sorrowful sentimental whooping cough due to foreign objects caught in the throat like fish bones, a deceitful silent scream or maternal machination. Was it his nation that was being led to the slaughter in Isaiah 53 or was it him? He would appreciate nothing more than to be able to get to the truth, the whole truth, and nothing but the truth, so help me, him, us, God.

"What is truth?" came a question out of nowhere. It was a soft sound and very quiet; it would be difficult to hear unless one was sensitively attuned to things considered spiritual. The body of it was contained in a cherub's bosom, some would say a womb, hanging mysteriously from an olive branch attached to the ceiling above an imaginary fire in the corner of Stuart's game room. After a few seconds its tenuous grip loosened, and it fell but not into the fire. It floated softly like a feather then landed softly onto the tile floor, slithered briefly on its belly unobserved towards an open window then disappeared like an imaginary ghost. Its voice had been heard by no one, except Stewart. A sudden gust of wind seemed to breeze through the room causing a communal chill. A subtle emotional shuddering lingered beneath the foundation of the home. The pink-cheeked vegetarian asked Stuart to put another log on the fire.

"So far, I believe everyone has been sincere, but passing the plate is not the same as passing the buck in search of a scapegoat. Is there anyone here who doesn't sincerely believe they have been guilty of misinterpreting statements held to be true, or to have intentionally misconstrued statements that were held to be false? Is there anyone here who has not suffered the pangs of separation based on the conviction of a guilty conscience? Is there anyone here who has not been guilty of fundamental attribution errors? Just as a tree is known by its fruit, so in like manner men are known by their behavior, but that behavior should never arbitrarily be attributed to a man based on his race, creed, color or religion, nor, for that matter, be based on a conditioned stimulus. Many sincere men have been sincerely wrong," Guy said sincerely.

"As opposed to being intentionally wrong, I suppose?" she said

"Well, Yes. That is certainly one way to put it" he answered. "But, can someone be intentionally sincerely wrong and think they are right? I think that is the real question.

"Can someone be intentionally sincerely wrong and be just as sincere as someone who is sincerely unintentionally wrong? Yes? No? Maybe?" she asked, then added, "This is not an oxymoron."

"Probably, but it goes to motive," the lawyer said.

"Exactly. It typically boils down to motive, and if there is an ulterior motive, we have the right to question the sincerity of the plaintiff" the magistrate said.

"What about the defendant? If his motive was pure, and he was sincerely bound by his conscience to do the sordid deed but had no ulterior motive, how should we find him?" she asked.

"If he was bound by his conscience, he had a motive, ulterior or otherwise, and would probably be found guilty, at least, to some degree. These types of acts are typically not done in a vacuum outside of the conscience, unless it had been seared by the proverbial hot iron," the psychotherapist said. "There may be a dysfunctional person hidden in the roots of that family tree's dysfunctional behavior. He or she may have left or may have been thrown out and is now running through an unfamiliar garden looking for just the right tree to climb. Or, this person whose mind may have been divided into two incompatible hemispheres, can be seen pitifully barking up the wrong tree. Also, please don't forget that "'A tree is known by its fruit.'" "Life can be a maze, you know."

"Yes, how true, and there may be no way out, at least not known to the prisoner, unless by supernatural intervention. I think this is where amazing comes in. This exit can be nothing short of amazing, but, not, of course, in all cases. There may not only be circumstantial evidence; there may be circumstances beyond one's control, and the fruit may have become spoiled because no one came along to pick it," she answered. Then she added, "On the other hand the tree may have been cursed."

"I think we should get back to the root of the problem, otherwise we risk becoming philosophically flowering clueless sleuths, who, at best, can issue citizens' arrests. The root of the problem or, if you prefer, problems, is always, or most usually, motive and the accompanying need to be affirmed, some refrigerator magnet motivation, as opposed to, of course, avoidance, and that is precisely why a man's past plays such an important part in his present as well as his future" Guy posed, then figuratively licked the plate clean, searching for some hidden fossils, some supportive causal evidence "Not one among us hasn't read Proust's "A la Recherche du Temps Perdue." Whether it is referred to as "In Search of Lost Time" or "The Remembrance of Things Past," fossils, real or imagined, play an important part in one's future."

"So then, have we not just zeroed in on the bullseye, confirming that such a fossilized root does indeed exist and can never be dated with absolute certainty? Unlike existence, emotions cannot be carbon dated. The seed will carry the day," the voluptuous secretary of the interior said while lifting her skirt above knee level. "I'm not saying you categorically reap what you sow, but you usually do. I typically tell my clients, which are somehow patients, to grow where you have been planted, and don't be ashamed of your Inner Ape if it is clawing to get out. There's nothing wrong with being a monkey's uncle."

"Did I just hear someone say, manslaughter?" the transgender asked moments before he/she popped the cork, unleashing the inviting center of a black hole with the power to permanently capture the curious in a gravitational collapse. "Or are you still floating in the gene pool behind closed doors dangling from a hanger in the closet? When they find my fossil, what gender do you think they will ascribe to my remains?"

"No, what you heard was someone declaring that the seed's responsibility to nature should not be superseded by the seed's responsibility to nurture," Guy answered. Then, to the astonishment of the guests he began to spin the priceless plate on his right index finger using his left hand to propel it. He was spinning it counterclockwise, of course, and it was spinning very quickly. The plate began to whistle. It appeared as if it was about to take off. This behavior could have been interpreted as Guy's attempt to go back in time.

"Guilt, contrition, confession and forgiveness do seem to be inextricably bound to one's sincerity, especially if cleansing is the desirable result, a psychological detoxification process designed to get you into the Z realm, a realm that transcends space and time characterized by profound feelings of spontaneity and harmony with the universe. No, I am not talking about self-actualization while on your merry oblivious way to a state of malignant narcissism. God forbid! Because as Stuart has kindly reminded us from time to time, " "'All have sinned and come short of the glory of God,'" Guy mysteriously and enigmatically added something to the equation nobody expected. He wanted to intentionally throw something common into the uncommon spinning pot being stirred by inquisitive minds, those involuntary bodily functions controlled by the autonomic nervous system.

"That sounds good, but it is possible to look clean on the outside and be as black as coal on the inside. Does the reference to whited sepulchers ring a bell? If so, guilt, contrition, confession and forgiveness are not necessarily part of the cleansing formula. An awful lot of clean looking hands have done an awful lot of dirty work and a great deal of that has been done in the name of

God," the thoracic surgeon said. "I've seen plenty of subluxations of the soul that could not be brought back to proper alignment, short of radical surgery. I've also come across quite a few yellow spines, hiding beneath muscle that has been hypertrophied by cowardly bullies flexing intimidation based on their physique. Yet, they have neither heart nor spine when challenged and beaten by someone considered their inferior. I do not approve of rejoicing in humiliation, but sometimes this act can lead to positive permanent change. Someone once said, "'The best apology is changed behavior.'"

"This is probably about as good a time as any to bring this up. This is something we learn the first day of nursing school. Dirty to dirty is dirty. Dirty to clean is dirty. Clean to clean is clean. Or, to put it another way, "'Who can bring a clean thing out of an unclean?'" Or, God forbid, if you want to get religious about it, "'Who can say I have made my heart clean? I'm pure from my sin.'"

"I wish you wouldn't have brought that word up. It tends to lead to a degree of introspection that could also result in spontaneous human combustion; the consequences, of course, being fatal. However, Plato did say, "'The unexamined life is not worth living.'"

"Very interesting. I wonder what Plato might have to say about the plate we've been examining. Or, better yet, the plate that has been examining us?" Stuart added coyly while examining the curious faces etched into the imaginary granite headstone hanging above the entrance to the cemetery.

"He probably wouldn't acknowledge the eternal impact of that three-letter word, but he did agree with Socrates that those regarded as experts in ethical matters did not have the understanding necessary for a good human life. Plato introduced the idea that their mistakes were due to their not engaging properly with a class of entities he called 'forms.' The chief examples were Justice, Beauty and Equality. To Plato, Justice, Beauty and Equality were accessible not to the senses but to the mind alone, and they were the most important constituents of reality. Plato developed the view that the good life requires not just a certain kind of knowledge but also habituation to healthy emotional responses and therefore harmony between the three parts of the soul: reason, spirit and appetite. In metaphysics Plato envisioned a systematic, rational treatment of the forms and their interrelations, starting with the most fundamental among them, the Good or the One," Guy added, then briefly continued, "That is precisely why I work at being good and have a desire to get even better. My reason, spirit and appetite are becoming my soul's habitation based on habituation. It will eventually become nirvana, a transcendent state in which there is neither suffering, desire, nor sense of self, and the subject will be released from the effects of karma and the cycle of death and rebirth. When I get there, I'll really be good, and that will be as good as it gets."

"Obviously Plato never heard this, "'Why do you call Me good? No one is good but One, that is, God,'" "However, had he had an ear to hear, he might have agreed with the plate's capacity to incapacitate defense mechanisms meant to bend the mind to be in agreement with aberrant salience's delusional and hallucinatory inclinations due to overactive dopamine's joy ride being turned into a haunted house where secret agents control thoughts that have been stolen by microwaves," the DJ, who hadn't played anything but Bach the whole night, said with the classical sound of a frustrated hortatory hornpipe that seemed to be blowing in the wind most of the gas filled evening. "I also believe that if you think really hard you will be able to come up with one example of the good becoming the enemy of the best."

"'If music be the food of love, play on,'" came a familiar voice out of nowhere.

"The singularity seems obvious but not to most people. That is precisely why they place such a great emphasis on fossils. They are convinced that the answers they seek in the present can be found in the past. One might consider that 'coming up short' but not sinful. It could merely be a matter of hieroglyphics like handwriting on the wall, but not necessarily that admonition meant for Belshazzar," the etymologist said. "Furthermore, one must remember that how and where one finishes is more important than how he begins, although a great deal of emphasis is placed on origins, especially words, since words are the most powerful of weapons. I wouldn't blame anyone who wanted to go fossil hunting, especially in their backyard, and most especially if they used a diving rod."

"So, the apple falls not only not far from tree, but the apple is the tree" the female impersonator said. "The best mirror you will ever have is the face of a friend."

"Someone once said, "'A man who has one good friend has more than his share,'" I wonder if anyone here has one good friend," the butler said as he wheeled in the dessert cart. His sudden, uncalled for remarks caught everyone off-guard. No offense had been intended, but, let us not forget that the remarks came from a butler. Not a butcher, baker or candlestick maker. A butler.

"In that case, perhaps you can tell us who did it," she quipped while sticking her finger into the hole in the dike to stop the flow of conventional thought, seeking to divert those more imaginative creative tributaries that could quench inquisitive thirst.

"I'm not sure if anyone can tell you who did it, because people are changing all the time, and, most especially, their minds. "Didn't Guy say, "Your body follows your mind. Where are you taking yours?" the shaggy-bell-bottom pants poet answered. "Don't mind me. I only came because I'd hoped to gather some meaningful metaphors or similes that might emerge from off-limit black holes, whose admonition to "Stay off the perimeter of gravitational collapse had been ignored." I had no idea we might be talking about substitutionary atonement in the guise of a fossil, and I don't mean expiation. I mean propitiation. Now, I am happier than you can ever imagine even if I'm turned into a human piñata before the night is over. On the other hand, my joy might be turned into sorrow when the subject of being sorry comes up, and I need to ask for forgiveness. I wouldn't think of using poetic license as my defense, but don't push, pull, or prod me. After all, I'm only human."

"All I know about time plus matter plus chance is that "there is nothing new under the sun," and that the shortest distance between two points is a straight line. Judge not that you be not judged," the butler, who hadn't even been technically invited, said with a geometric looking jaw that stuck out like a diamond emerging from the innocuous inviting rough. He didn't look at all like a butler should look, however that is. He looked more like a ringmaster. When he returned to the kitchen the cook asked him how the circus was going. "They are eating. They are drinking, but they are not very merry," he answered knowingly.

"But, would you say they, at least, appear to have become transparent? Is there, at least, one among them who looks like a piece of Swiss cheese? Or, based on what has transpired so far, do you think each, when he goes to sleep, tonight, might agree with Shakespeare and be categorized such as this, "'Infected minds, to their deaf pillows will discharge their secrets,'" the cook asked.

"The fossil you find may not be the fossil you have been looking for. So, don't be fooled while carefully dusting it if it crumbles in your hands and is lifted on the invisible wings of the wind then taken to the four corners of the earth. For it is in this mysterious manner that the architectural design of all life, Wisdom, is laid," the graphic designer said while fiddling with the compass dangling from his neck. He walked with an emotional limp, and his hip had been permanently placed out of joint while wrestling with his stepfather in the valley of the shadow of death. A replacement was out of the question lest he forget the paradigm shift's purpose, and his responsibility to read between the lines become blurred by ambition.

"Is what cries out in the streets beyond us? Is the fossil Guy will be searching for tonight to be found only in the future? Or is it to be found below his feet?" the African American professor of geology asked while exhaling a cloud of carbon dioxide that could kill an elephant.

At least two closet bigots questioned whether the geologist should have said 'beneath' instead of 'below.' One of these two bigots, also arrogantly quipped, "The last time I looked there weren't any Chocolate Cosmos on that tree."

"Yeah, and it wouldn't surprise me if he said the Cradle of Civilization was actually centered in the Congo and not Mesopotamia," the other said smartly. "Yeah, I agree. By the way, I certainly wouldn't want to insult him by bringing up evolutionary biology. He has carried himself well enough, tonight, but I guess you know he got in on a basketball scholarship. If it wasn't for basketball, he might have become a basket weaver. Or, if all else had failed, he'd have made an excellent chimney sweeper."

No one responded to the geologist's question. No one looked at one another. Their eyeballs rolled inward exposing the whites of their eyes, but not to each other, of course. There wasn't the slightest hint of transparency. Had sincerity been camouflaged by deceit? Had an intellectual opaque curtain been lifted without the knowledge of the cast? The most straightforward strategy when faced with an uncomfortable feeling or truth is to deny it, but it wouldn't be too long before gangrene would set in and expose the deluded bigot. The truth has an uncanny way of winning against all odds.

The atmosphere in the room had grown so quiet that you could hear the seconds ticking; they were coming from the Grandfather clock in an adjacent room filled with heirlooms Stuart had accumulated on his many trips abroad looking for the razor's edge, an edge he'd read about as a youngster but had never found. Guy told him it was because he tended to break everything down to the lowest common denominator, and what he had found, but didn't know it, was Occam's Razor. Guy had once said to him something like "For once in your life I wish you would free yourself philosophically from the dictum that entities should not be multiplied unnecessarily. I wish you would disregard your interpretation which requires that the simplest competing theories be preferred to the more complex or that explanations of unknown phenomena be sought first in terms of known quantities. If you do so you would be pleasantly surprised by the complex wonder of the universe that resides in your boobytrapped soul."

Suddenly, there was the sound of thinking being twisted into intellectual convolutions. A somewhat controlled scramble had turned into a free for all, and it was every man for himself. The inviting lips of the camouflaged kiss of death had produced a tongue-twisted group of Mensa Society wannabees into a menagerie of retarded over-easy eggheads. A very thin blanket of paranoia hovered above the room, and no one was outside of its impending descent. Fun, that clown that comes to town with the carnival, had been suited-up and had blown his horn, but he was about to remove his grease paint. Quantum leaps were knocking at the door, but they couldn't be heard because they were subatomic taps. Turkish taffy was everywhere.

All but one of the guests began to experience a full-blown lack of gastronomical jurisprudence. They had all become hungrier than they could ever remember, but there was nothing to eat except that which had been set before them. They weren't cannibals, however, and they had the common sense to question if any meat had been purposely left on the bone. Not a one, well, maybe not a one, loved to chew the fat. Some were meditative cud chewers who would take their books along with their predigested thoughts and sit below their favorite tree; they would read, think, assimilate, doze and dream; some would write, but, make no mistake about it; their bellies would have been filled and their inquisitive appetites satisfied.

"I hope nobody brings up creation," the beautiful, Irish catholic, belly dancer said. She'd left the nunnery after less than a year of unholy confessions.

"My good woman, it seems as if you just brought it up. Although, on the other hand, the subject presented itself in the first succulent bite of lamb. The Kashmiri Chile-Braised Lamb that Stuart served us this evening is a unique dish prepared for weddings and other special occasions. This classic dish is served as part of the Kashmiri feast called Wazwaan. The Wazwaan is comprised of 36 dishes; the majority being lamb. So, how can one possibly talk about Guy's foray into the forest without talking about creation? Could anything be more obvious?" The youthful looking Scottish priest asked kindly, then continued to elaborate on his take of one aspect of creation, the sacrificial aspect, the bloody aspect that turns a four-leaf clover into a prickly cactus that prohibits the right of passage to the presumptuous pilgrims who believed the world was not flat. "'Go west, young man. Go west.'" "The east is filled with too many sword swallowers and magic carpets, not to mention men sleeping dreamily on beds of nails."

"When Guy finds his fossil, do you think all he will find will be some familiar congealed sediment that has had the guts squeezed out of it by some inhumane pressure cooker, some force without a personality, who or which delights in the fallibility of man? Or will it have been something banged out of nowhere by something or someone who has always been? Maybe we're all just a motley group of punched out tin pieces, random artful artifacts that are continuing to evolve via a process of selection, some higher order of excaudate creature who has emerged from the green lagoon turned black. Maybe we still have a tail, but it's just stuck between our legs. Maybe it's just all talk," the youthful looking Scottish priest rebuked her with kindness. 'Talk is cheap, but the voice I'm talking about is continuously articulate. Sometimes it is as loud as thunder, and at other times it is the silent sound of growing grass."

"Furthermore, My Fair Lady, Richard A. Swenson, M.D. said in his informative book, "More Than Meets the Eye." "' No animal has been blessed with language, only man. The average adult has an 'active' or 'use' vocabulary of 10,000 words and a passive or recognition vocabulary of 30,000 to 40,000 words. For comparison, Webster's New International Dictionary defines 400,000 words, and the English language probably contains one million words-no one knows the exact number." "So, please excuse me but I'm sorry to say that your prehistoric thinking appears to have been fossilized by a sovereign spoken act of creation. No, not the hieroglyphic script of the ancient Egyptian priesthood, those enigmatic and incomprehensible symbols or writing, those coagulated voices subject to the sound of squeeze-box Velcro crackles," the frockless priest continued with great enthusiasm. He expected a response. When he didn't get one he continued by going to the book of Romans.

"No, no, no. No! "'For the wrath f God is revealed from Heaven against all ungodliness and unrighteousness of men, who suppress the truth in righteousness, because what may be known of God is manifest in them, for God has shown it to them. For since the creation of the world His invisible attributes are clearly seen, being understood by the things that are made, even His eternal power and Godhead, so that they are without excuse, because although they knew God, they did not glorify Him as God, nor were thankful, but became futile in their thoughts, and their foolish hearts were darkened. Professing themselves to be wise they became fools and changed the glory of the incorruptible God into an image made like corruptible man-and birds and four-footed animals and creeping things." "God could not have made Himself more obvious, unless He came to earth as a man, but men worshipped the creature rather than the creator," the priest continued. "I'd be curious if anyone has ever stumbled across the diary of a baboon."

"By, "all talk," are you referring to words at random or specific words whose meaning cannot be left to subjective interpretation, words that can stand alone, words that need no defense, words that have life and give life? Because, to me, even the purest words can be twisted into configurations that deny an absolute, a definition that implies a translation into any language results in the same, not similar, meaning. Nothing dangling like some participle by its neck at the end of a rope, words unlike a beached fish gasping for air," the retired professor of linguistics said with the voice of an absolutist.

"Furthermore, in the end maybe all we will have as a defense is a familiar bark that resembles all talk."

"If you mean to say, "Something out of nothing," then why don't you just go ahead and say it?" the big dwarf, who had become well known for his use of oxymorons, said in a rather loud whisper. He'd spent most of his life beneath The Big Top where his father was a lion tamer. He had a dream that someday he'd learn to read and write, but his father liked to keep him the dark. Well, his dream was answered when his father, for the last time, stuck his arrogant head into the mouth of a hungry lion.

"If I intended to say, "Something out of nothing," and meant "Something out of nothing," I'd have said "Ex-nihilo." I was merely issuing a warning, because the purpose of being educated is to defend our self against the seduction of eloquence, the mesmerizing sound of flamboyance coming from unthrottled throats designed to wash the brains of innocents," the professor said rather harshly.

"Frankly speaking, I didn't come to this party tonight thinking it was going to be an intellectual coming out party. I came here to have some fun, and furthermore, frankly speaking, I was hoping we'd be somewhat more salacious in our conversation. Do you know what I mean, boys?" the same She that had spoken before with uncrossed legs and bulbous lips was the same She now speaking. "There are many ways to get creative without having to speak about creation. All one needs to do is to do what comes naturally," She continued in a somewhat buttery and oily tone.

"What comes naturally to who, to you?" He asked.

"By all means, yes, that which comes naturally to me; even though to some my behavior might be considered unnatural. Maybe there's a fossil that can validate my behavior. Fossil is as fossil does. I suppose you haven't ever heard of the Big Bang Theory. No, no, don't say anything. I know what you're thinking. Sometimes those gutters can be very inviting, even to those who appear to be as pure as Ivory Soap," she said transparently.

"Don't you just hate it when you see foods advertised as being "All natural?" the lean baby-faced looking lacto-vegetarian asked. She didn't eat meat, but she did eat plants that had been fertilized by cow manure.

"Naturally, I hate that. Who wouldn't? That's like saying "All organic." It either is, or it isn't," the yoga teacher quipped with a distinct California suntanned voice. She'd always been afraid to go near the water, but now you couldn't get her out of the water. After a near death experience involving high tides and strangulating seaweed, she'd become obnoxiously evangelistic, and that is when she'd get herself into hot water with her relatives and friends. She looked like a pretzel, but she had the gait of a fish. After that flat earth paradigm shift experience, she renamed her studio "Living Water."

"Are you saying you don't think it is possible to have it both ways?" the petite librarian asked. She'd been balancing a book on her head from the moment she had entered. No one had expected her. In fact, she hadn't even been invited. Furthermore, she wasn't dressed properly, and she didn't even have common sense enough to be wearing glasses. "On more than one occasion I've eaten my cake and had it too. It has something to do with balance and a lot to do with how one thinks, especially how one thinks in his heart. To put it another way, perhaps a more profound way, every man is his own fossil, and 'a book is the only immortality,'" she added with the voice of regurgitation. She'd become somewhat notorious as a librarian because she liked to secretly recommend banned books to her young students. She also coined the phrase, "The only gift better than a book is time enough to read it." It had also been reported that she lounged around the house in nothing but a t-shirt. The shirt had the following quote from Voltaire on the front. "Books rule the world, at least nations which have a written language. The others do not count."

The party was moving right along just as Stuart had hoped it would. All the guests seemed to be engaged on more than one level, but their intellects were being challenged and stimulated. Mini brainstorms were breaking out everywhere; some came out of left field and left many of the players so flummoxed that their bats never left their shoulder. They struck out looking, and those who did swing were humiliated by a knuckle ball that left them dazed and confused. No end appeared to be in sight; it was more like, seize the moment and enjoy the banter but don't get argumentative. At a very light moment, there were a few, Stuart was tempted to ask, "Why is it that the electron follows the laws of nature because it cannot do anything else?" but he didn't.

"Both/And" will work nicely among these eggheads for obvious reasons," Stuart thought to himself. "This group doesn't have the fortitude to take an Either/Or position. If ever they are backed into a corner, they will paint it gray. This is their nature. I've known it for years, but if one or all had a similar Copernican experience, they'd certainly agree that Either/Or is the only way to go, but who, if any, among them would be willing to give up their free will?"

Stuart continued to analyze each guest who had been invited to the party. With a few exceptions he knew them well. They'd not been invited to this affair willy-nilly. "Surrender does not come naturally," he thought. "It is usually the result of a force outside of one's self. What benefit could there possibly be in surrendering, other than survival, of course? No, not of course, because understood in the proper context, total surrender is the only way to be totally free and eternally victorious. It didn't come naturally to me, and I don't believe it comes naturally to anyone; that is, if they are sincere with themselves, honest to point that their integrity becomes obviously transparent. Even though Guy seemed to agree that "All have sinned and come short of the glory of God," he really didn't believe it in the literal biblical sense of sin, the sin that condemns one to an eternity of utter darkness, a place called hell where a person's tortured personality exists after their physical demise, a place of eternal separation. Any reference to common transgressions could never logically be challenged since men acted according to an inherited selfish nature. No argument, there, but Guy believed in an institution of higher learning where intellect always superseded faith, a place where reason and logic reigned, and faith was in numbers, the concrete, the material, things finite in nature, equations that supported the fossils that preceded the Big Bang. He would say, "That which you can hear, see, smell, taste and touch." Even though he could never explain his imagination, he still believed it could be observed as an impression forged in a fossil, some antediluvian ancestor's femur, as opposed to "'The substance of things hoped for, the evidence of things not seen.'"

Stuart was tempted to bring up unmerited favor, pardon and/or mercy. He liked the Old Testament meaning of mercy: to stoop in kindness to an inferior. He had learned not to think of God's mercy as originating somewhere; it never began to be, because it is an attribute of the uncreated God, and therefor always was. He had a hard time controlling his desire to speak, but he hadn't recognized an obvious opening, so he said nothing. He'd learned early on to be sensitive to the Spirit's leading. In this realm he had also learned that one needn't be concerned about not "Striking while the iron is hot," because if God got the iron hot, He would keep the iron hot. Besides, he'd already opened one can of worms, and quite a few of them were still in the can squirming to get out.

One thing Guy wasn't, was a monster, the mythological tyrant-monster. At least, that is how he thought of himself, and others thought of him in the same vein. He was kind, compassionate, loving, generous, considerate of others' opinions and feelings, not given to intolerance or bigotry, and certainly, sincere. He didn't appear to have an inflated ego. He couldn't be accused of walking around in some hydrocephalous ego maniacal state that would portend an unbalanced state of mind prone to uncontrolled impulses of malignant narcissism. His speech and his behavior always seemed to match the size of his head; it never appeared to be swollen. But....

"The likelihood that the roots on the opposite side of the plate are related to the tree makes perfect sense, but how can we really know what the artist was thinking when he forged his design since no roots appear at the tree's base. Maybe he wanted us to assume that a connection existed, but a connection does not necessarily exist. What does exist is a man who seems to come and go based on one's concentration, undivided attention and focus. Is there anyone here who hasn't seen the man?" Guy asked.

"What man is that?" asked the last man standing.

"The man in whose presence you cannot remain standing," Guy answered. "Now, please sit down and look deeply into the past. Be sincere. Don't look in a presumptive fashion that permanently closes the door on contradictory assertions that are equally true, a door with only one handle that can only be opened from the inside. Let the eyes of your understanding be opened. Seek and you will find that out of the heart proceed the issues of life, but don't do anything yet. Remain seated," Guy continued, then stood up. For the first time that evening he looked vulnerable. Maybe it was his glass jaw that appeared to have some hairline, hard to decipher, cracks running through it. Maybe an impending, unrehearsed, fracturing moment was about to happen. Maybe the Trojan Horse was about to become a victim of humility. Maybe the sky would fall when every head was bowed, and Freud's depiction of the human mind as a fabulous haunted house would collapse under the strain of what Galileo calls, "'sensory experiences placed before our eyes or necessary demonstrations concerning nature.'"

"It surprises me that not one of you mentioned the man clinging to the innards of the trunk of the tree, those, not so obvious, growth rings. Don't misunderstand. I am not a judge. I have no desire to be a judge. I've never been a judge. I never will be a judge even if unanimously voted to take a judgeship deemed to be supreme. I just wonder how sincere we've been, tonight. I find it very hard to believe that not one person here saw the man in the tree, or, may have seen the man and said nothing. Admittedly his presence is not obvious, but he is there if only one were to look with his whole heart and not be ashamed to admit that they had seen him. Self-discovery can sometimes be very painful, but it is much better than to walk around in the guise of a hypocrite. I'm passing the plate, again. I'd like each one of you to look deeply into the trunk as if it were your trunk. This is your tree. These are your roots. What you do with them is up to you, but, remember, what you think and do can change the structure of your brain. This is essentially the definition of neuroplasticity. Don't fear change; welcome it. Don't be afraid or embarrassed to run into the phone booth to change, not only your clothes, but yourself. Be the Ubermensch you were born to be," Guy said with assurance and encouragement "Don't run with the herd mentality or morality." "'To lure many away from the herd-that is why I've come.'"

"And above all say along with me," "' Do not confuse me with what I am not.'" Nietzsche was one of Guys favorite philosophers, and he often quoted him.

"Once you find the man, look for the growth rings. Go deep. Peel the onion. Don't be intimidated by the truth. Be the naked emperor who knows he's naked and would still be willing to parade himself in front of the towns-folk unclothed, transparent and free. Face those unconscious patterns of thought or behavior that protect your conscious mind from thoughts and feelings that cause anxiety, discomfort and untold suffering. Thich Nhat Hanh said, "'People have a hard time letting go of their suffering out of a fear of the unknown; they prefer suffering that is familiar,'" Guy sympathetically encouraged the guests."

"Don't be captive to the carry-ons that don't fit into the overhead compartment. Relax your defenses.," he continued. "'Above all to thine own self be true, and it shall follow as the day the night that thou canst not be false to any man,'" Don't be afraid to let your guard down, lest your maladaptive defense mechanisms turn into neuroses. Divest yourself of your baggage, then, my god, please speak up," Guy continued. This exhortation caused a few of the guests to want to remove their clothing. Yet, he had to speak further to their silence. A compassionate compunction compelled him to add, "'Still is the bottom of my sea: who would guess that it harbors sportive monsters.'"

"Guy, it almost sounds as if you are encouraging us to make the proverbial paradigm shift, the 180 degrees about-face that will change, not just our direction, but our purpose. It sounds like an exhortation to move towards the light, a new light; it is something similar to what Plato said about fear, "We can easily forgive a child who is afraid of the dark; the real tragedy of life is when men are afraid of the light," the single mom said. Her father had abandoned her mother, and her husband had abandoned her, but she had not abandoned her faith; the pony was right around the corner. "'You'll never find a better sparring partner than adversity.'" Walter Schmidt." She added.

It was at times like these that Guy's nobility became obvious. It wasn't just his stature or his handsome, naturally tanned face. Guy was exactly 6 feet four inches tall and weighed 200 lean and muscular pounds. He'd always been a runner, especially long distance running that took him through fields, woods and dense forests. He'd been to places no one had ever gone to, places most people only dream about. One of his most memorable runs took him through the Black Forest mountain range of Germany known for its dense evergreen forests and picturesque villages. It is often associated with the Brothers Grimm fairy tales and is renowned for the origination of the cuckoo clock. Guy's nobility was in his blood, but he never claimed that it was blue. There were rumors of a family crest, but no one had ever seen it. Guy could easily sit upon the circle of the earth, but he wouldn't feel comfortable there. Neither would he feel comfortable living on the mountaintop; he'd rather be down in the valley with the peasants and the farmers. Stuart wasn't the only one of the two to have his own garden; Guy also had a garden. He also had a small farm on the outskirts of town where he raised rabbits, lambs and pigs. He never sacrificed these animals, but he did slaughter them and provide them as food to the needy. He absolutely loved to meet the needs of strangers; to Guy, no one was a stranger. He did claim that truth was stranger than fiction, but he never really embraced it with authority. Guy needed that fossil more than anything else in his life.

The Schwarzwald (Black Forest) gets its name from its dark slightly sinister canopy of evergreens. At high noon the rays of the sun were often occluded by this canopy of green, and the day was turned to night. When Guy recounted his visit to the Black Forest, he delighted in telling his friends that it was here that Hansel and Gretel encountered the wicked witch. He also said his most cherished memory of visiting the Black Forest was the privilege of visiting Calw, Wurtemberg, the home of Hermann Hesse, the Nobel Prize winning author of Steppenwolf, and other exceptional works. Hesse appeared in Guy's list of top ten authors. Guy once told Stuart that he could identify with Harry Haller, the protagonist depicted in Steppenwolf, as being torn between his humanity and wolf-like aggression and homelessness. He occasionally thought of himself as a noble savage. The savagery he dealt with must have taken place behind closed doors, because in the company of observers he always appeared noble. No sign had ever been given that Guy may have been bipolar, although he did disappear for days at a time and could not be reached. When asked where he had been, he'd always give the same response, "Nowhere." There was nothing dichotomous about his behavior in public. If anything, he had a botanical attribute that resembled repeated branching into two equal parts. He always appeared fair and balanced, tolerant, understanding, non-judgmental and given to compassion. He was never arrogant, and if he ever flew too close to the sun, he'd have a second pair of wings.

The room, once again, had grown silent. Each guest looked around the room at one another. It was like a parade of eyes circling the perimeter of fear with suspicion. Guy was about to start the plate around, again, when an anonymous ghost of a guest spoke up. He appeared to have been sitting at the end of the table, but one couldn't be sure. The food that had been placed on his plate disappeared, but his mouth was difficult to distinguish. He appeared to be a person, but he seemed to be coming and going. The obscure nature of his supposed presence had not been acknowledged; it was as if no one wanted him to exist, an Elijah who would never show-up, whose seat would always remain vacant.

"I thought my invitation said to come just as you are without an agenda. I'm certainly not prepared to dissuade Guy from going fossil hunting, although I do have a reputation for being quite persuasive. Had I known this party may have had something to do with me, I'd have had second thoughts about attending. If I wanted to be identified, I'd have stayed in the compound where I was just a number, a man of a thousand faces without tongues," this being that looked somewhat like a 'he' said.

"If I wanted to be dehumanized, I'd have come out long ago, and now I find that you, whoever you are, that you are trying to make me something I am not. How could I possibly be everywhere at the same time short of some incomprehensible miracle? Should the clay say to the potter, "Why hast thou made me thus?"

The room had become eerily quiet. There was little or no fidgeting. A few of the guests appeared to be playing nonchalantly with their desserts, but they were now hanging on his every word. He hadn't said more than a few words, but there was something about his voice that captured the hearer's attention, and it was riveting. He spoke simply, plainly, clearly, and with unmistakable fluency. It was as if they had become a church congregation, not newly formed, by any means, and he had become a ministering spirit, a deacon, a pastor, a missionary, an evangelist, a brother. This was the distinct sound of historical logos that, oddly enough, seemed to have neither a beginning nor an end, as it rolled off his tongue. He'd obviously realized, learned, and had been practicing, for what had seemed like forever, the salesman's motto, "Keep it simple, stupid," better known as the KISS principal, or it might just as well have been something like, "'Except you come as a little child, you shall in no wise enter into the kingdom of God."

Suddenly, Stuart rudely spoke up. "I hope you brought some fossil samples with you. I don't suppose you have the unmitigated gall to think your presence here has been an accident. It's not as if we have been patiently waiting for Godot. Your presence presumably had been predestinated before the foundation of the world. Show us the fossil!" This atypical remark from Stuart had the sound of a two-edged sword, drawn and made ready to thrust, and, furthermore, to pierce the conscience of his guests. This may have been Stuart's subtle attempt to divide and conquer, but it could just as easily produce the opposite effect. He sounded angry.

He sounded mean. Maybe he was upset with himself. Maybe he thought he had had the chance to pass the baton, and he'd just dropped it. Or, or he knew exactly what he was doing, and he was speaking somewhat harshly to camouflage his real intent. His intentions were that this night would not be like any other night, be well remembered and never forgotten, especially the sight and the smell of blood. He knew the ghost would be there, but he didn't think he'd take on flesh.

"Fossil, hell! Fossil! I'll give you fossils. I'll give you buckets, barrels, wheelbarrows, eighteen wheelers, boxcars, and even cargo containers jammed with fossils. But. But why would I bring fossils when I could instead bring the real thing? The only good fossil is a dead fossil. Now give me that duck-billed platypus of a plate," the ghost said while extending his muscularly wiry arm towards Guy.

No one at the party except Guy was startled to hear a reference to the duck-billed platypus. He'd studied the unusual creature and had found its evolution fascinating. It belongs to a group of mammals known as Monotremes. Monotremes are typified by laying eggs rather than bearing their young live. They are the only mammals that lay eggs instead of bearing their young live. On a trip to Tasmania Guy was able to view a duck-billed platypus fossil that was 100,000 years old. A fossilized tooth of a giant platypus species was dated 5 to 15 million years ago. Because of the early divergence from the therian mammals and the low numbers of extant monotreme species, the platypus is a frequent subject of research in evolutionary biology, one of Guy's favorite hobbies, and the platypus has been the butt of many jokes.

"Yeah, yeah, I know. You're saying to yourself, why duck-billed platypus? Well, because its appearance and physical composition generated a great deal of suspicion among scientists as to whether its attributes were that of an actual animal or a hoax being perpetrated on the public. George Shaw, an English botanist and zoologist, stated it was impossible not to entertain doubts as to its genuine nature, and Robert Know, zoologist, anatomist and medical doctor, believed it might have been produced by some Asian taxidermist. Obviously, no one had ever seen anything like it. Sound familiar?" the ghost quipped arrogantly.

"Oh, I'm so sorry for using such unorthodox language among a group of politically correct bibliophiles. I should have said something like, "Give me that presumptuous plate that hasn't a stomach for the serious challenges of the intellect, spiritual or otherwise. Maybe this plate was surreptitiously engaged in the beginning, behind closed doors, stained glass windows, closed curtains, beneath tombstones, above the law, and settled comfortably in the lap of the subconscious. I apologize because this plate does not represent an act of unlawful carnal knowledge; the plate is pure and innocent. We are the ones who turn the empty plate into a bottomless pit of gluttony, a cornucopia of obsessive fat laden compulsives driven by malignant narcissism," the ghost continued in a most denigrating way. "Furthermore, how would you like your doppelganger roasted? On a spit above an open fire or in a black skillet?"

For the first time that evening the ghost had suddenly become somewhat transparent. He could still be seen, but he appeared to be more of an outline, a corporeal anomaly, a voice that resonated with an irrefutable absolute. It wasn't exactly the voice of one crying in the wilderness, but it resonated with the sound of water breaking for the second time.

"Though rarely, profanity may be required to make a point; I never use it, and I never intend to. Resorting to profanity is like dumpster diving in a search for apples of gold in settings of silver. Profanity lacks power and is somehow impotent when used among Harvard educated men like yourselves. The F word, for example, can never rise to the occasion when presented with an intelligent logical argument. It lacks sophistication and sounds more like a cry for help coming from the mouth of a man drowning in ignorance. I'd like to add one thing, however, and it is an absolute. I'd rather hear the F word than to hear someone take the Lord's name in vain. Now grab your umbilical cords and don't let go!"

No one spoke, not a word, a sigh, or took a deep breath. Every guest was sitting as still as a mannequin. All hands were in plain sight, and then the table began to shake ever so slightly, and the lights began to flicker. Cobwebs were everywhere, but no spiders were in sight. The chimney began to whistle. The fat began to sizzle in the pan and then. Suddenly a tulip appeared in the center of the table. It had five distinct petals; each was a different color; yet, they seemed to come together as one. The balance of the night would not come close to a tiptoe through the tulips.

"Speak now or forever hold your peace," the ghost continued.

Every guest held their peace. It wasn't that they were afraid to speak lest they say something incriminating. It was just that their thoughts seemed to have become incarcerated. Yet, despite their inability to verbalize their thoughts, three of the guests opened their mouths very wide, as if they were having teeth pulled, but not a sound emerged, not even an incomprehensible mumble. They looked like gargoyles whose living waters had gone dry or clouds that held no water.

"What's wrong? Speak up!" he said somewhat loudly. "Perhaps the devil has got your tongue. He does have a way of doing that, but this is no time to take the Fifth. Even the most loquacious can become tongue-tied in his presence. Yes, of course; I get it. You certainly wouldn't want to incriminate yourself. Silence is golden, but not always. Sometimes you will be required to speak up even when you have no words to share, or you would like to speak but you just can't put two words together. Remember, the pen is not only mightier than the sword; it is the sword. There is a sword that is quick, and sharp and more powerful than any two-edged sword. The supernatural power behind the thrust and parry can divide the soul and spirit, the joints and the marrow, and is a discerner of the thoughts and intents of the heart. Furthermore, I would imagine that sooner or later if you don't cry out the stones will."

"Well, I wouldn't necessarily expect you to understand that, but perhaps you can more easily relate to this Robert Frost quote, "'No tears in the writer, no tears in the reader. No surprise in the writer, no surprise in the reader.'" The ghost had begun to move from one guest to the other while momentarily standing behind each chair. "This is about as quiet as it has been all evening. I feel as if I am in the midst of a bunch of "Tell-Tale Hearts." Maybe before the night is over, I will be "'poured out as a drink offering on the service of your faith.'"

"All this mumbo jumbo that has been bandied about regarding one's "false self" seems to have left us still hungering for a huge dose of sincerity, even though Guy did encourage us to not be a person who pretends to "BE" to avoid admitting flaws or internal conflict. I've come to tell you that it is not OK to be not OK" he continued with assurance.

"Maybe I should just go ahead and give you guys a fossil of a fossil. What do you think, Guy? Will that make you happy? Will that tickle your funny bone? Will that leave you pining for a dose of spontaneous human combustion? Or will you be content to dissolve into a mindless puddle of distorted hemispheres, cleaved personalities bleeding out?" he asked then began a traditional ghost dance, a dance that would make him impervious to harm of any kind, but, most especially, physical harm.

Every guest had become glued to his or her seat. They couldn't get up even if they wanted to or had to. Leaving was not only out of the question; it seemed impossible. They'd been welded to their chairs by some invisible force that had dictatorial powers over their free wills.

"OK, now I want everyone to remain seated. Don't get excited, panic or call the authorities. Eat the dessert that has been placed in front of you and don't say a word until I return. I'll be back," the ghost said with animated assurance.

Everyone did just as they had been told, which, of course, was easy because they couldn't leave. They methodically ate their dessert and tried to keep their eyes on the ghost without being obvious. The plate seemed to have become unimportant; it was now lying face down on the table with its roots exposed.

The ghost seemed to have left, but one couldn't be sure. His seat was as empty as it had seemed to be, but no less occupied as if by some chimerical being. Then, he just as quickly reappeared wearing a white sheet with openings for the arms. His head covering was a flowering garland of lilies woven rather loosely. He was wearing sandals that could be seen just below his robe.

His face had become the face of everyman.

"These are not the emperor's new clothes; they are a type of wedding garment suited more for a bride than for a bride groom, even though there would be no noticeable difference with respect to gender. It's kind of like "One Size Fits All." "'The earth laughs in flowers,'" as Emerson once said, he added as he humbly displayed his attire.

He then moved to face Guy and said, "Guy, we're going to find your fossil even if it kills us, and I want you to follow precisely in my footsteps. Before we leave, however, let me bring something to your attention. OK?"

"Sure, go right ahead. You've got my undivided attention," Guy responded, while all the while searching for the ghost's Adam's apple.

"All right. I'm going to be upfront with you. I plan to hide nothing, and I will appear so transparent that you will be able to see right through me. My integrity will be my covering, and don't be surprised or disappointed if I "'Bind the sacrifice with cords to the altar.'" He sounded like a tree hugger might sound.

All the guests were thinking the same thing at the same time. "Guy, don't go. Guy, please don't go. You have no idea what awaits you. Finding that fossil isn't that important. It's not all that it has been made up to be. That silly plate you brought out tonight was nothing more than glass. Sure, it was forged, fused, dipped baked and probably frozen below sub-zero with imagination designed to stimulate thought, theological, philosophical, spiritual or otherwise. In and of itself, it had no meaning or purpose, and it wasn't even signed. Don't go out into the unknown without an anchor, and most especially with a stranger, someone you may not be able to trust. We may never see you again, and you may be shattered into a million pieces and come back broken beyond repair. Your future is more important than your past. Besides, this man might be a wolf in sheep's clothing." But, no one spoke up.

Their strangulated voice boxes prohibited the enunciation of sounds that resembled known language; it was just as if their thoughts had become abandoned orphans in their collapsed throats. If their mouths were opened just wide enough, you'd be able to see a group of coagulated letters stuck together in meaningless formations striving to be released from the snake pit. This was no way to behave as watchmen who had been appointed to stand guard at the gate to warn anyone who might attempt to enter in the guise of a false witness carrying forged documents, but they did behave this way because they didn't believe that way. They believed that a cause does not necessarily precede an effect. Furthermore, on closer examination, they probably believed that it is better to have many worlds than one God. This presumption did not necessarily apply to every guest.

Suddenly, seemingly out of the rafters, the silent sound of fingers, sign language, came with this message to Guy, "'I shall return, with this sun, with this earth, with this eagle, with this serpent-not to a new life or a better life or a similar life: I shall return eternally to this identical and self-same life in the greatest things and in the smallest, to teach once more the eternal recurrence of all things, to speak once more the teaching of the great noon-tide of earth and man, to tell of the Ubermensch once more.'" Of course, once again, it was Nietzsche.

The ghost then left Stuart's mansion and motioned for Guy to follow him. Guy didn't hesitate; he didn't say, "Goodbye" to anyone, but he did catch a hopeful look coming from Stuart that seemed to offer assurance.

They made their way slowly through the ivory, sliding glass doors. They went around the pool, across the lawn, across the bridge, through the woods, across the river apparently on top of the water, then into an endless garden that looked and smelled familiar to Guy. The garden had neither a beginning nor an end; it had always been, and it always would be. Sure, it was a well-kept secret, but anybody who wanted to know where to find it, could find it in their own backyard.

Guy and the ghost walked for about ten minutes before they came to a fork in the road. The ghost didn't hesitate; he took the road less traveled, which, of course, delighted Guy. After walking through a world of wild flowers they stepped into an endless forest of colorful trees. The width and height of the trees varied dramatically. Some of the trees were as small as bonsais; others seemed to touch the sky. Some had hands that seemed to be clapping. When they got to the tallest tree in the garden, the ghost stopped, looked hopefully at Guy, looked longingly at the top of the tree, looked again to Guy, then asked him climb to the top of the tree.

Guy looked inquisitively at the ghost and said, "Now, wait a minute. On our way to this spot we could have turned over numerous stones, moved a few boulders, dug a few holes, and sifted some earth, but, on your advice, we didn't. Now, you want me to climb a tree. I don't think so. So, as far as I'm concerned this has been a poor excuse for fossil hunting. To be sure, it has taken me back, but not far enough."

"Guy, I like the way you bring the English language to life. There's always a hint of music in your speech patterns, and your audibility is exquisite. You have such a vivid imagination. Your voice has a special artistry capable of painting easily interpreted pastorals. It also has the capability of dissecting the surreal and making it as plain as day. For example, when you said, "'I don't think so.'" It had the distinct sound of a subtle exclamation, not the innocent tone of a response to a question. Is it any wonder people thoroughly enjoy engaging you in conversation?" the ghost said in a very complimentary way.

Guy did not respond. He seemed to be confounded. So, he thought it might be best not to say anything that might be interpreted in one way or the other, a position of neutrality inconsistent with his normal behavior. He put his hand to his chin in a rather obvious contemplative fashion. He looked inquisitively at the ghost then just stood there and waited for the ghost to say something.

The ghost confidently approached Guy until their bodies were within six inches of each other. He looked as deeply into Guy's green eyes as one man could without touching the other man's face. The ghost was about to ask Guy to go out on a limb that wouldn't support a Dragon Fly, but he prefaced his final directions with a biblical quotation. "Guy, "'Not many wise men after the flesh, not many mighty, not many noble are called, but God has chosen the foolish things of the world to confound the wise, and God has chosen the weak things of the world to put to shame the things which are mighty, and the base things of the world and the things which are despised God has chosen, and things which are not, to bring to nothing the things that are, that no man should glory in his presence."' "By the way, as a further point of interest, when Disraeli quoted this verse to Queen Elizabeth, she responded by saying, "'Thank God for the letter M.'"

"Is this the transparency you referred to earlier?" Guy asked while backing away slightly. "Is this what each of us would have seen reflected in the plate had we been searching with integrity rather than with an ulterior motive? Would we have seen our nakedness when we caught a glimpse of the man hiding among the roots? The wise, the mighty and the noble brought to nothing? I must confess I have a problem with that. I guess I just don't quite see it that way," Guy added quizzically. "Furthermore, didn't Disraeli say, 'I'm a self-made man, and I worship my creator,'" Guy continued.

The ghost did not respond to the Disraeli quote. "Yes, it is the transparency I was referring to, but I can understand your confusion; the rejection of something so absolute. But, now, let me bring it just a little closer to home for you. So, look at it this way, Blake's way. "'This life's dim windows of the soul/ distorts the heavens from pole to pole/ and goads you to believe a lie, when you see with, not through, the eye.'"

"Now, kindly climb this tree. I will give you a boost to get you started." The ghost said

"This is the craziest thing I've ever heard of," Guy answered. "But I've done much crazier things, and I've climbed much taller trees. Besides, what harm could possibly come of it? I'd be tempted to say, if it is good enough for William Blake, it is good enough for me, but that, though sublime, is still too simple."

Guy answered. "OK, let's go."

Guy got the boost offered and easily climbed the tree. His pride drove him almost to the top.

The ghost watched with great anticipation as Guy handily climbed up the tree. There was something so natural about the way he climbed, almost animal like. His agility and effortless behavior seemed to favor evolutionary biology. "'Is it any wonder that the kinship between human beings and the apes has been promoted in contemporary culture as a moral virtue as well as a zoological fact. It functions as a hedge against religious belief, and so it is eagerly advanced. The affirmation that human beings are fundamentally unlike the apes is widely considered a defect of prejudice or a celebration of trivialities.'" The ghost just heard the voice of David Berlinski coming from "The Devil's Delusion."

"Good job! Now, go out as far as you are able; go all the way to the end of the limb if you can. Don't be afraid. The limb will hold you," The ghost said confidently.

"That's easy for you to say. I'm up here; you're down there. You're on solid ground; I'm on less than shaky ground. Many may think I'm wise, mighty, and noble, but I'm not foolish. This limb wouldn't hold up a Dragonfly," Guy answered.

"Only the fool has said in his heart, "There is no God," and I know you are not one of those, however, until you realize that "'Right being is more important than right doing,'" you will suffer the loss of all things."

"OK, that may very well be, but I also believe that when I find the fossil in question I will have become as right as rain, and that all of my right doing will have resulted in my right being. Furthermore, not only will I not have suffered the loss of all things; I will have gained all things. Yet I cannot comprehend how I am supposed to find the fossil up a tree. As it is, I have listened to you and followed your seemingly foolish instructions to a T. Based on the compelling nature of your voice I am up a tree with no fossil in sight. I'm beginning to feel quite foolish. I guess this is what is meant by "Being up a tree without a ladder." Guy responded with an obvious hint of irritation.

"Well, not exactly, because you may feel like you are up a tree without a ladder, but you do have a ladder. You just don't know it. Furthermore, the ladder you have has nothing to do with head knowledge. If that were the case, based on the thousands of books you have read and the consequent brilliance of your intellect, you wouldn't be up, to put it another way, Shit Creek without a paddle. Sure, books are quite valuable, almost priceless, and many great men and women have come to worship them. However, books are not the be-all and end-all of life; they are not an end in and of themselves; neither are they a means to an end. I don't believe anyone has read more books than I have read, neither have they written as many books as I have written, but may I remind you of what King Solomon said about books: "'Of making many books there is no end, and much study is a weariness to the flesh.'" This verse from Ecclesiastes has always humored me, because I also love books and love to read and write. Someone once gave me a coffee cup that had this saying etched into the face, "You can't buy happiness, but you can buy books, and that's about the same thing."

Guy, who was standing close to where the branch hugged the trunk, began to see the ghost in a different light; he seemed to be almost human. Maybe he really did have something special to offer, some sixth sense or spiritual dimension that supersedes the flesh. Guy thought to himself, "Why can't we all be "People of A Book?"

"Hey, Mr. Ghost, while we are on the subject of books, Thomas Jefferson once enthusiastically said, "'I cannot live without books.'" "I feel the same way. You probably do too. Ralph Waldo Emerson said, "'When I read a good book, I wish that life were three thousand years long.'" "In fact, wasn't it Ilnicki who said, "'The only gift better than a book, is time enough to read it.'"

The ghost, the quintessential bibliophile, responded, "Emerson also said, "'Many times the reading of a book has made the fortune of a man, has decided his way of life.'" "And that may be true for some men and some books, but only one book has eternally changed the lives of thousands of men and women over thousands of years, and you know which book I mean."

"Holy Ghost! Didn't Franklin Delano Roosevelt say, "'We all know books burn, yet we have the greater knowledge that books cannot be killed by fire. People die, but books never die,'"

Guy quipped enthusiastically.

"Yes, he said that, and 'Fahrenheit 451' had not been published. Perhaps the president had a premonition. Yes, of course, all people die physically, yet, all people also live forever, somehow, somewhere, unless, of course, you do not believe in the existence of the soul. Furthermore, only one book lives forever. I'm sure he must have read "Holy Sonnet 10: Death, Be Not Proud," by John Donne, the ghost added as if he were conducting a "Fireside Chat.

"Speaking of books, writing and death, I find I may have been barking up the wrong tree, and now I am up it. I must say, I have been enjoying our conversation, but I think I'd be more comfortable if I were down there with you. Can I climb down and get back to earth, back to Mother Nature?" Guy asked, then added, "I'm beginning to feel like the King of Siam who sang, "There are times I almost think I am not sure of what I absolutely know."

"Mother Nature! Yes, Mother Nature. Now you're on to something supernatural, Guy. Listen to what Galileo said about Nature. "For the Holy Scripture and Nature both equally derive from the divine Word, the former as the dictation of the Holy Spirit, the latter as the most obedient executrix of God's commands." Add to this what Dr. David Berlinski, Ph.D. from Princeton who has taught mathematics and philosophy has to say. "Although inspired by the Holy Spirit, scriptures belong to the world of appearances, and appearances can be confused or misleading. With Nature, things are completely different. "'Nature is inexorable and immutable," Galileo writes, "'and she does not care at all whether her recondite reasons and modes of operation are revealed to human understanding, and so she never transgresses the terms of the laws imposed on her.'"

"Ghost, I have a pretty good vocabulary, but what precisely does recondite mean?" Guy surprisingly and humbly asked.

"Recondite means: hard to understand. Profound. Abstruse," the ghost answered.

"Guy, Galileo believed in the inerrancy of scripture when he said, '"Philosophy is written in this grand book of the universe which stands continually open to our gaze. But the book cannot be understood unless one first learns to comprehend the language and read the alphabet in which it is composed."

From Galileo's remarkable declaration, it follows that Nature is a book, and as stated previously, "nature never transgresses the terms of the laws imposed upon her." In Dr. Berlinski's words,

"These assertions imply that the Book of Nature is inerrant, so that the doctrine of biblical inerrancy, a staple of Christian thought, has not at all been discarded in Galileo's mind, but transferred. A new, greater, grander book now occupies his attention, but even though new, greater and grander, the Book of Nature-the Book-is nonetheless very much like the old book. It is inerrant." Berlinski goes on to quote Sir Francis Bacon who said, "'The book of God's word" and the "book of God's works, are not in conflict.'"

"Well, I must admit, you've got me thinking, but I'm still, in an absurd way, clinging to my geocentric, prehistoric, Ptolemaic view point. Maybe it's my pride, and I just won't admit it," Guy answered honestly. "You know what? I honestly think The Way to redemption you are referring to is a little too simple. Too easy. Too mundane. Too narrow minded. Too literal. Too orthodox. Too fundamental. Takes little or no thinking or imagination. Anybody can have it your way. Do you know what I think? I think you must not have been paying close attention to the individual responses of each guest when the plate was being passed around. Come to think about it, I don't ever remember you handling the plate. Am I wrong?" Guy added.

The ghost did not answer, at first, because his mind was on the brazen laver in the sky and the two turtle doves that he had just released into the wild blue yonder, but then he said, "Guy, when I met your sister, she told me you studied the life of Confucius. Here is what he had to say about life, "'Life is really simple, but we insist on making it complicated.'" "Sound familiar?'

"I want to come down, and I want to come down, now. I want to climb down. I need to get my feet back on the ground. May I?" Guy asked.

"Climb down? Climb down! No, you mustn't climb down. You must do what you intended to do when this night began. You must find your fossil, and you won't find it by climbing down. Your fossil will be found by stepping out in faith. You must go to the very end of the limb even if it seems foolish as well as hopeless. Remember how this all started with the wise, the mighty and the noble. So then, "'Faith is the substance of things hoped for, the evidence of things not seen.'" I'd like to add that you will see it when you believe it, not you will believe it when you see it. Merely as an aside, Einstein maintained that a "cosmic religious feeling" was the strongest motivation for scientific research."

Guy didn't respond. He didn't look down. He just looked straight ahead with one eye on the horizon and the other on the sparrow. He began a slow and very deliberate walk, placing one foot in front of the other while breathing deeply. About three quarters of the way to the end, the limb began to bend dramatically downward. The sparrow took flight. Guy was certain the limb would break, and he would fall back to earth. He was at least twenty feet up in the air, and he was certain the fall would kill him or cripple him, so he began to retreat. He made it back to where the limb met the trunk, and he held onto the trunk tightly. There, at the base of the trunk stood the ghost. No external stimuli had affected Guy's vision, but he either began to hallucinate or the ghost possessed a pair of broad, beautiful, and very colorful wings that resembled a sign of holiness. "I don't think I can continue; I'm feeling extremely fatigued," Guy said with the voice of exhaustion.

"Guy, you must go out again. Remember Vince Lombardi's admonition that "'Fatigue makes cowards of us all'" "Furthermore, Sarah Parish said, "'Living with fear stops us from taking risks, and if you don't go out on the branch, you're never going to get the best fruit,'" the ghost continued.

"Look, Mr., I've never lacked for the best fruit, and I always made sure to leave plenty of low-hanging fruit for the less fortunate. Risk? Risk to me has always been a Given. You seem to like famous quotes; here's one you may like: "'The biggest risk is not taking any risk. In a world that is changing very quickly the only strategy that is guaranteed to fail is not taking risks,'" Mark Zuckerberg. "Perhaps you may have never heard of him, although, I must say you do seem to have a rather peculiar degree of omniscience," Guy answered rather defensively.

"Guy, the last person in the world you need to convince about your life of risk taking is me. I've heard of the numerous risks you have taken, including risking your life for the lives of others. Nevertheless, I'm still concerned about your greatest fear; the fear of fossils that still paralyzes you when it rears its ugly head. This fossilphobia I am referring to is your fear that contradictory assertions that appear to be equally true are not true. You're afraid to get caught between a rock and a hard place because you might hit bottom and discover to your dismay that man is not the measure of all things. In this Valley of Despond, below which there no bottom, you will be keeping company with individuals whose I.Q's are much higher than yours, and you will meditatively be chewing the fat together that has been left clinging to the same ineluctable perfidious fossil, some innominate bone" the ghost said sadly.

"Guy, we know the earth is 4.5 billion years old based on radiometric dating, and that Mary Anning, one of the ten most influential British female scientists who discovered and sold fossils from the Jurassic Age, influenced the way the world thought about its pre-history. She discovered ichthyosaur, plesiosaur, and pterosaur and was the first to suggest that coprolites were fossilized dinosaur feces. Unlike you, however, Mary had no fear of fossils. She had no ulterior motive. She wasn't trying to prove anything" the ghost responded with both hands wrapped around a rainbow.

"I'm not sure why at this point in our discussion you have decided to bring up the Torah. As far as I know, there were no dinosaurs on the ark. Guy answered. "But something is very different about the situation I now find myself in. Nothing looks remotely familiar. I can't even recognize the path we took to get here, and I certainly don't see how we will ever get back. Could this be the wilderness experience I've often heard so much about, a place of testing, trials and tribulations? It's not as if I've never been here, but not for forty days, let alone for forty years. It seems as if there is a degree of primitiveness about it designed to make one helpless, hopeless, and worthless; the result, of course, being to make a person humble. I can't say I know for sure I'm in the middle of a desert, but I sure am suddenly very hungry. I'd do just about anything for a slice of bread. You know what I think? I think it is as if art has turned against me and has left me holding an urn full of ashes."

"Art turned against you! Preposterous! Why would you, of all people, make such an absurd statement. I'm glad none of the guests, and most especially, Stuart, aren't present to hear you. They'd probably Baker Act you. My, God, Guy, please let me remind you of what D.H. Lawrence said about art, "'The essential function of art is moral, but a passionate, implicit morality, not didactic. A morality which changes the blood, rather than the mind,'" the frustrated ghost said with outstretched hands reaching for the sky. "If I didn't know any better, I'd climb this tree and knock some sense into you. I'd take you to the "School of Hard Knocks," and impose my will, but that's not how I teach. Friendly persuasion has always worked best for me. There isn't a ransom too big that hasn't already been paid."

"OK, OK, Ghost, I wasn't thinking when I said that about art. You're right. I should feel embarrassed, and I do. You might as well have quoted Einstein, "Art is standing with one hand extended into the universe and one hand extended into the world, and letting ourselves be a conduit for passing energy,'" "Or Friedrich Nietzsche who said this about art, """You must have chaos within you to give birth to a dancing star, '"Guy retorted with self-deprecating hint of shameful arrogance. "I know. I know, I should have known better, especially based on the theme of this evening's party. I'm sorry I didn't give a better account of myself. I sincerely regret it."

"That is certainly understandable, but not necessarily something to be regretted. George Orwell said, "A man who gives a good account of himself is probably lying, since any life viewed from the inside is simply a series of defeats." Remember the discussion this evening that focused on motive? "the ghost asked.

"Yes, I remember," Guy answered. "I'm experiencing a certain uncomfortable disconnect, right now, and I feel very motivated to get my feet back on the ground. Can I come down now?" he asked hopefully.

"Not until you can plainly see what the hypocritical, judgmental, Pharisaical, white-washed Sepulchers didn't see. The same religious zealots who famously said, "Do as I say, not as I do."

It's what's on the inside that really counts, or to put it another way, Jesus said, "'It's not what goes into the mouth that defiles a man. It's what comes out the mouth that defiles a man.'" "Guy, my Guy, the proverb says, "Even the fool may be considered wise if he keeps his mouth shut."

"Based on that proverb and the perspicacious insight of the most famous rabbi who ever walked on the face of this presumed fallen earth, I'm going to rest my case on something Will Rogers said, "'Never miss a good chance to shut up.'"

"Well, I certainly can't disagree with that advice. It has a profound spiritual ring to it," the ghost said hopefully. "I think we may finally be getting somewhere regarding origin, meaning, morality and destiny. In fact, I might even be so bold as to say, we're making considerable progress."

"Ok, Ok. Who knows? Maybe we are making some progress, but I wouldn't bet on it. So, don't suddenly take me for another Blaise Pascal or

John Bunyan. However, I'd like to add just one more thing before I shut up," Guy added quickly.

"Yes, of course. Why certainly. Be my guest. Far be it from me to prohibit freedom of speech. Holy cow, even "'The heavens declare the glory of God; and the firmament shows His handiwork. Day unto day utters speech, and night unto night reveals knowledge. There is no speech nor language where their voice is not heard.'" Please carry on," the ghost joyfully said.

"OK, but far be it from me to say anything denigrating about a being I've never met before. What or who gives me the right to judge another? All species of organisms arise and develop through the natural selection of small, inherited variations that increase the individual's ability to compete, survive and reproduce. "'Judge not, that ye be not judged. For with what judgment you judge, you will be judged.'" "I've never met the likes of you, and I don't suppose I ever will again meet the likes of you, at least, not on earth, but I'm certainly not going to judge you," Guy said.

"Furthermore, Mr. Rogers said, "'I never met a man I didn't like,'" but I was just wondering where that might leave you. You know what I mean. You know. Heck. I'm just curious. Your origin. You know? Anyway. By the way, and more importantly, I just realized that you forgot to bring the plate with you. Or, did you leave it behind on purpose?" Guy said with genuine kindness and a sense of humility.

"Now, just what plate do you suppose that might be?" the ghost asked quizzically.